POWER SLIDE

POWER SLIDE

A DARCY LOTT MYSTERY

SUSAN DUNLAP

COUNTERPOINT
BERKELEY

Library of Congress Cataloging-in-Publication Data

Dunlap, Susan.
Power slide : a Darcy Lott mystery / by Susan Dunlap.
p. cm.
ISBN 978-1-58243-542-8
1. Women stunt performers—Fiction. 2. California—Fiction. I. Title.

PS3554.U46972P69 2010
813'.54—dc22

2010008580

Series design by Kimberly Glyder Design; cover by Domini Dragoone
Top cover photo by Judy Davis
Interior design by Megan Jones Design
Printed in the United States of America

COUNTERPOINT
2117 Fourth Street
Suite D
Berkeley, CA 94710

www.counterpointpress.com

Distributed by Publishers Group West

10 9 8 7 6 5 4 3 2 1

To Megan and Sean

POWER SLIDE

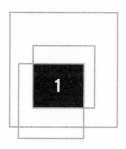

1

"Where the hell is Guthrie?"

"He'll be here by call. He always is, Jed."

The second unit director nodded, and I subtracted a big bite from my account in the Stunt Doubles Bank of Trust. This gag was part of a sequence in the planning for over a month. I'd been to the preproduction meeting, noted the storyboarding, and choreographed my part. My name would be in the credit roll. I always want gags to go right, but this one was special: it could make or break my future. Not to mention my neck.

We'd had a top-notch wheelman in on the planning and ready with his truck, but he'd downed some bad crab last night and it'd been all he could manage to lift the phone this morning. So I'd called Damon Guthrie. I'd vouched for him, promised he was a quick study, had a good resume, and, most important now—was reliable.

"You've known him a long time?"

"Never missed a call." *That I know of.* "He's on his way."

"Driving the rig?" A flash of fear—economic fear—whitened Jed Elliot's already pale face. I'd worked with him before—turned a busted fire gag into a showstopper and left him grinning ear to ear. Still, every time I saw him I was struck by what a worrier he was. So, I swallowed a retort and went for over-the-top reassurance.

"Guthrie'll get here. Listen, he's the best. He's modified that rig of his till it's like a Swiss watch. He hits a button and the payload swings like a salsa dancer's butt. He's invested everything in that truck. He's not going to blow this chance to recoup."

"Yeah, but rehearsals—"

"Tell him what you want and he'll make it happen."

"Minimally, he's going to need to scope the layout."

"Sure. But we're on a loading dock here. It's an easy drive. He comes full speed around that corner onto the pier, starts toward the ship. I'm riding the bike, catch the tire in a rut, and do a fall, go into a power slide. He jackknifes and I go straight under his truck. He'll handle it."

Jed shot a glance at the second unit crew—the camera operators, lighting guys, wardrobe mistress, and landscapers making final adjustments to an arbor that would hide a camera—along with everyone else hanging around, waiting for the truck to arrive and the day's shoot to finish up. If Guthrie threw off the schedule and sent the shoot into tomorrow, paying the Port of Oakland for an extra day would pretty much blow the entire second unit budget, *if* we could get the dock at all.

Already the lighting tech was eyeing the bank lights he'd used for a dusk shot, and it didn't take a mind reader to know he was gauging how long he could stretch "daylight" without losing continuity. We might squeeze out another quarter of an hour if we shot against the beige buildings rather than the cargo ship, but then there'd be no point in being on the dock.

The photographer from the *Oakland Tribune* who'd been clicking away when I did the first half of the gag had left, but the woman from the *San Francisco Chronicle* was after the city angle: San Francisco Girl Makes Good. She wanted to catch me coming out of the slide, and I wasn't about to turn down publicity.

Jed was staring at something on his clipboard. "I don't know, Darcy. It's a split-second gag. If he screws up, there's no leeway. Without rehearsals—"

"We'll handle it."

Jed looked dubious, as well he might. A moment passed before he said, "It's your head. The rate this fog's flooding in, we're not going to get more than one shot."

"I need to do a final run-through." *Need to get out of this conversation and hope to hell I'm right about my good friend Guthrie.*

I loped toward the end of the pier. Mo Mason, in the camera cart that would be running next to me for the close-up, tooled it alongside me now. At the end of the dock, he cut in front and started bitching about Guthrie. "You sure about the guy?"

"Never seen him fail."

"You know him . . . well." It wasn't a question.

I thought we'd been more subtle.

"Listen, I've worked with Guthrie before," he went on, "but that doesn't mean I know him. Nobody does . . . except maybe you?"

I stared down at him. "He's always shown up, right? Always aced the gag, right?"

"Yeah, but used to be he'd cut it close, then pull out the gag, and afterwards he'd take the crew out for a beer. By the end of the night he was everybody's best friend and no one remembered that half hour cooling our heels. But the last couple of times, it was just shoot and I'm out of here. No drinks, no jokes, all business . . . like he was a different guy, you know?"

"Actually, I don't. Haven't seen him in a year."

"But you're the one who vouched for him. Aren't you two—"

"No." I forced a grin for him. "It's complicated. And anything but full-time. But I love the guy even when he's off my radar. Uh-oh, look at the fog!"

The startling wall of white was banked thick and high behind San Francisco across the Bay. Only the Sutro Tower was holding it back. Jed Elliot was right: in a few minutes it'd stream over Twin Peaks and flood down the hills into downtown. Then, in a flash, it'd be across the Bay and turning our shoot into mush.

Where the hell are you, Guthrie? No problem, you said. You'd be on the road by ten, here by four.

I understood there was a wildness about him. But I'd always been a sucker for that in a guy, something I wasn't about to admit at this particular juncture. Guthrie's intensity burst out full force when he plotted a stunt, tossing out ideas like Frisbees to see which would be caught and brought back in, hunting down the cable with the least give or the most, finding an angle no one had tried, pushing the limits with each gag. But he'd always kept that wildness under some control, like a thoroughbred in a fenced pasture. And as far as I knew, he had never, ever, blown a gag or held up production.

Until now. *Where are you? It's my neck on the line here!*

And it'd be my body if I didn't do just what I told Jed I'd come down here to do—mentally run through the gag one last time. I had the feeling Mo was thinking similarly. Driving the camera cart wasn't the same as doing the stunt, but it wasn't tooling along the freeway, either. You had to be alert for obstacles, figure where to move in close, gauge your speed, all the while keeping your target front and center. More than one cart guy had ended up on the paramedics' gurney.

Enormous metal cranes stand at this end of the Port of Oakland loading docks as if ready to take the Bay in three steps and devour San Francisco. I'd see them when I drove the Bay Bridge; I thought of them as Trojan birds, though the last thing they could have done was hide anything in their bellies. They hadn't eaten the city, but they'd made a meal of its port. Now San Francisco piers held shops and restaurants, while lowly Oakland sported the fifth-largest container port in the country.

My ride, an old fat-wheel bicycle, was lying at the tip of the dock where the last scene had ended. I balanced astride it, let my eyes go blank, and felt the wind snapping my hair, icing my bare neck. I heard the slap of the Bay, the whoosh of water as distant boats cut through the briny smell. For a moment I didn't name the sounds or smells, merely met them, as I'd do on the cushion in the *zendo*. There, it wasn't a centering technique but an outcome of *zazen*, for no purpose but itself. Here, though, it shifted my focus away from Guthrie—away from Guthrie and me—to the gag.

It was a timing gag. Easy. Guthrie and I had done this kind of thing together three or four times before, made it look deadly. Then celebrated after. And the next morning before dawn, one of us would be gone.

I glanced down the dock, at the massive ship alongside, the boarding slips, the train tracks and, above it all, the giant gantry cranes. Twenty-two stories tall, with one guy in the cab up there grabbing and plunking down containers, thirty to the hour. From a distance they'd been Trojan birds. Now, from the ground, all I saw was two huge white metal slabs twenty-five feet long and the same distance apart.

I'd already done the first part of this sequence in two sections—jumping on the bike, going across the tracks, and riding up to and around the base of the crane. It had taken four days—an hour or so for four afternoons. Today I'd redo that ride, but only as lead-in for the payoff, the straight shot from the crane to the truck and the power slide underneath. I would have felt a lot better if I could have eyeballed the truck.

The first part was in the can. Still, I needed to visualize the whole thing. I put down the bike, stood against a pillar, let my eyes close, and pictured—at first pictured, but almost instantly *felt*—myself at the starting point five yards behind the bike. Me doing a shamble run to simulate the desperate heroine, then a mini-pause, a glance behind, a stumble-and-save, before the double take at the sight of the bike. I felt myself lunging, grabbing the handlebars, yanking up the bike, running to get momentum to fling my leg high over the bar. Next my legs were pumping the pedals, my head down apparently oblivious to the crane, the bike weaving, me looking over my shoulder, tires catching in the track, making the save. Suddenly, the reversal: a major double take when I saw the crane, a quick cut to the left to skirt the crane, dropping my shoulders in an exaggerated "Whew!" Now right the bike, lean hard forward into all-out speed position. I could "see" Guthrie's truck rounding the corner, feel my gaze drop to spot the track, see Guthrie jackknife, feel my shoulders thrust left to catch the tire on the track. I'd fall off the bike, shooting it left as I shoved right to land in the middle of a pad that would be a yard from the truck. As if it were happening, I felt my hands grab the raised back edge of the pad and push off, sending me straight ahead under the truck and midway between the tires. The entire business would take less than a minute, the portion we were shooting twenty seconds.

I did another mental run-through but wasn't reassured. Stunt work is illusion, relative safety masquerading as danger. But it only works that way with meticulous preparation. I'd done mine; I wanted Guthrie here to do his. If he blew it, he'd be sorry.

I'd be dead.

"Can't even see San Fran any more." Mo was staring across the Bay at the thick white cover hiding everything but the tops of a couple of high-rises and the tip of the Transamerica Building. "What do you figure? Fifteen minutes?"

"Max."

Together we started back toward the crane.

We heard the cheer before we saw Guthrie's truck.

A second later he jumped down from the cab, looking like he always did. And all the doubts of the last half hour might never have existed.

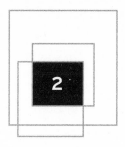

GUTHRIE COULD HAVE been born in that big semi-trailer truck of his, at least that's how he looked. Red plaid shirt, lined; white T-shirt, jeans, boots. The only thing missing was a signature hat. He'd been vain about his hair, admittedly, then worried, and now the whole issue had receded— into an ear-level rim of brown fuzz and a silly-looking ponytail. But, it all just seemed background to those startling dark brown eyes that searched me out as if to say there was us, and then, way down the ladder, everything else. For a guy pushing fifty, he looked damned good. "Sorry! Really, sorry," he said. "Accident on 980. Two rigs. I didn't think we'd get the one guy out at all. Ambulances took forever. There still light?" He meant for the gag.

"Just." Jed looked like he was downshifting emotional gears, from fourth to third and now first.

"You want me to do a slow drive around the corner to the mark, so you can get the oncoming shot?" And so he could do a slo-mo run-through for himself.

Jed gave a curt nod. Even with doing that to check for angles, trolley speed, lighting, it'd be asking the camera crew to perform a miracle. The run-through was what he'd have ordered, but *he'd* wanted to give the order. Jed was a good director, but he wasn't a saint, and Guthrie had turned more than one director into a martyr. He usually didn't start this soon, though.

He loped over, bending as he hugged me, muttering, "Thanks." He was back at the cab before he had a chance to feel me go stiff.

The dim light veiled changes in Guthrie's face, but his ribs were bony to the touch in a way they hadn't been the last time I'd had a serious feel of them. His heavy shirt flapped around him all too freely as he darted across the pier and sprang up into the cab.

Till that moment I hadn't realized how tense I was. Jed had wanted to give him the order; I just wanted to smack him, heroic performance on the freeway or not. What were cell phones for?

Don't get into that! This is a dangerous gag. Concentrate!

He backed up the big rig as if it were a VW Bug. Driving slowly forward, he rounded the corner and jackknifed the trailer before he came to the stop mark. I ran through my gag, factoring in when I'd spot the truck, where it had to be when I skirted the crane. Then there was the angle of the trailer when I tossed the bike and the angle when I slid forward under it, between the rolling tires. Most of the reasons for rehearsing are aimed at bringing the unknown into the light before it's too late. No one wants to do a gag cold.

"How'd you manage that, man?" One of the gaffers was staring at the tires on the trailer. "It's like they skidded, but they couldn't have."

"Trade secret," Guthrie said, grinning.

"Okay," Jed snapped. "We need to get this in one take. Fog's to the end of the dock. Darcy, Mo, there just isn't time for rehearsal. Can you handle it?"

I need you to, he meant.

I nodded and headed for the start mark. Behind me I could hear Jed giving Guthrie his start signal.

The bike still lay at the end of the dock. The start mark was a couple yards away. In the few minutes since I'd stood there the temperature had dropped sharply and now the damp of the fog brushed my back. Ahead, lighting techs did final checks and Mo revved the camera cart. He'd be running mostly a couple yards in front of me. If he ended up in the still camera shots, he'd be edited out later.

"Ten seconds!"

I inhaled, then exhaled with care to pull in my attention.

"Live on the set! Action!"

I ran, scooped up the bike, swung on, hard-pedaled toward the container ship, overcompensated, and skidded back right. Straightening with my head down over the handle bars, I thrust my body with each downward push. Mo's motor ground ahead: doin' good, doin' good, doin' good. At the crane I jerked into the double take, swerved, did the "relief" shoulders drop, looked at the truck, and did a bigger double take—a real one.

The trailer was out of position!

It hadn't jackknifed.

It wasn't in front of me. No way could I do the easy slide. The cab was almost at the stop mark.

No time!

Mo's cart engine roared; he was cutting right.

I jerked, tossed the bike, hit the pad, caught the raised edge, and flung myself to the right as hard as I could. Then I skidded toward the front tire, caught the lug, and swung myself under the trailer.

Not hard enough. The truck was moving. I was sliding ever slower. The rear tire would crush my feet. I needed to grab, but I had no leverage.

I crunched my abs, lifted, caught a pipe—hot!—pushed off harder than I'd ever done, and shot out the far side of the truck.

The rear wheel ran over my hair.

13

I was clear.

Usually, after a big, final stunt, there's a moment's silence and then the whole second unit crew applauds. Now they stood silent. They looked as stunned as I was. I glanced over at the cameraman. He was still on his dolly a couple of yards in front of the truck. Fog had dampened his shoulders, but he seemed oblivious. Jed was eyeing him questioningly. The only sound was the click of the newspaper photographer's camera.

Guthrie jumped down from the cab. In an instant he was standing over me. His face was dead white. "You okay? I'm sorry. . . I . . . shit. I don't know what . . . You okay? Omigod! Your hands, they're burned!"

The camera clicked again. This was *not* the picture I wanted in the paper! Not in a field where reputation is everything. "Shh! They'll be okay."

"I . . ."

"Shut up! I'm fine. Just shut up! I vouched for you, dammit. Don't blow it!"

Guthrie was still staring at my hands. The camera clicked again.

"Give me your jacket. Now!"

He nearly ripped the thing getting it off and trying to wrap it around my shoulders. I didn't dare think about the wheels, how close—I couldn't feel my hands; didn't dare look at them. I jammed them through the sleeves and into the pockets. Then I turned to the photographer and grinned.

"Great shot!" Mo yelled. "Way better! And that last grab, Darcy: terrific! I thought you were being sucked into the chassis. It's gonna make the scene!"

"Thanks!" I yelled before anyone could disagree. "Mo, you're the best!" I eyed the cameraman, still standing behind his camera on the cart, hoping to pull him in. But he wasn't committing. He was heading to the monitors, where Jed was already running the coverage from the dolly. The other guys crowded in behind, and we all watched each camera's take. My hands were burning. "This a wrap, Jed?"

"Unless we're going to do it in the dark. You're shivering. Check with me in the morning, just in case, but I have a good feeling about this one. Good work, Darcy. You'll be at dinner?"

I glanced over at Guthrie. "We might be late."

□ □ □

"What the hell happened, Guthrie? You were supposed—"

"I could have killed you!" The words exploded from him as soon as the crew moved off. His face was stiff with horror. "Omigod, I just can't— You know I would never, ever—"

"Of course, I do. It's over. Fine, now." I looked away, blocking out his fear. I couldn't go there. "Could have been killed" will kill you. Mistakes are for learning. "But still, how come—"

"Stupid! You're lucky to be in one piece." He hoisted me into the cab and thrust my hands into his ice chest. "I blew it! They all know it. No reason to drag yourself down with me!"

"They knew it when you blew the jackknife, but once the shots were good, you're the great wheelman again. Maybe Jed noted me reacting mid-gag and making it work, and that can't hurt. So, all good."

"Yeah, 'cause they'd be thinking you're using your balls for brains."

"So to speak." I caught his eye and grinned. It was an effort, but when his mouth twitched and he fought back a laugh, I relaxed.

Suddenly he looked almost like himself, the guy always ready with the quick comeback, up for the next impossible challenge, ready to go all out, then shrug it off if he failed.

"Using *my* balls for brains?" I said. "I must really be losing it, or else you are?"

It was the wrong thing to say, and I saw him just as quickly sink back down. I felt bad, puzzled, worried, and then just pissed. My hands throbbed. "The hell with you. What do you have for burns?"

"Lemme see those hands."

I'm not superstitious, or at least no more than anyone else in the business, but now I had to fight the urge to shut my eyes, as if refusing to see my scabrous red palms would keep them from being reality. I held them up to what was left of the light. "Backs are fine. Skin's still on the palms. Fingers are better than I thought, as long as I don't have to bend them. Won't be too bad. But I'm glad I don't have another call for a few days."

He looked closer. "You could take those hands to the emergency room, but you happen to be with the all-time expert on undercarriage burns. When something's gone wrong in the middle of a shoot, there's no time to wait for things to cool."

"Yikes."

He shrugged.

"Yeah, I know. You gotta do what you gotta do. But still . . . So, welcome to the Guthrie cut and burn clinic. Healing faster than the eye can see." He laid my hands gently on his own and bent close. "You must've let go fast."

"Well, yeah!" I kind of snorted, but it turned into a laugh and then he grinned, too. I couldn't tell whether he was truly coming out of his funk. I'd forgotten how tender he could be, how seductive in the way he cupped my hand as he moved it closer to his eyes. But I did have a good idea where all this was headed.

"I've got some good stuff in the back."

"Burn ointment?"

"That, too."

The odors in the cab seemed homey, as if welcoming me back into our past. There was always the smell of gasoline—I liked that—and the wood chips he kept handy, and the pistachios I'd seen him shell with one hand while driving. A bottle of Plymouth gin had been a staple behind the seat till a close call with the Highway Patrol made him stash it in the trailer. But enough had been spilled over the years, in my presence alone, that the smell of juniper and fruity aromatics hung on. And coffee, good strong coffee brewed in one of those old metal drip pots.

An aspiration of Zen students is to be not so much *in* the moment but an integral part *of* the moment. There was no such blending with him. If the Zen student were a dollop stirred into the mix, Guthrie was a marble added to the bowl, touching everything but still the marble, banging around, popping up, instantly recognizable as itself and nothing else.

He'd pulled into a parking slot near the dock, turned off the engine. "I wasn't kidding about the ointment. Your hands don't look bad, but that stuff'll have 'em working fine tomorrow. You won't even remember you had a worry. Step this way."

In the trailer it was, of course, dead black, and the lamp cut a small circle in the dark. Carefully he slipped palm-only gloves over my fingers. "I told you this was the best clinic." He got out a jar of salve.

"You sure about this stuff? These are my *hands* here! My career!"

"Trust me. I've burned my mitts on this truck more than any sane guy should and all ten fingers are still working, sensitive as ever." He grinned. "Let me show you."

I had questions—big questions—about the stunt, about my hands that now felt cool, and about him. In the end, though, as I leaned back against his shoulder and he bent over for the first teasingly soft caress to the back of my neck, I decided to postpone them.

17

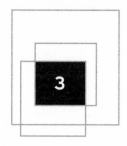

3

IT WAS LATER, when we were still in the back of the truck, leaning against the pillows, his arm around my shoulder, that I said more pointedly, "So what happened with the gag? I mean, why didn't you do the jackknife?"

He shrugged.

"Did the gear jam?"

"Hell, no!"

"Electrical—"

"No. The truck's always ready. I make sure of that."

Whoa! I'd sure hit a nerve there. Any decent stunt double keeps his equipment geared up; it's an insult to suggest otherwise. But if the problem wasn't the truck . . . "Then what was it?"

"Just a bad day."

"Come on! We're both pros. Bad day equals last day."

"I got distracted."

"Distracted by what?"

"I don't know. The traffic, the cranes, the containers."

"The shipping containers!" I couldn't believe he'd more than glanced at something so peripheral to the gag.

"Doesn't the script have a stowaway? Hides out to where, Shanghai?"

"That got cut."

"Too iffy?"

"No, something financial." I shifted away so I could look at him. "And this, is this another distraction? From my question? You're not getting a pass from me!" *I could have been killed!* "I have to know I can trust you the next time."

"Let it go. I'm dealing."

"Not very well if—"

He pulled me to him. "I thought we had something special."

"We do. Odd, but special. We see each other as often as the geese fly south and it works fine."

"Birds of a feather?"

"I guess." When he was gone I thought of him with more of a feeling than with specific memories or hopes, much less plans. I rarely called. And vice versa. But when he was here—like now—it was like the return of the hero in the last reel—heart pounding, *Gone with the Wind* music, a slo-mo race to embrace. And it was more than that. There was something unspoken, not thought out. The other men, the ones who'd loved me, ended up complaining that I was preoccupied, that there was a wall between us they couldn't breach. But Guthrie understood. He had a wall of his own, and that was fine with me; I'm not big on dragging forth secrets. I leaned back against his chest. "You know, I'm into Zen."

He laughed. "The number of times you've sprinted out of this very truck before dawn to go meditate, a lesser man would be insulted."

"The focus of Zen is the present, this moment, perpetually this moment. The past is stuff in the mind, the future illusion. But now—"

He ran his hand down my back. "Yeah, now!"

I had meant to say that that was the allure of being with him. We never talked past or future. The time with him was the intense now, magnified by its isolation. By knowing that, demands would never come. But this time that didn't hold. This time I needed to know. "Jed's toying with using us for another gag here, the one up on the crane—"

"How come they're not blue screening that back in the studio?"

"You'd think having me, or even the lead, trot across a beam on the ground and them plunk in the background later would make sense. But Jed's hot to see what more we can get out of it live."

"Great! More work for us!"

I nodded. In a shrinking profession, with animation taking big bites out of the live gag action, any chance we got to be indispensable was one we had to take, for ourselves as well as every other stunt double. "My point is, if you're driving below that crane arm, I need to know you're not going to be distracted. That happens and your rig taps the base of the crane, I'm dead."

"Look, today was a fluke. I wanted to find out . . ."

"So there wasn't any accident on 980."

"Nah. Sounded good at the time, right?" He seemed hesitant. *Shit.*

"Find out what?"

"Nothing."

"What, dammit?" *I'm not letting you off the hook.*

He pulled his arm back, skidding it along my shoulder, chafing my skin as it went. He turned to me, his eyes narrowed in an expression I couldn't categorize—shock, sorrow, calculation, fear? "My old phone died and I needed to call a guy. So I had to pull off the road and then I had a helluva time getting back on."

"It took you *hours* to get back on?" In the realm of no pressure, I'd gone from zero to a hundred! He was looking at me as if I were a stranger. I felt like one now, for sure. And so did he. "What is it? You've never let anything get in the way of work! Are you okay? What could possibly be so important?"

"I can't tell you. I don't want to keep making up excuses—not to you! But right now, I just can't tell you."

"You can't *not* tell me." I pulled away, now kneeling on the bed, facing him in the dimming light.

"Dammit, Darcy, lay off."

"No!"

A horn honked. He jumped for the door.

I grabbed his arm. "No! Tell me!"

"I can't talk about this, not yet." He sank back. "All the time I've known you . . . I've been as close to loving you as any woman ever . . ." His voice caught. "I've never asked anything. But now, can't you just trust me? I will never put you in danger again. Please . . . please trust me."

Could I? If I couldn't . . . I had to. "Okay."

He leaned over and kissed me in a way he'd never done before, so hard and sudden he pressed my lip into my teeth. I could feel him shaking. Then, as suddenly, he let go. "That nagging horn out there for you?"

"Omigod, is it eight already? That's my sister. If I don't move, she'll be in here in a minute."

"Don't you have a car?"

It was such a California reaction. "I live downtown. Couldn't find parking if I had one."

"Go, then. I'll call you tomorrow," he said, getting up to open the door. Then, with a glance at my injured hands, he swung me to the ground.

Automatically, I headed for the driver's door of Gracie's old station wagon and almost said, "Shove over," as I and any sane person who'd driven with her did. But no way could I drive with my hands burned and covered in goo. "Pop the passenger side, will you?"

"Hey, there's a handle." But she leaned over and shoved obligingly.

I slid in and closed it with a yank that was over before I felt the pain. "We should move before the fog gets worse," I said, to keep her from noticing my hands. Gracie's a doctor, an epidemiologist. If she saw my burns, her only question would be which emergency room. She'd have the best intentions; she'd dig her heels in halfway to India.

She'd stand over the ER doc. I'd get the best medicine in the Bay Area. But on this I was trusting Guthrie, the guy who knows what it takes to be back on the job in a couple of days.

In the rearview mirror I could see him sliding behind the wheel of a big black convertible. *Where'd he get that?*

"Stunt go okay?" Gracie asked.

"Single take. In the can." In fact, she hadn't asked her real question: *Are you okay?* But we were doing the kind of stylized greeting that, were we Japanese, would have been a series of ever lower bows. In her mind, stunt work was akin to walking naked into a level 4 lab. She didn't want to know the details—they just made the danger more blatant. And yet, in a way she could never admit, she was impressed.

But she didn't sound impressed now. "Didn't you hear me honking?"

I didn't answer, but instead just eyed the rearview mirror, watching Guthrie drive off. "Are you going to sit here, or are you going to drive?"

"So give!"

I stared out the windshield at the slabs of port buildings across the vacant roadway, trying to figure how to divert Gracie from whatever details she was after. Most of the second unit guys had already cleared off, but Jed Elliot was headed in this direction. "That's the second unit director. I'd better see what he wants."

Opening that wretched door sent a new wave of scalding pain through my hand. I shut my eyes against the pain and when I looked up, Elliot was almost in front of me.

His normally creased brow was rutted deeper, his jaw tight. "That's it for Guthrie. He's not worth the risk."

"What? But the gag was a take," I said, stunned.

"No thanks to him. I only called him on your say-so. We could have lost a whole day. You could have been run—"

"But I wasn't. I'm fine. The gag's fine. We're on schedule. We've just got the clean-up end to do."

"I can't chance it with him."

I couldn't let Guthrie get canned, not in the middle of a shoot. Not now! "At least talk to him. It was fluke. You'll see. You've got to give him a chance to explain."

"There's no point—"

"Hey, I trust him with my life! You want a rerun of the gag tomorrow, I'm ready."

"I don't . . . Okay. But he calls me. ASAP. Gives me the kind of explanation that lets me sleep tonight."

"Sure." Before he could reconsider, I turned, hurried back to Gracie's car, and slid in the still-open door.

"That your guy, in the convertible? He waved," she added.

"Yeah."

"Not half bad."

I couldn't let him get canned. Word would spread like a virus. Then no one would hire him without a triple-check. A career killer, and not great for me either. I pulled the seat belt as near to buckled as I could manage.

"What?" Gracie prodded. "What's going on?"

That was the last thing I wanted to discuss with Gracie. I felt like Guthrie ten minutes ago when he'd been facing me, reaching for excuses.

Suddenly the words just burst out of me. "Omigod, Gracie, he said he was as close to loving me as any woman ever."

Gracie jolted back in her seat. "You close to loving him, too?"

"Maybe. Probably. I have to catch him."

Gracie shot me a look like I was a teenager, and grinned.

"No, listen, this is serious. He's going to get himself canned. I don't have his new cell number. When we called this morning about the gag, we had to use his land line. Now I don't know where he's going. We've got to catch him before he gets out of here, before he's on the freeway and gone."

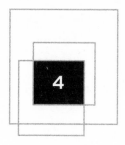

4

GUTHRIE WAS ON the freeway on-ramp before we cleared the port gate.

"He's heading north. Can't you make this thing go any faster?" I demanded, though I knew the answer only too well. Gracie downshifted—somewhere she'd heard that lower gears produced more power. The car lurched and we shot onto the freeway.

"He's up there, second to left lane." He was six or seven car lengths ahead. "We're lucky it's rush hour." Otherwise he'd have been long gone.

She nodded.

Ahead, Guthrie veered west toward the converging lanes of the toll plaza for the Bay Bridge. Why was I surprised? Guthrie's having some private thing to do in the city didn't bother me. What struck me was that black convertible. Where'd he come by that car? Surely he didn't tow it up here, though it would explain why he'd gotten to the set so late. Ditto, driving it into his truck and then having to find a loading dock to off-load it before using the truck in the gag. And chance holding up the entire production? I just couldn't believe that. But it sure would explain why any lame excuse beat the truth.

If the convertible wasn't his, what did *that* mean? There was more I didn't know about this man than I'd realized, and that was already a lot.

Gracie's car was no match for his, but she knew the tricks of the bridge plaza. By the time we cleared the toll booths we were only two cars back, though three lanes apart. "Get closer so we can honk."

"Relax. There's nothing we can do till we clear the bridge. Meanwhile, what's with your hands?"

"Just a little burn. No problem. I've got salve—"

"Let me see."

"You're driving!"

"I'm a doctor, let me—"

"Keep your eyes on the road!"

Gracie's number five in the Lott family. I'm number seven. All my older siblings view me as a daredevil whose risky ventures end up affecting them. Gracie sees me as a potential disaster for her to clean up, stitch up, or pull out of a hole. John, the cop (number two), is personally offended at my challenging any law, even gravity. And Gary, a year older than Gracie and a lawyer, sees me as a way to find out what he can't. Only Mike, who's four years older than me and was my buddy and protector the whole time I was growing up, totally approved. He disappeared twenty years ago, and none of us has really gotten over that, least of all me.

"This guy we're so busy tailing," she said. "He's something special, huh?"

"Yeah," I informed myself as much as her. "He is."

"So, then, this guy"—she was choosing her words with a lot more care than normal for my mega-hyper sister—"this guy . . . is he like Mike?"

"What? You think I'm trying to—"

"Incest? No. I just mean, is he, well, like Mike?"

"No!" What was she driving at? Why bring up Mike, now of all times? This conversation was going from bad to worse. I looked three cars ahead and a lane over at Guthrie, one hand on the wheel, his arm out the window, his silly ponytail flapping in the wind. She couldn't be right. I was *not*, sub-consciously, trying to replace the brother I'd adored and lost. So, how was Guthrie different? "Well, when you explained something to Mike, it was like he was the one person who truly understood, and cared. He was end-lessly patient—"

"Are you kidding? Mike, the kid who couldn't wait to be older? He begged Mom to get him into first grade early. He wrote up a new 'birth certificate' in crayon with a fake date."

"He did start early, though, didn't he?"

"Hardly because of that! Dad had done a favor for the priest and . . ." She shrugged. "Bad idea because now all his friends were a year ahead, so he really wanted to be older. When driver's license time came he just about drove Dad crazy—surely he knew someone, there had to be some way, some angle— But, it's Guthrie I'm asking about. So, what's the scoop?"

"Similar, yeah, but he's not Mike. He's all stuntman, a guy's guy. Everybody likes him because he's so into the gags and he'll take any chance this side of death. I mean sensible chances."

She shook her head. "Why? I've asked you before, repeatedly, and you've never given me a good answer. So this guy, what is it about look-ing into the void as a career choice that attracts him?"

"He's shifting left. Can you—"

"He'll be sorry. Trust me."

I didn't. If only I'd insisted on driving, burned hands be damned. I eyed his back, as if my gaze were some kind of virtual leash. "I can't say for Guthrie, but for me it's the next best thing to meditation."

"Pretend-meditation?"

I shrugged. "In zazen the idea is to be aware of everything without judging. Just noticing, not being the center of the noticing, you know?"

"Hmm."

"It's really hard. You're aware, then you're aware you're aware, then you're thinking about that, and soon you're thinking about dinner and sex."

"In that order?"

"But when you're doing a balance gag forty feet about the street, it's easy. No wandering mind; you're focused, totally at one with everything you're doing but also with everything that plays into it. You're not thinking about the wind; the wind is part of the whole gestalt of the gag, and so are you. When you get to the other side, you're high."

"I felt like that when I did the surgery rotation."

"Right. It's not meditation, but it's, well, clear."

"Damn!"

A car shot across our lane to the left-hand exit. Brakes screeched. Traffic stopped in all lanes but Guthrie's. The black convertible sailed right on.

"Catch him!"

"How? Fly?"

If only I were driving! "Cut left. Go!"

She rumbled left. Brakes squealed. A horn blew long and loud. But we were moving and Guthrie was still in sight.

"Good work, Gracie!"

She grinned. "He's heading for the Marina. He'll be in city streets. We'll get him there." She was leaning forward, looking lane to lane, checking the rearview.

As soon as we crested the hill, I saw the fog blowing thick from the Golden Gate. "Keep close. Don't lose him!"

"Not to worry."

Was Guthrie like Mike? The very thought made me squeamish, but I forced myself to deal with it. "Okay, here's the thing. When Guthrie turns up, he's totally focused on happy-to-see you, I mean me. But then we have the kind of weekend you don't want to consider in light of your brother. When we're talking, it's about the business, about gags he did, gags we could make better. Really focused. Hey, he's going to cut left."

"Where's he going at this hour? The Golden Gate?"

"Or the Palace of Fine Arts?"

"I've just about burned out my engine chasing him over the bridge and across town so he can feed the swans?"

There were only two cars between us now as we headed into the area of narrow streets and few outlets. The Palace of Fine Arts would be a good place to talk to him, a good, calm, bucolic spot for him to be in when he called Jed. It had been designed by Bernard Maybeck for the 1915 Pan Pacific Exposition and appeared to be a Greco-Roman temple. Maybeck had made it to crumble. But he hadn't counted on San Franciscans loving it too much to let it go. So, it had been restored early on and again in 2009. I'd catch up with Guthrie at the lagoon in front. It'd be quiet.

But it wasn't quiet, not hardly. Despite the fog, the street in front had been closed off and there seemed to be some kind of party or rally going on, spreading from the park lawn in front of the lagoon into the street. "No way we're going to get through here."

"Where's your guy? I can't believe this. I lost him!"

"No! You can't—"

My phone rang. I shrugged—this little venture was shot anyway—and answered it.

"Darcy?"

"It's him!" I mouthed to Gracie.

31

"Darcy . . ." His voice was muffled under the crackling of the phone, but still I could hear his hesitation.

I waited.

"I need to ask you something."

He was a jump-in guy; he never foreshadowed comments like this. "Okay?"

"I don't want to do this on the phone. I need to be with you. It's a big step."

What, dammit? Spit it out! "Okay. I live above the Barbary Coast Zen Center on Pacific by Columbus. Why don't you meet me in the courtyard?"

"How fast can you get there?"

5

"SLIDE OVER, GRACIE."

"You can't drive. Your hands—"

"I'll use my elbows." I pulled the driver's door open. "Move!" I didn't even feel pain when I grabbed the gear knob and smacked it into reverse, did a three-point over the curb, and cut back through the warren of the Marina.

Gracie braced her hands against the dashboard. "This isn't a set; it's a city street. Slow down. What the hell did he say?"

"He wants to ask me something—needs to do it in person!"

"Interesting."

I glanced at her but didn't say anything. I couldn't. Instead, I concentrated working out the fastest route across the city. Suddenly it struck me that Gracie wasn't saying anything either. I sneaked a peek at her. She looked like Guthrie'd sounded on the phone, like she had something stuck in her throat she couldn't cough up. "What?"

"This guy's important to you, right? Even if you've never mentioned him to *me*. It's obvious."

"Yeah."

"You haven't been excited like this, not over a guy, not since you moved back here anyway. You'd be happy if he stuck around?"

I nodded. "I guess that's true. I would."

"So, Darce, how many months till he'll be gone, like all the others?"

I gasped. I heard the sound before I realized it came from me. "Who the hell are you to talk—divorced and back living with Mom." It was a low blow.

But not low enough. "I'm one who knows, and so are you. Don't let this be the same old routine. You've got to give this thing—this guy—a chance."

"I intend—"

"You *intended* every time you met a guy, right?"

"Yeah, but—"

"No, listen, there's only one way to make the change. You have to get past Mike. We all do. For the lot of us, time stopped when Mike left. We went on and found things we could escape into, careers that don't give you time for extra thought. With your job, your mind wanders and, bang, you're dead, right? All of us, we look like we've moved on, but emotionally, we're all still sitting in Mom's living room waiting for the phone to ring or Mike to walk back in. And Mom, it's worse for her. Darce, it's got to stop."

"What do you mean?" She sounded like she'd rehearsed in front of a mirror. It scared me.

"We have to give it one last shot—all of us, throw everything into finding Mike. The difference is . . . that this needs to be the *final* search."

"Final, like what? Like the next time we get a lead, we blow it off? Are you crazy? What're we going to tell Mom then—'Oh, I heard Mike's living in Toronto, but it's too late to bother now?'"

Grace put a hand on my arm. It was shaking. Or I was. I slowed down so I missed the light, sitting there while cars shot across in front.

"Of course, after this we'll never ignore a lead. But then there'll be a difference: we'll admit the lead probably isn't going anywhere. We'll track it down, all right, just not with the desperate belief Mike'll be there. What I mean by the final search is, we pull out all stops, and if we don't find him, we admit to ourselves Mike's not coming back."

"That he's . . ." I couldn't bring myself to say it.

"Dead."

"No! I can't do that. No. I can't believe you're saying this. Maybe you didn't care as much—"

"Darcy, stop! You're a Buddhist. You're supposed to deal with life as it is, with what's real, not live in your own illusions, right? Mike is where he is. Your being desperate to have him back doesn't change that. It only screws up your life. Maybe he's living in Stockholm or Tashkent and he doesn't intend to come back. Maybe he's . . . well, any of the places we've endlessly considered. And maybe the most likely thing is true, that he didn't come right home that Thursday because he got killed then. Something happened to make him dead. That's reality, and we have to deal."

The light changed. I focused on traffic, shot through the light as it was turning. Mike had been *my* buddy. Grace had had Gary; I'd had Mike. The rest of them were all so much older—they'd been teenagers when I was a toddler. Only Mike had been my real family. She didn't understand. There was no way I could abandon him. "I've spent most of my life searching for him. I don't even know what I'd be without . . ." Without Mike? Without the search? I didn't even know what I meant. "What does Gary think? You talked to him, right?"

"It's taken him three wrecked marriages, but he gets it. He's got to be able to move on."

"And John?" I asked desperately. Surely, John, the cop, wouldn't close the case on his own brother.

"I haven't gone around lobbying for this. But I know how things are for every one of us, and for Mom. Look at her: she still lives in that ramshackle house; she never goes anywhere for more than a day; she always answers the door no matter how late—because she's afraid he'll show up once and then disappear again, and she couldn't forgive herself for missing him.

"Darce, Mom's got a chance now. Her friend Jess has got a timeshare in Hawaii in January—the whole month of January. Mom could go, instead of freezing here."

"Wow!"

"She's over seventy. She's spent the last twenty years waiting for a knock on the door that never happens. A chance like this, it may not come again. She can't give this up to sit home waiting for the call that's no more than a dream."

It was a moment before I could get out the words: "And if we do this and"—I swallowed hard—"the result is . . . bad? Then—"

"Then . . . then, it'll be even more important for her to get away, to not sit in that house knowing he's . . . he's never coming back."

"Here's the thing, Darce: you're the one who was closest to Mike, the one most destroyed by his disappearance. We all watched you tough through it. You had to wall everyone out; it was the only way you could deal, we knew that. You think no one noticed? We all noticed, especially Mom, but she insisted you had to handle things your own way."

I didn't dare look at her. We'd held back all these years; if we let go—

"So—" Her voice caught. "So, it's your call. The final search won't happen unless you say so."

It was a moment before I could say, "And if I do?"

"It will."

We were two blocks from the zendo. I pulled over to the curb, got out, and strode off before she could say anything else. If I tried to say anything,

I'd lose it entirely and everything I'd managed to control all these years would flood out. I needed to get inside and sit facing the wall, watching my breath until the barrage of thoughts became just thoughts again, until I could see what was extra and what was reality. How could I ever say Mike was dead? If there was the slightest chance—

Reality! Gracie hadn't said to ignore chances. But no way could I make the decision for everyone. *Reality*—she didn't mean that either.

I turned the corner onto Pacific, walking fast past Renzo's. I wasn't surprised that Gracie was sitting in her car outside the zendo when I walked up. I knew, as if I'd known for a long time and hadn't realized it, that she was right. As if I'd already mentally gone through all my protests, already done all my grieving for Mike. "Every moment we are born; every moment we die," Leo had said in his last dharma talk.

She'd already rolled down the window.

I said, "Okay. Do what you have to." Then I turned and walked into the courtyard. Behind me I heard her pull away.

I sat on a wooden bench in the semi-dark, oblivious to the damp cold. And by the time Guthrie arrived, I'd forgotten he was coming.

He walked up behind, lifted me off the bench, and pulled me against him. It was as if he was allowing me time to shift out of my barely conscious blame of him for the prospect of giving up my beloved brother. *Reality! Dammit, deal in what's real!* Reality was his warm, firm body against mine. I turned, ran my fingers behind his neck, and guided his head down to mine. He pulled me tighter against him, kissed me hard. And when he eased out of the kiss, he still held me there. I felt both great closeness and great distance.

Was it coming from him, or was it me?

After a moment, he asked, "Is this it, your Zen place?"

That sure wasn't the question I'd been expecting.

"The zendo?" I said, pulling myself together. "Yeah."

"The priest lives here, too?"

"Right. Our rooms are upstairs. They're really too close together for me to—for privacy."

"Is he here now?"

"I don't think so, but still I don't—"

"Do Buddhists have confession? Absolution?"

Huh! Boy, had I been misreading his intention here! "You mean like Catholics?"

He nodded.

"Why?"

"I'm asking for myself."

I slid my hands off his back and caught his in mine; despite the pain from my burns it seemed vital not to lose our physical connection. "We have a Bodhisattva ceremony, but it doesn't cleanse you of your sins; in fact, what we say is: 'All my ancient tangled karma, from beginningless greed, hate, and delusion, I now fully avow.' You're not cleansed, but admitting your part in the chain of events is, in its own way, cleansing."

When he didn't respond, I added, "Things are as they are. When you stop trying to pretend otherwise, things are clearer, and also easier. But you shouldn't be dealing with the assistant; you ought to be talking to the abbot."

"The guy who's not upstairs?" For the first time since he'd gotten here, he sounded like his normal, ironic self, for whom nothing was ever make it or break it, except when it came to work.

"Leo should be back by ten. I'm sure he'll see you if that's what you want."

"But it won't make any difference."

Even in the dim light I could see how edgy he looked, as if he'd been piloting a getaway car instead of merely driving across the Bay Bridge. "Then just what *would* make a difference?"

He slid his hands free. "I don't know."

"Guthrie, what is going on?"

"I can't—"

"Tell me. You say you're near to loving me." I shot a glance at his face, wary for a flinch that would show me he hadn't really meant it, but he stayed steady. "So, trust me. I'm near to loving you and whatever you tell me isn't going to change that."

"You don't know."

"I don't know events, but you and I, we've been close ever since we first laid eyes on each other. I do know you. There's something we share— I can't put it into words, but with you I'm at home in a way I am with no one else. There's a reason for that and it's beneath the surface of who you are. I'm not about to give that up. No event is going to change it."

He slipped behind me and wrapped his arms around me again. The warmth of his body felt good but when he spoke, I understood why he didn't want to look at me.

"I did . . . something . . . a long time ago. I didn't give it any thought, not then. Now, it's always with me."

So that was why he understood my own preoccupation. "If—"

"No! It doesn't matter about the absolution. Some things are beyond that."

I pulled loose. "Not true. Things change. All things. And you don't know how that's going to affect you. But look, Leo—the abbot—will be back in forty-five minutes. Let's walk up to North Beach and get a drink or some pizza. I'll leave him a note so he'll expect you."

It was a moment before he said, "Okay."

As we headed out of the courtyard I felt more like I was leading him than walking with him. I ached to ask what he could have done that left him in this shape, and yet I knew not to.

"The ceremony," he said as we turned onto Columbus toward the cafes of North Beach, "when do you have it?"

"The Saturday of the full moon."

"Tomorrow?"

"Right, tomorrow morning."

"I'll try that then, and see." He hugged me, turned, and strode back downhill. When I got back to the zendo, his car was gone.

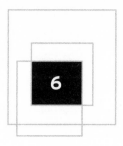

6

MOST ZEN STUDENTS greet the passing out of the sutra cards for the Bodhisattva ceremony with surprise. In the old monasteries, monks performed a long version of this acceptance of the fruits of their actions twice a month. They, surely, knew the ceremony by heart. Here, we do it monthly, and most students forget the date and are surprised to see the *zabutons*, the two-foot by four-foot mats, turned lengthwise to the altar instead of toward the wall. They are surprised they won't be sitting cross-legged on a *zafu*, facing the wall, but will be standing, bowing, kneeling as they do the call and response.

I was surprised only that Guthrie was not here. Still, I had to admit, not very surprised. A strange ceremony in a strange place is going to be less appealing when you're actually faced with it. As we chanted *All my ancient tangled karma, from beginningless greed, hate, and delusion, I now fully avow*, I kept wondering what was this thing that Damon Guthrie did years ago, without much thought, an act that now haunted him as much as Mike's disappearance did me.

We chanted three times, following with the vows. Afterwards, Leo bowed to the altar and to us in the zendo, and walked out, followed by his attendant of the day.

It was only then that I saw Guthrie, near the door. Without looking at me, he turned and followed the two of them.

Had it been someone else, I would have wondered if he'd tracked down Leo's phone number and scheduled an appointment. But Guthrie? He'd be trotting right up the stairs behind them, charming the shocked *jisha*, and making his case to Leo. Before I finished putting out the candle and straightening the cushions, he'd be sitting cross-legged in Leo's room, telling him . . . what?

I wanted to plant myself at the foot of the steps to snag him . . . to ask Leo . . . or at least to see Guthrie's face. But by the time I trimmed the candle and sifted the ash for the incense, I was lucky to catch him as he ran down the last step into the lobby and turned toward the outside door. "Hey! Where're you off to?" *What did you say upstairs?*

"To walk."

"Want company?"

"Later. I need to think."

"Oh. Sure."

He turned, then turned back, hugged me hard, and said, "Leo's right. But it's a lot to take in."

Right about what? What was hard to take in?

"You free for dinner?" He'd loosened his grip but was still holding me against him.

"Yeah."

"Come to the truck. It's parked where it was last night." He plunked a kiss on the top of my head, pushed a spare key into my pocket, and was gone.

The whole time I hadn't seen his face. To a stranger, his voice would have seemed normal, but not to me. I tried to rewind the reel of the last twenty seconds but didn't have enough information. I had to stop myself from racing upstairs to ask Leo, which would have been a really bad idea on a bunch of levels. Instead I walked into the courtyard, poured a cup from the after-service tea table, and introduced myself to a pair of newcomers. Then I went to the gym, spent an hour in the weight room, and took a yoga class. I left my phone on, bad luck as that is when you want to hear from a guy.

The only call was from my brother John as I was walking out.

"You're serious about this?" he demanded. No pause for pleasantries. Not that I'd expect it from "the enforcer."

"About what? Do you mean the all-out search for Mike?"

"All or *nothing*?"

Was he furious, frightened, or merely affronted? After all, he was the professional, the police detective who'd been on the case for two decades. "Nothing's what we've got now. Much as this may terrify us, we've got to do it for Mom."

"Do you imagine there's any hint of irregularity I haven't investigated?"

"Listen, you've turned night into day, you've followed every lead, you've probably spent more money on p.i.'s than Gary has on alimony. And time! John, I think no person on earth could have done more."

"Well, I'm not the only one," he said, clearly taken aback. "Gary's been under my feet the whole time re-interviewing leads because he thinks he can do it better."

Because you're a heavy-handed cop and Gary's had years of negotiating settlements and charming juries.

"And Katy's kept Mike in the news. Like coming up with the earthquake retrospective year," he pointed out.

Katy had used all her newspaper connections to keep Mike's story alive the entire time since he disappeared. The twenty-year anniversary of the Loma Prieta earthquake was a natural for a newspaper series. Weaving Mike's story into newspaper stories had become natural for my oldest sister. "She's behind the review of all the buildings in the Marina?"

"No. That's from the building trades unions. Big waste of time. Dad did some of the work there. Had me on the sites with him the summer before I went into the academy." He paused. "Even Janice checks the missing persons' sites."

Even Janice. What did that mean? I'd done that only once. Once was plenty. You stare at the dead whose pictures were taken in the morgue, or at faces reconstructed from their skeletons years after their bodies had been tossed in the woods. Janice—referred to as "the nice one" of my older sisters—was sure tougher than she seemed.

"I'm telling you, we've covered every lead. But now—I'm not going to say this in front of Mom—but now if we find Mike, it'll either be by some crazy fluke, or because he just walks in the door."

I nodded. Not that he could see that.

"Guys his age who go missing—and late teens, early twenties is the most common—they're naïve. They think they're invincible. They hitch a ride; it doesn't occur to them they could be climbing into danger. Girls, they ought to know better, but the boys, they figure they can take on anyone. Makes them easy marks."

I couldn't believe he was saying that, not about Mike. "Do you really think that's what happened to—"

"No. I don't think that. I'm telling you what any Missing Persons division guy would. And if it was someone else's brother, I'd think that, too." A muffled noise came through the phone, possibly my brother's attempt to get control of himself. "It's the easiest thing in the world for a con man to take in a decent person. But to get a kid who's angry, depressed, distracted, not paying even normal attention—no contest. If you—"

"I get the picture!"

"So, I don't see how a big family meeting's going to do anything but upset Mom."

I let out a long breath. "We've done everything. At the same time we missed something. Obviously."

"Okay. Be there at seven."

"What? Tonight?"

"Yeah."

"I can't."

"What do you mean?"

"I have a date."

"A date that's more important than finding Mike?"

"Can't we reschedule?" I felt like shit.

"No. Gary's got a deposition in L.A. in the morning. He's cutting it close as it is. Like you said, we're doing this for Mom. Just be there." Then he hung up.

I hit number three on my speed dial and got my sister's answering machine, which was just as well. "Dammit, Gracie, how come *you* insist we have this final search for Mike, but now it's billed as *my* meeting, and it's set for seven tonight, and if I miss it to go have dinner with the guy who thinks he loves me, then I'm a traitor to the family! No wonder only children are more likely to marry."

I called Guthrie. No answer. I was about to leave a message but couldn't, not with things like they were with him, and with me. I rounded the corner on Columbus, coming abreast of Renzo's Caffè. There, at a table, sat my brother Gary, looking ready to pounce.

I glared at Renzo. Renzo's an old hand in this part of town, a guy with a lot of opinions and no hesitancy in sharing them. Now he said nothing, finished making an espresso, and set it and a frittata in front of me.

"This meeting." Gary leaned toward me, as if anything could be a secret in such a tiny space. "It's a bad idea, very bad."

"Postpone it! You're the one—"

"I can't. Guy I'm deposing's leaving the country tomorrow night. Anyway, it's not the time, Darce, it's the meeting. Mom'd never admit it, but Mike was her favorite. Lucky for the rest of us we were too old to be jealous much."

"But?"

"But there're things Mom doesn't want to know. Things you don't."

"What do you mean?"

"Exactly."

"What is it I don't want to know?"

"If you hadn't set up this powwow, none of this would be happening."

I grabbed his arm. "Tell me, dammit."

He exhaled and leaned back as if to balance on the back legs of his chair, a trick I'd seen him use to distract opponents before. Now, in the café's metal chair, he reconsidered. "Lore is that you were the wild one. Okay. Mike, meanwhile, was the happy one and was happy to keep you from breaking your neck. Everyone believes that because he made it easy for them. But I was the brother nearest him, so he wasn't quite the little kid to me that he was to John and the older girls and to Mom and Dad. Here's the thing, Darce. Your wildness gave him cover."

I sipped the espresso, for once barely tasting it.

"How many times did he take you downtown and stop in some place you couldn't go? How often did he say he'd meet you in an hour? And you'd never have told anyone, right?"

"Yeah, but it was just head shops, or porn—teenage boy stuff."

"Maybe. No, really, maybe you're entirely right. I'm just saying that's an example. Until now there's never been a suspicion he wasn't with you every moment he took you anywhere."

"Are you saying that I—"

"Not you. Look, here's how it was. When I was a kid John drove me crazy."

"He drove us all—Mr. Enforcer. It's only now that I'm beginning to get past it."

"Me, too. But being three years younger than the enforcer made me what I am."

I laughed. He was the best defense attorney in the city. He could outwit any D.A., impress the judge, and charm the jury while doing it.

"It took me years to master getting around John. When Mike came along, I taught him all I'd learned. It wasn't till near the time he disappeared that I realized he'd done me one better. He was getting around John and me, too."

"Doing what?"

"That I don't know. But if this comes out, John's going to be hurt, and Mom."

Stop! Don't make me choose! But when it came to Mike, for me there was never any question. "Gar, it's Mike's life we're talking about. If some of us get our feelings bruised, so be it."

"If, suddenly, after twenty years of each of us chasing every tiny lead, *if* this unearths him, yeah, fine. But here's the likelihood—we don't find him, and the only thing that changes is the scabs we pull off each other."

I stared down at the table. Each of the siblings had a tag: John, the enforcer; Janice, the nice one; Katy, Numero Uno; Gary, the Can-Do-Kid; Gracie, the scrapper; me, the wild kid. Only, Mike, I suddenly realized, was untagged. He was Mike—no need to say more. Or maybe it'd been that each of the rest of us viewed him differently, so one label couldn't suffice. Maybe Gary was right about Mike. The notion seemed at once shocking and yet so right, I had to wonder why I hadn't seen it before.

Still, it unnerved me that Gary, Mr. Optimist, saw nothing but bad coming out of this search.

I needed to be at that meeting to protect . . . whoever. I was going to hear what my brothers and sisters had been unable to say before. They were right that I was the one who cared most about Mike, and dammit, that made me the one responsible for seeing that this time, once and for all, we got the search right. If there was any chance at all of some clue, lead, something Mike had said that could be interpreted differently now, I had to recognize it.

But I needed—wanted . . . longed—to be with Guthrie. All the years of our odd, intermittent relationship had led to this moment when he was ready to face his past, and do it with me. It was the only time he'd ever needed me like this. I couldn't blow him off.

Cut off your right arm? Or your left? How could I—

I reached across the table to Gary and said, "Give me your car keys."

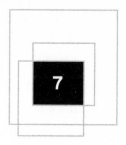

7

ON THE WAY to pick up Gary's car, I called Guthrie again. Still no answer. Any other time—but this wasn't any other time. I wanted to go back and knock on Leo's door and have him tell me Guthrie was okay, that now, after their talk, Guthrie was going to be feeling better and better. But Zen interviews didn't work that way. They're not salve. Often they pull back the scab and say, "Look!"

I hit redial. Again, the call went to his recording. There could be a dozen good reasons for Guthrie not answering or—

I left a message that I was on my way.

The wind was whipping down Montgomery Street, pushing handfuls of fog into my face. If I got across the bridge to Oakland in half an hour, I'd have at least a few minutes, see that he was okay, spend a little time before I had to tell him why I was abandoning him at the one time he really needed me. *If* I did.

But how could I leave Mom and everybody sitting around a table waiting like we'd all done day after day when Mike disappeared?

I turned the corner to the garage—the wrong garage! What was I thinking? Gary kept his big client car here, not the Honda he was lending me. The Honda was in a lot across from his office half a mile away. Talk about not focusing! Now there'd be no time to do more than say sorry to Guthrie.

In any other city I could hail a cab! I turned and ran full out, beating the pavement so fast I couldn't think. Sprinting, I made the light at Broadway and in twenty minutes was poking the key in the ignition. The heel of the key jammed into my hand. Pain shot to my elbow. I shook it off.

The Bay Bridge was crowded. I weaved in and out of traffic. The bandages cut into my palms. I loosened my grip, but in a minute I was back clutching the wheel.

Traffic just about stopped in the Treasure Island tunnel, and when I finally got onto the eastern span of the bridge it wasn't much better. Cars were shifting right. In the low-slung Civic I was practically sitting on the roadway; every van and SUV that cut in front of me blocked the view. If there was an accident ahead, I'd never spot it. I was almost to the toll plaza before I saw the smoke spreading up, coming from the Port of Oakland.

Omigod, fire! No wonder he hadn't answered the phone.

Was it anywhere near his truck? Too hard to tell.

The van in front of me slammed on its brakes. I swung left inches in front of a truck and kept moving. The fire looked huge.

The port's loaded with imports—cloth, plastics, stuff that'll burn.

At the gateway, I waved my production company card as I raced through. Sirens blared, but I ignored them, and the smoke, too. I didn't look at the plume. Instead I kept my eyes down, retracing the route I'd taken yesterday. It didn't matter where the fire was; all I cared about now was Guthrie.

A giant red fire truck swung around me. I hadn't even heard its siren in all the distraction of my panic. The smoke turned thicker. I could barely see anything but the fire engine's flashing lights. It swung left onto the pier. *Our* pier.

I stared in horror as it raced to the burning white mass—a big light-colored eighteen-wheeler. Guthrie's ride.

A police car came out of nowhere, blocking me. Red lights flashed.

"Get that car out of here!" It was a bull-horned voice. "Back up! Now!"

"Guthrie!" All I could do was scream his name.

The cop jumped out, instantly in my face. "Back up!"

"My friend!" I pointed to the burning truck.

"There's no-one—nothing—in there. Nothing but gas. Understand?"

I got it. No one could be alive in a fire like that. If he was—but he wouldn't have been. No way! "He's not there!" I said aloud. "Not there."

Before the cop could shout at me again, I shifted into reverse and shot back up the pier.

Something was behind me! I braked with a screech mere feet in front of a big white truck cab.

This was Guthrie's truck! *Thank God!* I jumped out and raced for the cab door. "Guthrie!" I pulled myself up to look through the window. "Guthrie!"

The cab was empty.

I raked my pocket for the key.

Behind me the cop was yelling.

Where was Guthrie? Was he in the back? I blinked hard against the smoke. "Guthrie! Are you in here?"

I felt for the flashlight beside the door, sprayed the room with the light. Empty. "What the hell are you doing?" a fireman yelled. "We got a blaze to fight here. It's moving this way. You're blocking our access. Get your truck out of here or we're going to push it off the pier!"

It's not my truck! I don't know how to get the damn thing in gear! I said, "Yessir!"

I jumped into the driver's seat, balled up a jacket I found, and crammed it behind my back so I could reach the pedals. Then I switched on the engine. My heart was hammering against my ribs. Turn the wheel wrong in a truck and you're sunk. I could barely breathe. *Think!*

Another fire engine swung around to my left. The sirens reverberated off the building on one side and the huge cargo ship on the other. *Think!*

Where was Guthrie?

Focus! The truck!

In the gag, he'd driven the truck around the corner, but I didn't have to do that. I just needed to back out straight.

Tentatively, I shifted and very slowly let out the clutch.

The truck inched forward.

I slammed on the brake. Too hard. I stared at the gear stick. That had to be reverse. Had to! I shifted again, let out the clutch again. The truck jolted backwards.

What was behind me? Where was the rearview? I checked the side mirror and inched the truck backward, clutching the wheel as hard as I could.

Sirens screamed. The guy was yelling again. I didn't have time for him. I let the clutch out a little more.

He yelled louder. "What the hell are you doing with my truck?"

I concentrated on the clutch.

"Get out of my truck!"

"Guthrie?"

He was black with smoke. Tears streaked down his cheeks.

He slid in the driver's side and we passed the pedal so smoothly the engine didn't even cough. In less than a minute the rig was on its way out, and the fire was receding behind us. The first thing he said was, "I gotta spend some time teaching you to drive."

"Hey—" Then I was coughing.

"Listen, you were great. But when we've got a production company, we can really ramp up the truck gags. I've been thinking . . ."

Suddenly, his attention snapped back to the smoky landscape around us. "I gotta put some more distance between those flames and this rig."

He was in his element, feet on the pedals, arms curved into the wheel, eyes straight ahead, an unconscious smile playing on his mouth. Like the fire never existed at all. Like we were on to the next scene. I was so relieved—giddy with relief—I almost slipped over onto the driver's seat with him and snuggled under his arm.

He took the corners fast but nothing like he'd be doing in a shoot, moving through the gears the way I did with a standard four on the floor. I was making mental notes of the sequence, of his timing, of the pull of each gear.

"Always learning, eh, Darcy?"

"No novices in Lott and Guthrie!" It was way too early in our sudden relationship for that kind of commitment, but I didn't care.

"Listen, this isn't pie-in-the-sky stuff. There are great drivers—not like me, but, you know, good ones—"

I laughed.

"And there are great high fall artists—not up to your standard—" Even at this speed, his eyes never left the road. "But the combo—no one's doing that, at least not like we can. We can cushion the roof of this baby so you could hit it at forty feet moving—piece of cake."

He pulled over near the gate. In the side mirror the fire looked like a funnel cloud, just not moving. He gave me a quick kiss, and then, as if choreographed, we both jumped out to check the rig for fire damage. All stunt doubles are careful—at least those who have a long life in the business—but no one's more obsessive than those of us who do high falls. One loose tie-down overlooked, and splat. We've all heard the tales of catcher failure, wind not factored in, or more bones broken than we even realized we possessed . . . of death. I surveyed the trailer shell with that same professional obsessiveness while Guthrie squat-walked underneath where an ember could still be smoldering near a gas line and blow us into the Bay.

Even with my help, the check took an hour. By the time he declared the rig okay, the fog was moving in for the night.

"Another couple of minutes and I'd've been working by flashlight," Guthrie said, emerging from under the bed. He straightened so slowly it looked like he was being cranked up by gears.

He slipped his arm around my shoulder and we leaned back against the siding. We stared at the fire's black plume against the gray fog. The heat of his body flooded into me so only my right hand was still cold and I reached up to slip my fingers through his.

"You're a different man than the guy who was so down on himself yesterday."

"You suggesting I'm unpredictable?"

"I'm applauding."

"You've got your guy Leo to thank."

What did Leo say? I can't ask. Tell me!

As if intuiting my thoughts, he repeated the sutra, "All my ancient, tangled karma I face up to."

"Avow."

"What?"

"You fully avow the karma, but I guess it's the same thing."

"I don't know. It's hard to believe I wasted all this time avoiding it. I sweated for weeks at a ranch in a hole in the desert trying to deal with it. And then I have one chat and all of a sudden it seems so clear that facing up to it is the answer. How could I not see that before? It's crazy."

"But us, being together, that's crazy, and yet it's not. It's like you run toward a cliff for an hour and then in one step you're over."

"Pleasant analogy, that."

I shrugged, scrunching closer under his arm.

"Whatever you—"

In a split second he'd shot a foot away from me. "Whatever I did? You want to know?"

"I didn't say—"

"But you do, don't you?"

"Hey, where'd this come from?"

He turned, strode off toward the fire. *Really unpredictable!*

I raced after him, grabbed his arm, turned him toward me. "Yeah, I want to know. Because whatever it is, it's okay. No, wait! Don't start that business of my not being able to say without knowing first, just fucking tell me. Did you kill someone?"

He looked down at me and our gazes locked. "I used to think that 'worse than death' was hyperbole. Now I know better."

I just buried my face in his chest and pulled him tight to me. I realized he was shaking. In that moment it was as if I was both present and also looking down on the scene. And then, providing the backdrop to his grief, like an over-the-top movie set, were the fire and the sirens and the flashing lights, and it was almost too much. "How?"

"I let him die."

You stood there and watched him die? "How?"

"I walked away."

"So, you were a bystander?"

"I was in it up to—as high up as you can go. I could have . . . but I didn't. If I had . . . but I didn't. Because, see, I wanted to save my own skin. It's the old story about guilt. A thousand plots make this point. My ancient twisted karma."

A deafening bang came from the pier. Fire shot up.

"Lucky you got my rig out of there when you did. That fire's going to eat up the pier. Look how fast it's coming—"

"Omigod, Gary's car! I jumped out of it to get the truck. It's still back there! Gary's Honda!"

"Flip me the keys!"

"They're in the car." I ran full out, but he was taller, faster. Smoke was filling my mouth; I could taste it. By the time I rounded the corner onto the pier, Guthrie was nearly at the door.

A police car—light bar flashing—sped toward us.

"Deal with them!" I yelled.

The cop screeched up five yards from the car. Guthrie was at his door before he could get out.

With a last burst of power, I dashed for Gary's car, swung in, and did a 180, pushing the passenger door so it popped open right next to Guthrie. He leapt in and I hit the gas.

We rounded the corner, laughing.

He leaned over and kissed me sideways. I could just see over his ear to drive. "We're going to make one helluva team!"

I pulled up next to his truck and reached for him.

My cell phone rang.

I shrugged it off and pulled him to me for a long, giddy kiss, the kind we'd be sharing a lot after triumphs by Lott and Guthrie.

The phone started up again. I shrugged and clicked it on.

"Darcy!"

My brother John, I mouthed.

"There's been a—"

"Do you have any idea what time it is?"

"—a fire—"

"We all waited for you. We sat around the table, Darcy, waiting for you. You get us all here and then don't show."

"I can still—"

"Too late." The phone clicked off. I could picture him stabbing his thumb into the button and slamming the phone shut.

"Oh, shit, it's after eight."

Guthrie was staring at me. "What?"

"I was supposed to be at Mom's at seven. Shit. There was a family meeting; they all think I arranged it. They're . . . pissed doesn't begin to describe it." I squeezed his arm. "I've got to go."

"I'll come with you."

"No. Trust me, you do not want to face this scene."

□ □ □

He was deciding where to move the truck as I headed for the freeway. I made it almost to the gate before admitting I needed a few minutes to get myself together before heading onto the bridge. I pulled over and checked messages and got an earful.

7:46 P.M. "Darce, you okay?" Gary asked. "Call me. My car, is it okay? If you haven't driven it into the Bay, you're still in deep shit with everyone. Seriously."

7:48 P.M. "Jeez, Darcy"—it was Gracie—"Jeez! I hope you're okay— I know you're okay—but where the hell are you? Call me before you call anyone else." I heard what sounded like a snort. "You're not going to want to talk to anyone else in this family. *Believe* me. Jeez!"

8:00 P.M. Mom: "You know I trust your judgment and don't worry about you. But Darcy, you call me right now and tell me you're okay."

I called. Then I headed across the bridge, deposited Gary's car in the slot by his office, and checked messages while I trudged back to the zendo.

Only one: 8:10 P.M. From Guthrie. "Listen, your brother's a cop, right? I need to meet him tomorrow, first thing. Early, before there are people around. Palace of Fine Arts. 6:00 A.M. I'm turning off my phone. Sorry to be . . . Love you."

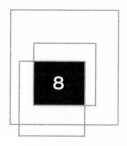

8

JOHN SQUEALED TO a stop by the zendo at 5:45 and I slid into the passenger seat. Fog lay over the city like foam on a crash set. His lights were on, but by the time he reached the corner he was out-driving them.

"Gonna be worse in the Marina," he grumbled.

"Guthrie's not from here; he wouldn't have known."

"He could've checked. Hell, he could've just hauled himself over to Mom's last night when we were all there."

Outside, the world was gray, momentarily broken by spots of white as a car passed. The fog muted out so much that in the vacuum the engine roared.

"Why not your zendo? Why didn't he come there instead of dragging us across town?" My brother was clearly at his grousing best. "Is he staying in the Marina and just making it easy on himself?"

"He wouldn't do that."

"Why are you so sure? What do you know really about him, anyway?"

I was asking myself that very question.

Trying another tack, John asked, "What is he when he's not working?"

"I don't see him then."

"Not even curious? Give me a break. But of course you don't ask. You care about him, so you need to believe in him. How many times have I pointed out, when you care about someone, in your mind he can do no wrong?"

"Not true," I protested. "Not any more."

He grunted, and I was happy to let it go. He was entitled, I figured. Hadn't he dragged himself out here for me? Besides, I knew he was right. I was always trying to be objective about people I cared about . . . but, damn, it was hard. How could I *not* jump to their defense? Hell, I didn't even let people badmouth him, despite the litany of good reasons.

But he'd set me to worrying. I'd assumed Guthrie slept in his truck, at the set. *Don't assume*, Leo always said, meaning look at any event with fresh eyes.

"Fog's going to be so thick at that end of the Marina we won't be able to see the Palace from the street. We'll be lucky to make out the lagoon. Whatever made your boyfriend choose there of all places?"

Why *was* Guthrie focused on this area? "Yesterday, Gracie and I followed him over here, but we lost him behind a party or demonstration of some kind."

"Swans."

"No, it was people."

"Swans," John repeated. "What I said was what I meant. City's threatening to relocate some of the ones in the lagoon again. That always sends the fur and feathers wackos into the streets with signs. It's been going on for years. Don't you remember? Mike dragged you to one of their protests—I chewed him out good."

"Hey, Mike didn't drag me. He went along because I needed a ride." I couldn't help but smile. "He never told you that part, huh? Not that there was any danger. A hundred or so people, high-end houses behind us, swans and ducks in front. Biggest danger would have been falling in the water and that's probably two feet deep. Mike ran into a girl he'd met when he worked with Dad a few blocks from there the summer before. I had to hunt him up to get my ride home."

My oldest brother was shaking his head. "You just never can see him as less than perfect, even now."

"What?"

"There you were, a kid taking honors classes, into track and gymnastics and dance and God knows what else. Half the time you didn't even make it home to dinner. How'd you have time to get so passionate about swans? Was it Mike who fed you stories about the swan danger? So he could run into this girl?"

"I may be naïve, but you are the master of conspiracy theory. Why would Mike go to all the trouble of doing the setup and carting me over here, on the chance of meeting a girl he liked? He was star quality. All he had to do was pick up the phone."

"But he didn't. How do I know? Because that demonstration was a couple of weeks before he left. I scoured the city for the girl. I'm surprised you don't remember me asking you what he said about her. You never saw her, remember? You took his word about her. But there was no girl."

"No girl *you* found."

"Will you stop! Stop believing your picture—"

Don't assume! Had I assumed about Mike? How much? Omigod, had I always assumed? It was too much to deal with, especially now, in the car with the brother who'd be only too ready to pounce. "You're right."

"What?"

"You're right, John." It shocked me as much as it did him. "Maybe there was no girl; maybe he just got sick of me and the swans."

"Or maybe something else."

"Yeah." *Game over.*

Finally he muttered, "Damn fog."

At least he'd stopped bitching about Guthrie. Worried as I was about him, I was thankful for this small respite. The fog was blowing thick across the windshield. The wipers were on high but couldn't push it back fast enough.

"Those were the days," he said, "working with Dad. He didn't run his own business yet, and so he was pulling in a lot of overtime. Man, were we wiped out by the time we rolled into the house. But, I'll tell you, it was the perfect summer job. Dad offered it to Gary but after one summer he was too good to smudge his hands."

"Gary said he didn't want to be accused of working a job that ought to be union."

"He was nineteen! And clueless! How'd he ever know he was gonna be a hotshot lawyer back then?"

I wondered but let it drop and John seemed glad to also. For him, reliving happy family memories was a peace offering. But it was also an idealized picture of the family. I'd heard a lot of this before, but I was glad to let him settle into a better frame of mind.

He turned into the maze that made up the Marina district. I gauged we were blocks away from our destination, but it was just a guess.

"But by the time Mike got there, Dad was top dog. Those were the days! Running three or four crews, heaviest thing he'd be hoisting was a clipboard. You just about had to make an appointment to catch up with him. And you know Mike," he said in that way we fell into talking about him, as if we'd seen him yesterday and he'd be dropping by tomorrow. "He gets along with anyone. He liked it so much he took the fall semester off. By the end of his time there, before the quake, he could have handled any job on the site, maybe not journeyman level, but well enough. Dad was figuring he'd be an engineer or maybe an architect. He took it hard when Mike just walked away . . . I mean from the job."

As opposed to when he walked out the door and disappeared. Dad had taken that hard, too, but what with all the reconstruction after the Loma Prieta quake then, he was gone working dawn to dark.

"Did your guy bother to mention what corner he'd be on? Unless he's got himself surrounded by light bars there's no way we're going to see him."

The thought had struck me, too. The park's two blocks long and another wide with a lagoon in the middle and the reconstructed Greco-Roman temple behind that. "He'll be looking for us."

We turned left. The fog suddenly seemed less compressed, as if it were released from the narrow passage between buildings and was spreading over the lagoon.

"This is it. Let me out."

"Hang on. Let's see if we see him."

I reached for my phone. Before I could peer through the contacts list, John recited Guthrie's number. "Amazing." I dialed. He lowered the windows, but there was no ringing, only icy gusts. "Maybe he's got his phone turned off."

"So it doesn't disturb the people across the street inside their houses? Dream on."

"Hell, just let me out! We've gone the length of the park. I'll start back on the path here and meet you back at the far corner."

"We'll drive back. If he doesn't show, then we get out."

I nodded, though, of course my brother didn't see me. Out the window, I knew, was the lagoon with its demonstration-worthy fowl tucked sleeping among the grasses at the scalloped edges of the water. Bushes sprouted around the building and the water. Trees overhung. A walkway followed the water's edge. Not a place where noise carries.

John slowed. "You hear anything?"

"Zip." Still, Guthrie couldn't miss our car.

"This guy . . . How do you know—"

"If he's reliable?"

"If he's anything."

"If he wasn't reliable, he wouldn't have work. Movie companies don't waste money on stunt doubles who oversleep." Guthrie'd always been dependable. Except yesterday. Except now. "Let me out!"

"Wait, I'm turning around." He hung a U, his headlights shining off the cars parked beside the park, showing the white of the fire hydrant, the chrome of a car on the grass.

I was out in an instant, staring at the black sports car on the grass that had to be Guthrie's.

"On the grass!" John came up behind me. "Does he park on his own lawn? But, of course, you don't know." He shone a flashlight onto the dashboard, the floor, the wet seats. "Looks like he got out and closed the door. What kind of guy doesn't bother to put up the top in this kind of weather?"

"Give him a fucking break, will you? It's six in the morning. Maybe he didn't stop to make himself more comfortable so he didn't hold us up. Did you even consider that?" Before he could retort, I yelled, "Guthrie! Guthrie!" I strained to hear his voice, his shoes slapping the macadam. Silence. "I'll go this way"—I motioned north toward the Golden Gate— "you go around the corner and on."

"6:10. Meet back here by 6:30 no matter what."

I started off, but he grabbed my arm. "No matter what. Agreed?"

Where could he be? This was crazy.

"Darcy, you know he could just be in the bushes taking a leak."

"Sure. You have another flashlight?"

He gave me his. I didn't wait to see if he had a spare. I ran down the sidewalk by the street. "Guthrie?" I stopped, straining to hear any kind of response, then ran on another twenty yards and called again. It wasn't night any more; the world was a dirty gray. At this hour on a Monday morning, cars would be pouring in from Marin County to the north, flowing along Doyle Drive onto Marina Boulevard fifty yards beyond the park. But right now there was no rumble of trucks, no sounds of brakes or horns. Across the street no lights shone from houses, no cars pulled out of driveways or away from the curb. And no one walked, ran, or called out from the park.

I started back, this time cutting across the grass to take the path next to the lagoon. "Guthrie!"

Water lapped softly, stirred by the wind. I thought I heard ducks or swans fluttering in their nests, but it might have just been the water. I aimed the light under the bushes. No birds and definitely no Guthrie. Where was he? I checked my phone again, even though it had been on since the last time I looked at it. "Guthrie!"

Had he had a heart attack? He was too healthy. But seemingly healthy people drop dead. The stress? Was he lying there collapsed on the grass? I arced the beam low across the lawn. Or worse, could he have fallen in the water? That was absurd, not Guthrie, the guy who'd done a forty-foot-high fall last year. He'd broken ribs then. Maybe they never healed, or pierced his lung, or bled or—

He couldn't be in this shallow lagoon, but I shone the light across the water anyway, then down into the water along the side of the raised edge. A couple of birds squawked. I almost dropped the flashlight. "Guthrie! Are you here?"

The light hit something white. Round and white, like a shoulder, or a butt, or the top of his head. "Oh, God!" I stepped up on the ledge, leaned over the water. It couldn't be— The light was shaking in my hand, the wind icing my sweaty face. It just couldn't— I leaned far over, bracing my foot on the side of the ledge to keep from falling in. The light shone brighter, clearer—on a stone.

Relief flooded through me. For an instant I forgot where I was and almost lost my balance. Then, as suddenly, I was livid. Where the hell was he, anyway? Did he get lost in the fog? Forget his phone? Goddamn him! Maybe, like Mike, he'd walked off to a new life. Maybe he was in a cab on the way to the airport.

"Guthrie!"

I was almost back to the middle of the park. I heard John's voice calling his name and getting louder. Our flashlight beams crossed in the water and then on the lawn.

"Did you see *anything*?" I asked. "Anything at all?"

"No. We're going to have to wait for better light. We might as well go hunt up some breakfast and—"

"John! He *said* he'd be here. If he changed his mind he would have called. He's got to be here. Or maybe he went around to the temple and got lost."

"I was there."

"Can't you call the crime scene techs and get some light here? Or a dog. I could call Mom and she'd bring Duffy."

"Cool off. It's already dawn above the fog. It'll be light soon."

"Maybe he got sick and knocked on the door of one of those houses across the street and—" I knew I wasn't making sense.

"When he had a phone? And his car's right here?"

"But if he was really sick—"

"He'd call 911."

"And they'd come and take him to the hospital and that'd explain his car here."

"You can call the hospitals while we eat breakfast."

"I'm not leaving here!"

My brother sighed. "Suit yourself. But . . . look, I've been at hundreds of scenes like this. I could get backups and techs here, but the only thing they'd do would be to walk around in the half-dark and trample any clue that might be here. If you want to walk around the lagoon again, I'll go with you, but I'm telling you now, it's not going to make any difference."

He was right. But I couldn't just leave. I didn't know what to do. All at once, I felt empty and exhausted. I stood on the sidewalk, grimly looking back at Guthrie's car on the grass. I could barely bring myself to say, "We should pop the trunk."

"You're absolutely positive it's his car?"

I shone the light down on the license plate. A blotch of mud covered the first number. I moved in closer, squatted. "Omigod!"

"What?"

"Feet. Look." I raced to the front of the car and aimed the light underneath. This time the white shape was no stone. What I saw was a pale white scalp with a fringe of brown hair around it.

"Guthrie! Are you okay? Damon! Answer me! You don't need to move, just grunt. Or something. Anything! Please, Guthrie!"

I shoved myself under the bumper.

Something was pulling me back—John.

"We've got to get this off him."

Sirens cut the air. My brother said something.

"Help me!" I screamed at him.

The car was so low. The grass was wet, the wheels sunk down into it. The undercarriage had to be pressing on Guthrie. And he wasn't answering me. "The side. We can lift the side of the car and flip it. Come on, here!"

John's arms were around me, imprisoning me. I shoved but I had no leverage. Brakes squealed, doors slammed, shoes hit the sidewalk.

"Backups," my brother said. "We've got three more nearby. Do you hear the sirens? In a minute we'll be able to lift this car up off him. In just a minute . . . you tell him that, okay?"

I bent, face against the grass, reached in, and took his hand in mine. I didn't dare shine the light in his eyes. Was he breathing? I couldn't tell from his chest. His hand was cold. I pressed his finger between mine, the way we'd done in the trailer yesterday. "It'll be okay," I reassured him just as he had me about the burns on my hands. "We ought to have some of your magic burn cream, huh?" My voice was cracking. I had to swallow, but there was nothing but dryness in my throat. "Just another minute. Backups are coming. Hear the sirens? You know my brother's a cop. He'll have the whole force here to get you out." I wriggled under the chassis. My head was near his shoulder, but I couldn't hear his breathing, couldn't see anything. Somewhere I'd read that people in comas can still hear. "I've got your hand. Don't let go. Hang on. Guthrie, I love you. I love you."

"You gotta move, Darcy. They're going to lift the car."

I slithered back, but I didn't let go of his hand.

I didn't dare.

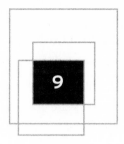

9

THE FIRST TIME I saw Guthrie's face was when they plugged him into the ambulance. His cheek was streaked with grease and soot, and his nose had been mashed down to the side. *How can he breathe?* I lunged toward him, but someone was holding me back.

"You'll be in the way." My brother's voice was shaky. "You gotta listen to me."

"His shirt's sooty, but I didn't see blood, did you?"

"Uh-uh."

"That's good, isn't it?"

"Hard to say."

I stiffened. *Hard to say because you don't want to hear?*

Sirens were burping off; flashers battled red; squeals echoed at each other and the guys guarding the scene were yelling at civilians to stay on the far side of the street. Guthrie's car had been halfway across the grass, but the scene supervisor was closing off the street and the entire park.

Across the road, lights had come on in the houses. People in bathrobes were standing on a front lawn.

A cab pulled up just as the ambulance shot off. I leapt in. I wasn't surprised the driver was Webb Morratt, the cabbie John used for personal and off-label runs. I tried to interpret his appearance as positive, that John called him for me because he knew Guthrie was headed to the hospital, not the morgue. He squealed off through the fog-dense and empty streets and caught the ambulance at the third intersection.

I couldn't bear to think of Guthrie in the vehicle ahead, charging up the steep rise of Divisidero that made even Morratt downshift. Instead, I focused on the black convertible. Someone had driven that car over him. Carefully, so it covered his body. Someone had laid him on the grass when he was unconscious and then driven his car over him. In the dark. In a place it would be discovered as soon as it got light. Therefore they must have wanted him to be found before long. It made no sense.

"I spent a lot of time sitting around there," Morratt was saying.

"The park? For John?" The ambulance raced over the top of Pacific Heights, through the intersection on the red light. Morratt followed. He must have been doing 80.

"Maybe."

A city park with tree-shaded nooks. "Drugs, fights, kids, and liquor?"

"Sure."

"What else?"

He hesitated. "Cars boosted, burglaries. Cat burglaries."

"Huh?" We hit the congested part of Divisidero. The ambulance slowed. I leaned over the seat, peering through the windshield, willing the ambulance faster. Now it was behind a bus. *Go around, dammit!* If only Guthrie'd been driving! I squelched a sob—wanting him here to laugh at the irony.

We were closing in on the hospital. The ambulance cut into the ER. Morratt started after, hit the brakes.

I jumped out and ran inside. A clerk handed me clipboarded papers with questions I couldn't answer. His address? I'd only called him, never written. Date of birth? Close to fifty years ago? Next of kin? I'd never given it a thought. Insurance? Probably, if he'd been paying union dues.

In way too short a time, a doctor motioned me in through the double doors.

I didn't need to wait for words; I could read his face. "He's dead, isn't he?"

"Yes."

The air went thick. My words sounded like they came from someone else. "How can that be? It was just his nose. There wasn't even any blood on his shirt, was there?"

He hadn't seen the shirt, I could tell that, too. He was saying it didn't matter. But it *did* matter, how could he not get that? "His shirt was fine, just dirty. There was no damage to his chest, was there?"

Doors whished open; metal rattled. People muttered, moaned, screamed. A woman was yelling into her phone, "Just get your lazy ass over here." The walls—beige or that shade of pale blue or green or yellow that's the same as beige—evaporated. Nothing made sense. "It's just a broken nose! How can he be dead of a broken nose!"

More words. They made no sense. Then I heard, "Do you want to see his body?"

His body! I longed to see *him*, not his body, his empty body. I nodded and was led down the hall and into a curtained-off slot, the kind of place Guthrie would hate. Like a work cubicle in an office—a death cubicle with curtains.

He lay there, his face cleaned now, his nose caved in to the right, his head propped up on a pillow in mockery of his last hours. I had to fight not to think about sitting with him in the cab of his truck talking about my burns, or in the trailer, leaning against that shoulder that now stuck out from the sheet, bare, already dry-looking, but with every muscle still visible. I wanted to reach forward, to rest my hand on his skin, but I just didn't dare. Barely audibly, I said, "How?"

The doctor lifted Guthrie's shoulder and turned him on his side.

The back crown of his head was caved in as if it had been hit with a pipe. Blood matted his hair and the bleeding had spread down his neck onto his back. It looked like his head had exploded inside.

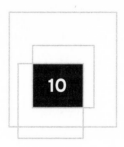

10

WHEN MIKE DISAPPEARED I went into a funk that only eased back to normal years later. Now, I could tell that Gracie and John and, particularly, Mom were worried about how I'd deal with Guthrie's death.

But one of the things I've learned is that you can grieve wholly when you sit zazen. No interruptions, no one cheering or offering ineffectual comfort, nothing between you and every memory or hope, every pang that leaves your chest hollow and cold. Leo offered to sit with me, and we sat period after period. In normal zazen we let go of thoughts and come back to the breath. But this time I let the thoughts linger, memories of the set outside San Diego where we'd met doing car gags, the time I'd run into him at an opening and barely recognized him in a tux, the nights and luscious afternoons together in the truck, the plans he and I'd just started making. The feel of his body against mine.

After a few periods of zazen, thoughts start to arrive more slowly and they're easier to see. The back and forth between the thoughts and the cold hollow in the chest becomes clear, each beholden to the other. In its starkness the pain is easier to face as what it is—fear—and feelings in my chest that I wanted to call grief or regret but that were in fact just feelings there. I might have loved Guthrie, but I hadn't known him. What I loved was the acceptance we had each allowed that preserved our own secrets.

If he'd kept his secret, would he still be alive?

I went to bed exhausted, slept till ten, and then got the streetcar out to Mom's house and picked up Duffy for a walk on the beach, one of the places Guthrie and I had never been. I think of Duffy as my dog even if my mother thinks otherwise. He, I'm sure, figures he has many servants. A Scottie, he's not a beach dog. The slap of the waves on his low-slung stomach irritates him, but he trotted along the sand and when we came to the grassy dunes beyond the Great Highway, he was in his element, barking and burrowing. Later I ate some of Mom's beef stew and was back in bed in shortly after sunset. I felt like I could sleep forever.

The next morning I woke up angry. Now all the energy someone else might spend in grief surged into fury. In zazen I could barely sit still, barely wait till the bell rang me free. I wasn't through mourning, but I was done with moping. Dammit, I had to *do* something. I could have gone for a long run. Instead, I sat on the steps between Leo's room and mine and called John.

"What did the medical examiner say about the wounds? That bruise? What's the report on the crime scene? Did the neighbors see anything?"

"It's not my case any more."

"Couldn't you even—"

"Not my choice."

"But you have to be running it. No one's in a position to know as much about Guthrie as you are. I can give you inside stuff, the people to talk to, tell you what makes sense and what's just blather. Gracie talked to the ER docs and she—"

"Right. But here's the irony. After the last Lott-related blowup—the one *I* orchestrated—the department's got new rules."

"That's crazy! None of us is going to be as free with a stranger—"

"She won't be a stranger long. She's probably on the horn to you this minute."

He was right. The instant I hung up, the message light blinked.

Half an hour later an unmarked car disgorged a thick white woman in a blue slacks suit. She had blonde hair pushed behind her ears, but it was too short to stay put. Clumps hung in front of her ears like surviving trees in a clear-cut forest. She strode across the zendo courtyard to the bench where I was drinking an espresso. There was something familiar about her.

"Darcy Lott?" She had one of those voices that isn't loud but cuts through all other conversations. She stared down, assessing me in a guilty-till-proved-otherwise way.

Now I recognized her. Remembering a trick I learned in an acting class, I thought of a pineapple, *saw* the pineapple with its rind mostly green though beginning to go to yellow at the top, its leaves thick and healthy. My face showed nothing when I said, "You're an inspector now, Higgins?"

"Damon Guthrie. I need to know everything you know about him. You were his girlfriend?"

"I guess."

"You don't know?"

"Girlfriend is such a kid term."

"You tell me what your relationship was, then." She pulled a notebook out of her purse. "Is there a more private place?"

"No." Quickly, I added, "This is very private." I could have asked if she'd like me to get her coffee. But, no, I couldn't. The most I could manage was not to take a swallow of my own. Higgins had been on guard at an apartment when I'd used my police connections to push past her and chat up the detective in charge. And when she left I'd sneered—to myself, I'd wanted to believe—at her large, square, and sagging butt. I'd figured her for a rookie, but either she'd flown up through the ranks, or I'd erred. Maybe my sneer had had an effect. She had the look of not only having lost weight but of going the all-out gym route. She'd lopped off her pony tail and bleached the remains. I wondered how much she recalled of our encounter. Too much?

"You know the deceased through stunt work?"

The deceased! How could that be Guthrie? "Yes."

"How long have you known him?"

"Ten years, give or take."

"And you've been intimate how long?"

I made myself respond. "Six, seven years."

"The address on his driver's license is no longer valid."

"Why is that?"

"He doesn't live there. Ms. Lott, where does he live?"

"I don't know."

"You've been intimate with him for years and you don't know where he lives?"

I pictured the pineapple. "Yes."

"Who is his next of kin? Parents, siblings, wife?"

Wife! "I don't know."

"He never mentioned any relatives at all?"

"No."

"Friends?"

"I'll have to think about it."

"You do that."

I gave up. "Look, I'm being straight with you. I'm going to do everything I can to find out who killed him. I was the one holding his hand when they lifted his car off him; I don't just want to find who did it, I want to bludgeon him. But I have to tell you, Guthrie and I had an, uh, unusual relationship. Part of its appeal was that we didn't ask questions. But here's what I *do* know. He did something years ago and the guilt was eating him alive."

"What was that?"

"He said he let a man die."

"He killed him?"

"No! He walked away."

"Give me details."

"I've told you everything."

But she wasn't buying that. "You have to know more—"

"Like I just said, we didn't ask questions."

"Uh-huh."

"Twice in two days he was at the Palace of Fine Arts. He was to meet me there the day he was killed. The day before that I followed him and lost him—"

"You were following him? Why was that?"

I told her about Jed Elliot's demand. "I said I'd have Guthrie call him."

"Did he do that?

"For chrissakes, get off this! His job prospects don't matter. He's *dead*. Look, we were working at Port of Oakland. It's not next door to the Palace of Fine Arts. He doesn't live in this area. Here's what's important, that something drew him to that spot twice."

"What?"

"I don't know."

She checked her pad. "His guilty incident, when was that?"

I was ready to snap back again, but I stopped. "Good question. He didn't say, and he'd never mentioned it before. I mean, it's the thing that he kept secret. There was some kind of wall around him when I first met him; he didn't suddenly change one year or another. So, my guess is that it happened well before I knew him."

"Did he talk to anyone else about this?"

"He was going to meet John, my brother."

"Inspector Lott?"

She uttered his name with such disdain that if I'd had any doubts about which side she'd picked in the departmental wars, it was sure gone now. "Right. But Guthrie didn't meet John. By then he was dead."

"No one else?"

I hesitated. I'm careful to protect friends, but this time I couldn't let any stone go unturned. "He talked to Garson-roshi, the priest here."

She did a flash-reveal. In acting it's a hard thing to learn, showing your true emotion just long enough for the audience to get it, then shifting into a different, usually neutral expression. In front of the cameras you have to hold the flash longer than seems reasonable, to allow time for the audience first to see it and then to register what it means in relation to what happened before. Higgins did it normal speed. She flashed frustration, then tried to cover by busying herself with that pad of hers. She was thinking Leo's talk with Guthrie would be privileged, as if it'd been in a confessional. I wasn't sure where Zen fit into the world of legal privilege, but I didn't disabuse her.

At that moment Leo opened the zendo door. Turning, Higgins saw a bald guy with features too big for his face, dressed in sweats and sandals. He grinned at us, waiting for an invitation from me.

I hesitated. Three things were in play here: I was desperate to know what Guthrie had told Leo. But I hated to involve Leo more than I already had. And Leo had an unfortunate habit of answering questions truthfully. He's not naïve; it's just that his commitment is to the dharma rather than the exigencies of the moment, and in the past some of his responses have led to exigencies in custody.

Still, it had worked out. He'd survived fine. "Inspector Higgins," I said, "this is Garson-roshi."

She did another flash-reveal before saying, "Sir, I need to ask you about your conversation with Damon Guthrie." Her tone had the brittleness of uncertainty. It made me uneasy.

But, as always, Leo took her as is. He smiled, which made his features seem even larger. It was a disarming expression and Higgins—involuntarily, it appeared—smiled back. He pulled up a chair and took a moment to settle himself comfortably in it, as if this conversation would be important and he wanted to be prepared to give it his full attention. "Guthrie was at the point of balance," he said, "that's very unstable. If you've ever been in a handstand and suddenly you're there, you're terrified because you've lost the leverage to move forward or back. You're dead still, but you're out of control. See what I mean?"

Higgins nodded, but almost certainly to move things along rather than from any personal understanding. He'd been looking at her, but I knew the explanation was for me.

"That moment of ultimate uncertainty, when all normal paths seem closed, when you have to give up . . . when everything's closed, everything's open." His cheerful expression implied that this basic Zen understanding was a bit of wisdom shared between the two of them. Her expression said she was humoring him.

"That's the moment when a person is open to learning, so it was very good Guthrie came then. Here's what I told him—it's a koan, a story with a question. The story is an old Chinese ghost tale. A girl, Seijo, was betrothed to a distant cousin when she was an infant. She and her father and the cousin's family lived in a village by a river in China. Seijo and the boy grew up together and were happy with the marriage plan. But"—Leo grinned, as if to say his listeners would know there was a "but" coming—"when Seijo was just about marriageable age, her father realized he could do better by giving her to another man. When Seijo's original fiancé was told, he was indignant. He lit out, got a boat, and headed upriver.

"Day turned to evening, but he kept moving. Evening turned to night. The sounds from villages he passed grew intermittent, then stopped entirely till he was alone in the dark. Suddenly he heard a voice on the bank, excitedly calling his name. It was Seijo. She had run after him. She'd run away to be with him. This is China almost a thousand years ago; what Seijo was doing was very daring. Her fiancé was delighted. He helped her onto the boat and they kept going upriver till they came to another village where they married, had two children, and lived happily.

"But"—he grinned again—"after a while they became homesick for their families and decided to take a trip back home.

"When they tied up the boat at their original village, Seijo stayed in the boat while her husband went to make apologies to her father for taking her away. But the father stopped him mid-sentence. 'What are you talking about?' he said. 'My daughter's right here where she's been all along.' He pointed to a bed where Seijo was lying unconscious. Not a hallucination, but a real girl.

"Of course, her husband was shocked. He ran out of the house back to the river to the boat. And there she was, the real Seijo. He grabbed her hand and ran back to the house. Seijo was still in the bed.

"There were two Seijos.

"When the Seijo from the boat saw the figure in the bed, the Seijo in the bed awoke and got up, and the two embraced and melted into one." Leo paused. "It's not the ending that you'd expect, right? Guthrie was surprised, too. He had the same expression you do. See, koans ask a question. It's what gets you thinking. It allows you to see an issue in a different light, and that was what Guthrie needed to do then. What this koan asks is, which Seijo is the real Seijo? Most people would say the one living her life. But see, Guthrie already knew that, even though it appeared he was living his life and living a good life in a profession he loved and was tops in, he really wasn't living it. He was just going through the motions." Leo shot a glance at me. I knew he was thinking of me living my life still caught up in the question of Mike. "Guthrie had done something so terrible, at least in his mind, that he was immobilized."

"The girl in the bed," Higgins said.

"Exactly. Except that he was still living his life. I think this story could help you understand where he was if you take a stab at the answer. Which is the real Seijo?"

For a moment she seemed to consider the problem. "What's the answer? Just tell me."

"That's just what Guthrie said, though not in those words."

And not in that tone, I'll bet.

"There isn't 'the' answer, Inspector; that's what I told him. No, wait, I'm not avoiding your demand. In a koan there are two parts: the question and you. So, your answer would be subtly different than his. Having said that, there is the easy answer, the answer before the real answer."

Higgins was afraid she was being played; I knew that look. I said, "Seijo is real when the two parts of her come together."

"So, you were telling Mr. Guthrie to take initiative?"

"Why—"

"That's the only time this girl does something on her own. Otherwise, she's got this husband dreaming she's running after him. And this father figuring he's still got his property home in bed. And the girl, she's got no life of her own. Like these battered women who get beat up time after time and won't press charges because their boyfriends cry about how sorry they are and how they're going to change."

Spoken like a cop who'd spent too much time catching domestic violence calls. Still, I was impressed at how much Leo had drawn her in and, I had to admit, by her answer.

"But who is she, then?" he said. "What does 'real' mean? That's the underlying question. When these two parts come together, what do you have?"

"She got up, she brought her halves together, and I'll bet she'd got some things to say to both of those men."

I laughed.

"Inspector, Guthrie's answer wasn't the same as yours."

"What was his?"

"Of course he saw that the key was when the two parts came together. His guilt was the Seijo in the bed. In the story, what is it that motivates the girl in the bed to get up? Excuse me for asking. I know you're here for answers, but this is just my way."

"Omigod."

They both turned to me.

"It's the sight of her other half coming back from her happily-ever-after life. Her realizing maybe she's just made that up." Like Lott and Guthrie. Like our "almost loving." Was all that a fantasy spawned by the hyper-emotion on the set? Had he lived, would we both be giving it second thoughts by now? I'd never be sure, because, dammit, I didn't know who he was, not really.

But Higgins wasn't dealing with such considerations. "So, what was Mr. Guthrie going to do?"

Leo hesitated. I wondered what he was considering. "You're aware that he planned to talk to Inspector Lott. But before that, he said he had to go and face his guilt. Maybe, he told me, he'd return something."

"What?" Higgins demanded.

"I don't know. What he said was that it had been given to him but no one would believe he didn't steal it."

Higgins rolled her eyes.

"I'd believe him! You believed him, didn't you, Leo?"

He shifted uncomfortably in his chair, something I couldn't remember him ever doing before. "I believed he believed that was true."

"You think he fooled himself?"

Leo said simply, "We live in delusion."

He meant that Guthrie was no different than the rest of us. I nodded. But Higgins's jaw was tightening. She had the look of believing herself the last sensible person in a room of babblers.

"In Buddhism," he said, "we see our problems are caused by greed, hate, and delusion. Whereas, you think your problem right now is caused by me being flaky, right?" Before she could respond, he added, "This is the one hard fact I can give you. Guthrie intended to go and return the item before he met with Inspector Lott."

"Before six in the morning?"

"I left him at his truck in Oakland around 8:00 P.M." I said. "Omigod, was he lying dead in the park all night?"

Higgins looked at me as if I were an idiot. Closing her notebook, she hooked her pen on the spiral, slipped the combo into a compartment in her purse, and checked around in there as if searching for something she couldn't name.

"If you need anything more, ask now," Leo said. "I'm going to be out of town for a couple days, at the monastery." He waited a minute, letting her dismiss him, and left.

When he was out of sight, she rose and said, "There's another hard fact you didn't give me."

I stared at her.

Neither of us said anything for a minute. Then she sighed.

"Tell me," she instructed, with ill-disguised contempt, "how, all that greed, hate, and whatever aside, did you manage to forget that Damon Guthrie's got a sister living across the street from where he died?"

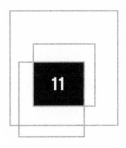

11

"GUTHRIE HAS A sister? Across from the Palace of Fine Arts?"

"Are you going to tell me he didn't mention her either? Living in the house his parents bought in 1965? He hauls himself across the Bay twice in two days to go there, tells you to meet him across the street at an hour that says he wanted to creep out the door without waking her, and you're claiming he never mentioned her?"

"Yeah." My voice was barely audible. I had no answers. Higgins was asking what I was thinking, and it was a whole lot more incriminating coming from my own self. Guthrie had a sister here in the city? How could he *not* have told me? A sister who lived in one of the toniest neighborhoods in town? Did he grow up there? His whole person screamed, No! Topeka, Spokane, Medford, Roanoke: those, I could believe. El Cajon. Places like that. Or smaller towns where eighteen-wheelers are big deals. Places where you drive to get where you're going, where cruising the main drag, low-riding, wheelies made for a big weekend. The Marina district just didn't compute.

"You thinking up a better answer?"

"No." I had to project calm. "As I said, I'm the one who most wants to find Guthrie's killer. You say he grew up here, so now I'm wondering: who were his friends, what did they say about him? Who've you—"

"We don't reveal evidence."

You mean, we don't have any. "What were the autopsy findings?"

"It's not scheduled till—"

"He's been dead for two days and you people haven't taken him out of the drawer?"

She just stared. She didn't have to tell me a damned thing and we both knew it.

I tried another tack. "The sister, she must have identified his body."

"Of course."

"So? She must've said something about him."

She didn't bother to respond at all.

I could have smacked her.

But I didn't have that luxury, not even the comfort of rolling my eyes. I had to make one last effort to create cooperation. Mustering every bit of control, I said, "This is San Francisco." I chose my words carefully. "When I was a kid my brother was already on patrol, and there were kids who called me piglet. I know—"

"We're not buddies, you and I." She was almost sneering. "This is a police investigation—"

The hell with it! "I'm done here. You need me, call my lawyer."

"I repeat—"

"Repeat till they give you a cracker. I'm going to talk to Guthrie's sister and I am going to find out about him. What matters to me won't be what you want to know."

"Do not—" She looked like she was going to bite me. "You've already got a reputation at headquarters. You're not special. Cross the line this time and your brother won't be able to save you."

I laughed.

□□□

"What the hell's the matter with you?" John demanded.

"Higgins got word to you this quick?" I'd barely gotten back upstairs to my room above the zendo before he called.

"Did you go out of your way to piss her off?"

"No, it was a straight shot. The woman's an ass—"

"A well-connected ass. Don't let her looks deceive you—"

"She looks incompetent, and like she's happy to screw John Lott and family."

"Incompetence is a dangerous quality in an adversary, particularly a well-connected one."

I snorted.

"Listen, Darcy. I'm the department straight arrow now. Have to be. Everyone's eyeing me—guys who care about the department look up to me, guys with grudges watch for me to cross the line—any line. It's not my case and I can't barge in."

"Fine! Forget it. I'll find out what I need to."

"Going to see the sister?"

"Right. I told Higgins."

"She warned you off, right?"

"So?"

"Exactly. Don't you hear me? You've got a reputation going. She knows you'll barge ahead. That warning—she's just baiting you. When you get to that door, she'll be watching. When you walk out, she'll be waiting. And you'll be sitting in a soundproof room downtown till dawn."

"I'm sure you—"

"Haven't you heard me? I can't. Even for you. Especially for you. I . . . cannot . . . bend . . . the rules."

"Fine. Forget it!"

"Don't be a patsy. At least take a lookout."

I laughed. "What? With tin cans and string?"

"I'm serious. Take . . ."

"Right. Not Gary—too well-known. Gracie? Spare me. Mom? Think I should take our mother to help me impede a police investigation?"

"Or Janice, now that'd improve your chances. She'd be so wowed by the Palace she'd forget all about you."

I'd had enough of him and his straighter-than-thou-ness. "Give her a break! No wonder she moved away."

"She's my sister; I'm certainly not—"

"Yeah, right. Forget it. If you don't hear from me, I'll be in jail." I clicked off.

I eyed the brown silk slacks I'd been planning to wear. Maybe I'd better go with something sturdier now. Black chinos, black jacket, black T-shirt, pale green scarf. Shoes that could leave Higgins in the dust.

I opened my door and found Leo in the hallway between our rooms.

"Coffee?" he said, extending a paper cup and sitting down on the top step. There was no way to refuse to join him short of leaping down three stairs. For an instant I thought he'd overheard my snapfest with John. But that wasn't what he was waiting to discuss. "I was truthful with the inspector."

Truthful meant responding honestly, but not blurting out everything you knew or suspected. "So, what else?"

"I gave her all I knew."

Uh-oh. "Did you? How'd Guthrie seem when he talked about return-ing the item? Nervous? Relieved?" Hard as it was for me to picture, I added, "Scared?"

"Curious."

I smiled. "I can believe that. I first met Guthrie doing a car gag adapted from Yakima Canutt's classic one in *Stagecoach*, where he's trying to stop the horses, runs out over their backs, appears to fall down between the first team and then works his way back underneath all three teams and the stagecoach, climbs up and over, and saves the day."

"Live at full speed?"

"Oh, yeah. *Stagecoach* was 1939. Now there'd be parts they could blue screen and a lot of animation they could slip in. But even for anima-tion, there has to be some template to draw from. They need to know what the real stunt should look like. And Guthrie, when they wanted a similar gag in a car chase in a Duesenberg, he made it work."

"Surely cars are more reliable than horses."

"Also lower to the ground. He had to figure out how to jimmy the Dues's suspension without screwing up the handling and wrecking the car. The guy who tried before him ended the day in traction. Guthrie told me later he starts with the idea that it's going to work; he's just got to figure out how."

"Hmm."

I shot him a glance. One of the very appealing things about my teacher is that he always gives you his full attention. It's his practice. But he sure wasn't focused on me now. "Leo?"

"This is how Guthrie was," he said, as if we'd been discussing "this" all along, "like Seijo coming back into her father's house. She already knew she wasn't going to get bawled out. The way had been prepared for her.

She walked in not knowing what would happen but having been given the feeling it would be surprising in a good way."

"Because for Seijo meeting her father was incidental on the way to seeing her other self?"

"Exactly."

"Because," I mused, "what Guthrie had to do was an event already concluded in his mind on the way to the important one."

"And that was?"

"Talking to John, I assume. He wanted to see his sister, give her some warning that he was going to go to the police about what he'd done. Maybe he wanted her to get him a lawyer. Maybe he just wanted to say goodbye because he was"—my breath caught—"going to jail. Maybe he wanted to give her some family heirloom he had with him before he turned himself in. Ah . . . return it. That makes sense."

He just shook his head.

"But here's the thing, Leo, the state that Seijo was in as she ran past her father to the thing that she cared about—her other self—that state was lovely for her, but it must've infuriated her father. Even if he was stunned for the moment, pretty soon he'd have been offended about her leaving her comatose self for him to care for all that time. Plus, if there'd been talk about calling the police, no one in Seijo's family would have been happy."

"All you know is that he wanted to return something and seemed calm. Don't create delusion."

"You mean extra delusion?"

"Right. At least stay within the realm of the default state."

I reached for my coffee and realized it was empty. "The thing is, my whole relationship with Guthrie may be a delusion."

Leo nodded. He meant that since we all see people through our own eyes, how could it be otherwise? He was talking absolute.

I was thinking relative. "Guthrie works in illusion within illusion. In the fiction of movies and within the illusion of stunts. But it's not just that; stuntmen have their own schticks. Mr. Tough, Mr. Ready, Mr. Don't-Feel-Pain. So even what guys on the set see isn't reality. If Higgins goes stomping in there, she's not going to get anything. And she will, as cops say, contaminate the scene. Guthrie lives in a truck—"

"When you see him."

That stopped me. "Right, when I see him." I stood up.

"You're leaving?"

"I may not be back till tomorrow."

"Should I ask where you're going?"

"Not hardly."

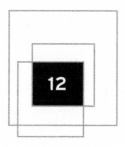

12

THE HOUSE WAS two tall stories with a peaked tile roof and decorative masonry around the edging. The paint hadn't peeled but rather faded into a paleness that forced me to look twice to imagine its original pink color. It had the look of a place let go as much as possible without arousing the neighbors.

I'd found the exact address online and had walked from the zendo, assuming I'd come up with a plan of action on the way. But au contraire. It was nearly noon. The fog was thinning, promising it would lift within the hour. People were staring up at the Greco-Roman temple, shooting pictures, strolling toward the lagoon, tramping over the spot where Guthrie died as if it was just mere grass. The whole thing undid me more than I could have imagined.

I pushed the bell but couldn't hear it ring inside. Then I banged on the door like a bill collector. And, finally, when a woman opened it, I said the worst possible thing: "*You're* Guthrie's sister?" It was virtually an accusation.

"And who are you?"

"His friend. A close friend." I waited for her reaction. She really was nothing like him. She was short, thin to emaciation. Everything about her just looked dried out—skin, eyes, long dark hair.

"I'm Gabriella," she muttered.

What was I doing? I could feel my face flush. "Listen, I am so sorry. I didn't mean to sound like that. I'm just, just— I'm so undone by all this, Guthrie dying, here, like he did."

Her tiny body stiffened; she looked even more unnerved.

I put a hand on the doorjamb. "I was his friend! Tell me about him."

"I told the police. I identified his body. What more do you want?" Her hand tightened on the door. She'd only opened it a third of the way and she looked like it was fifty-fifty whether she'd slam it without realizing my hand was still there.

"I want—I need—to know who he was. I mean, as close as we were, I figured there'd be years to ask the unimportant questions, like rocky road or pistachio? But then, all of a sudden, he's dead and . . . Please!" *How could he end up dead here?* Edgy as she already was, I needed to start with something easier. "What was he like growing up?"

Her expression didn't change.

Too broad a question? "What sports did he play in school?"

"Sports?"

"Football, baseball? Did he run track? Race cars, motorcycles?"

"I don't know. I don't remember. He was older; I was a kid. I don't know what he did; he was just gone."

"He's your older brother?" Looking at her, I sure wouldn't have guessed it. Over her shoulder I could see a pile of newspapers, magazines, mail interspersed with clothing. She hadn't even left the house to take out the recycling. I eased to the side, trying to see farther into the house. Was this the single spot of clutter, or was the whole place crammed with papers ceiling to floor? Was that why Guthrie never mentioned her? "What kind of kid was he? Was he a brat? Did he—"

"He was just an older brother!" Her hand tightened on the door. "Look, I haven't seen him since before the earthquake."

"The Loma Prieta? You haven't seen Guthrie since 1989?" I could barely believe it.

"No. No calls, no letters. I would have thought he'd been killed in the earthquake—I would have been worried to death—if it hadn't been for the Highway Patrol. Pulled him over for speeding in Marin the day after. You want to know how I know? Because he didn't bother to pay the ticket. I was so furious. He was lucky he didn't come back then."

"Kids do that kind of thing."

She shook her head. "Damon was twenty-eight. A speeding ticket's hundreds of dollars, and he just blew it off. So, yeah, I hadn't seen him till . . . till the morgue."

"Till he came here the day before, you mean. He was coming to give you something. He told me that."

She looked up suspiciously. "Give me what?"

"Return something, that's what he said—return."

"Return something to me? I can't imagine that. Returning things wasn't Damon's strong suit."

"Huh? No wait, don't shut the door. I'm asking because, listen, I know him. He's been gone and you haven't seen him, but I have. Don't you care what happened to him in all that time?"

She pulled back. She didn't look curious, but instead afraid to find out what he'd done. Finally, she said, "It doesn't matter because he never came here."

"But I followed him here, to this corner on Saturday. He was going to meet me across the street the morning he died. I found his body."

"Then he must have still had whatever it was you think he was going to give me, because I never saw my brother."

95

"But he came here! That night, the day before his body was found. You had to—"

All of a sudden I saw things as she must have. "Omigod, I am so, so sorry. I can't even imagine—so many years he was gone, and now to know he came back, he was right here on your doorstep and you missed him. He died without your seeing him at all! That's so awful!" If Mike were dead and I had missed my one chance— No wonder she was so undone. Instinctively, impulsively, I reached out to her.

"Get away from me! I can't go on with this. First he just leaves, leaves me to deal with everything. And now all this."

I grabbed the door. "He grew up here, right?"

She looked terrified.

I didn't care. "Let me see his room."

"No! No, I'm not letting you in to see anything. Let go of my door."

"Wait, I'm the only person you know who cared about him . . . Or maybe I'm not. Do you have sisters, other brothers? Are your parents still here? Other relatives? Who were his friends? Give me their names and I'll leave you be. Or one, just one person to tell me about him. You're his sister; you have to know someone!"

"People move."

"But parents, sisters—"

"It was only us two."

"Just one name! Now that I know he grew up here, I can check his yearbook and track down friends. My brother's a cop so he'll have resources, but that'll all take time and—"

"Okay. Okay. Pernell Tancarro. I'll call him. Wait here."

I pulled my hand back just in time before she slammed the door.

Pernell Tancarro? Why was that name familiar?

A six-foot wall surrounded the grounds on both sides of the walk. I hoisted myself and peered over. The yard was a field of weeds. It looked like she hadn't considered mowing since he'd left. As I lowered myself back down I shot a glance across the street and noted the patrol car waiting. In the back of my mind I'd planned on being invited inside, on taking tea and talking of Guthrie, holding my position till the patrol shift changed. Now I was going to have to come up with another escape route.

I moved closer to the street and hoisted myself high up on the fence on the other side of the walk. The yard on this side of the walk was a different world from the mess I'd just seen. It was a garden with potted geraniums and a camellia bush in the corner by the street. Surely there would be a gate in the back, leading somewhere. I leaned in, took my time peering toward the back. Let the cop wonder if I'd make my exit from the side or back. If he took the bait and drove around the corner, I could sprint across the street into the park and vanish—all perfectly legal. Or, if I could get Gabriella's friend to let me go through the house or the yard somehow, better yet.

I dropped back down on the path.

A hand grabbed my shoulder.

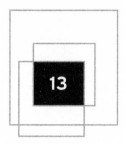

13

"WHAT THE HELL are you doing?" A man pulled me off the fence from behind.

I turned, shoving free of his hands. I was expecting to be face to face with an enforcer, but what I found was a solid guy with dark hair gone gray around the temples and a pissed-off expression. "I'm trying to find out about Gabriella Guthrie's brother."

"Behind the fence?"

"Touché. Look, Guthrie was murdered across the street from her house and she's carrying on like 'so what?'"

"There's plenty here besides her house—the park where he played as a kid, the temple pillars where grass, and who knows what all, was sold. There could be people on the next blocks he knew. Lots of connections beside a sister who hasn't seen him since the earthquake."

"If you're Tancarro, you're the only one she gave me. She said *you'd* tell me about him. How could he be here less than a day and end up dead?"

"I don't know! Look, I've barely thought about anything else since I saw the police over there. I haven't seen him in twenty years, and . . . He was gone for so long, he was nothing but a memory and then, suddenly, he's here again, but dead. It's unbelievable." He stood, slowing shaking his head. "Tell me again who you are?"

"Darcy Lott. And you're *Pernell Tancarro, the poet!* We read you in high school. I've been out of the loop a lot since, but I remember you're a native San Franciscan, right?"

"Fourth generation."

"And you're still writing?"

He hesitated a moment. "My focus has changed. I enable others. On the board of the Arts Commission, the museum, the Palace of Fine Arts, of course. But about Damon, we were no more than friends of convenience, neighbor kids. There were years we'd barely nod in the street."

"What about other friends—"

"Gone. Houses sold and resold. If I weren't on the neighborhood committee, I'd hardly know anyone here but Gabi."

"So, there's no one for me to ask but you—or her. Look, I found him lying there with his nose smashed in and his head—" I had to swallow hard to keep from losing it.

He put a hand on my shoulder. "Sure. Of course I'll tell you what I know, but just be prepared that it's not much and definitely not recent."

With that hand he was steering me along the path onto the sidewalk. Across the street the patrol officer started his engine—ready to hustle me down to headquarters to explain to Higgins? I moved a bit closer to my new friend, the neighborhood committeeman.

"Growing up, Gabi was smart, focused, hard-working—Little Miss Perfect. Damon was a fuckup."

Was he talking about the same people? Gabriella was Little Miss Perfect? And Guthrie a fuckup? I would never have believed that before last Friday on the set. But now I had to wonder. "Like how? What was his most recent escapade?"

"Hmm. Well, the year before the quake, he and I, and a couple of other guys spent too much time in the bars on Union Street. We'd already carried out some pretty dark deeds."

Dark deeds? What was this, high school? "Such as?"

"One time we broke into a neighbor's basement and lifted his porn collection."

Junior high! "And the guy went public?"

"Worse. We were in our late twenties—way too old for that kind of shit. He called my father. 'This is San Francisco,' he told him, 'people don't care about porn, but burglary—they care plenty.'"

"What about *Guthrie's* father? What'd he—"

"Dead. Both parents. Died a couple years before. Car went off the road on Route 1 somewhere around Big Sur. Shot over the cliff. It was awful."

"Omigod! Poor Guthrie!" Without thinking, I reached out for him. "How'd he take it? I mean, was that the cause of this second adolescence? That he couldn't focus? Or did it—"

"Poor *Gabriella*! She just about fell apart. But him, no," he said, in a tone of disgust. "Suddenly, he was totally focused. He had one goal and that was to get his inheritance. Their parents left Gabi in control of everything. The porn thing was probably just to embarrass her. He just about drove her crazy—well, the truth is he *did* drive her crazy. He called day and night till she never answered the phone at all. He'd bang on the door, peer in the windows, everything but pop up through the toilet. By the end of a year she was so undone she put those wretched bars on the basement windows, double-paned the rest of the windows, and walled off the fireplace. Paneled over it and the bookcases in the living room—pine paneling from a rec room in some tacky suburb. Then she got those blackout curtains. I told her the house is so dark at night, people'll think it's empty. But she's beyond listening."

"Why didn't she call the police?"

"What, and sully the Guthrie name? Not likely. Her parents expected her to take care of her brother. Naught is so potent as the dictates of the dead!" He shrugged. "She'd never have gone public, not if it hurt the family image."

Never do anything to hurt the family. I sure knew that one. "Why didn't you—"

"Hey, I do have my own life! Besides, I didn't know what-all was going on back then." He'd been walking slowly and now, at the corner, he paused. He had to live close by, but clearly he no more intended to invite me in than Gabriella had.

"I just can't believe Guthrie was like that! You knew him years ago, and people change . . ." I was thinking aloud and Tancarro seemed fine with that. "And he did feel really guilty about something—"

"He had plenty to choose from. You saw Gabriella now. But you can't imagine what she was like before. She used to be an up-and-coming attorney."

"She was a *lawyer*?"

"Hotshot prosecutor. But you can't lose your concentration in the courtroom. Now she doesn't leave the house."

"Ever? How does she live? Off the trust?"

"Right. If she hadn't had that money . . . Now, no one goes inside there. Even I haven't crossed the threshold in ten years." He stopped in front of a yellow stucco house that looked like the loved cousin of Gabriella's, and turned to face me. "Damon did a lousy thing."

"He really did feel terrible. Maybe that's why he was coming here. He talked about returning something."

He slowed his pace. "What thing?"

"That's *my* question. You knew him. What—"

Now he stopped dead. "Twenty years! He held onto something for twenty fucking years and then all of a sudden he's got to return it? I mean, there is UPS. God, it's so Damon."

"But what could it be? Why? What got him killed?"

"I'm sorry, honestly." He strode on, faster than before, as if to distance himself from his unseemly outburst. "I wish I knew the answer, for me as well as you. I'll try to remember if there was anything, any*one* who might know. If I come up with—"

"What about those guys he hung out with on Union Street? Where are they?"

"They won't remember. You'd be wasting your time."

"It's the one way you can help me. Our only lead. Who are they?"

He shrugged. "Okay, but— The guy Damon was closest to is Luke Kilmurray."

"Where can I find him?"

"Thailand."

"What's he doing there?"

"Drugs."

"How long's he been there?"

"Years. I wouldn't even know he *was* there if a friend hadn't run into him on the street in Bangkok."

"Do you have his number? Or an address?"

"I might."

I could hear the patrol car behind us. "Do me a favor? Let me go through your house and out the back."

He turned, looked at the patrol car, and for the first time he smiled. "The fast getaway, huh? You really are Damon's friend."

In two minutes I was in his kitchen by the back door, slip of paper in hand.

"It's not a private number," he said. "Luke's landed in a strange situation over there. The time I tried, I called and they had to go find him and then he phoned back. You know, like it's restricted usage or a hostel or something. It was such a hassle I only did it once."

"I'll deal. What about the other guy? Didn't you say there were four of you in the bars?"

"Ryan Hammond? I have no idea where he is."

"Will you check around?"

"I'll let you know. And vice versa? Do me a favor, too? Let Gabriella alone. Call me if you need anything, okay? Damon could be a pain in the ass, but there were times when he was my friend. I don't want some idiot to kill him and walk away free."

□ □ □

Flights to L.A. aren't quite like having the airlines call to ask you when it might be convenient for you to depart, but close. I got a seat on Southwest boarding in half an hour, which meant I just had time to call Thailand.

I found the quietest noisy spot, and punched in the number, hoping but not believing I would get through. Fuzz and crackle, squeaks and metallic scrapings suggested a squirrel racing along the wires.

"Anja Chak," a female voice said.

Of course I didn't know whether Anja Chak was a greeting, a person, or a place. Risking rudeness, I went with the straightforward. "Luke Kilmurray?"

The line crackled. She repeated his name, I think.

"Is he there?"

"Here? Yes."

"Yes? Can I speak to him?"

"Oh, no. He will call back."

"When?"

"Later. In daylight, yes?"

I took that question as a very polite way of saying, "It's the middle of the night here."

"When?" I insisted. But she'd already hung up.

I headed back to the boarding line. There was just time to call and leave an update on John's machine—what I'd learned, not where I was headed.

With a stunt man there's always someone who knows the skinny. I'd given Higgins Guthrie's L.A. connections. She'd approach them sooner or later. When she did, she'd piss them off. But I would have gotten there first.

My flight was boarding. There was one seat in the bulkhead row and I grabbed it.

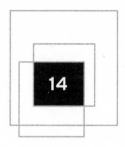

14

"I KNOW REX isn't expecting me. *I* wasn't expecting to be here. Trust me, he's going to want to see me."

The dark-haired, long-lashed, fat-free, wrinkle-free, concern-free young woman at the desk looked at me as if I'd ridden into Los Angeles on a load of cantaloupes. "Mr. Redmon is very busy."

Agents are always busy. I leaned closer. "In a few minutes the police will be on the line to him. He's going to want to know what that's about. I'm here to tell him."

She nodded, sending a wave of hair over one eye. "That's a good one. But, as I said—"

The phone rang.

"Better not answer it unless you want to be lying to the police."

Her hand paused over the receiver. Her expression said she didn't believe me. The phone rang again.

"Or you could put the call through and let Rex take it cold."

She punched another line. "Rex, there's a Darcy Lott here. She says it's about"—she lowered her voice—"the police." She listened and then mouthed a question to me.

"No, not drugs," I said.

Behind her the door opened. Holding it was a wiry guy whose hair was as red and curly as my own but whose angular face was so at odds with it that it was a moment before I could focus on his annoyed expression. And another before I spotted his crutches and the cast on one foot. "From kicking ass?"

"Bruised up to the collarbone." He swung back, around a glass desk, and onto a green leather chair. "Darcy Lott. You're Guthrie's girl."

Guthrie'd talked about me with his agent? "You've got a good memory."

"You looked sharp in the high fall off the cupola in *Barbary Nights*. Things are good with you?"

He meant agent-wise. So, Rex Redmon hadn't heard about Guthrie. No reason he would have. I had given Higgins his name, but not that of his agency. Anyway, Jed Elliot, the second unit director, and Mo Mason, the camera cart guy, were on the scene and it was a no-brainer she'd go for them first. "Guthrie's dead," I announced.

"Drugs?"

"Why'd you guess that? Was he using?"

"Safe guess. But I never heard of him wasted."

"Come to his place with me. I want to get it in order before the cops tear it apart."

"Cops are on this and no one's notified me? He was killed? How? You involved?"

"If I were a suspect, I'd be in shackles."

"Guthrie?" he said. And it was as if the reality of it had just hit him. "Damn! He's always been so careful . . ."

"But?" Suddenly I remembered having that same feeling on the set. Guthrie had always been reliable, always on time, walking the gag first, triple-checking his truck and every other vehicle and prop involved. Always.

Until suddenly, he hadn't.

"Nothing." He clamped his teeth together but couldn't hide a quiver. "Damn! Guthrie's the best!"

"Has he been with you long?"

"Whole career. Fifteen years."

I'd been in the business over twenty, and Guthrie was older. "What did he do before?"

Redmon shrugged. There was no reason it would matter to him. Then he surprised me with, "College, I guess."

"And between?"

"Hey, he was just twenty-two when he signed on."

I nodded. But, in fact, that couldn't have been right. Guthrie must have cut years off his age. Not unknown in Hollywood, but you don't usually keep your agent in the dark. There really was a lot I didn't know about my guy. A lot no one knew. "Look, you're busy. Going to his place isn't going to be any fun for either of us. Let's do it before the cops are on the phone."

"Hey, what kind of accident was this? Elliot knows his business. With him, I don't worry. It was Guthrie's truck. How could— What the hell happened?"

I sat down. "I don't know. One minute we're fighting a fire, a real fire, on the dock, worried about getting the truck out, he's talking about our future—"

"Guthrie, talking marriage?"

"Nah, starting our production company. Lott and Guthrie."

"Oh," he said with obvious relief. "He have backing? Or you two talking dreams? Can't believe he— What gave way?"

I stood up. "I'll tell you in the car. If you don't get out of here, you're going to find yourself waiting in line for an interview booth downtown."

"Get out of here where? I'm not taking you to Guthrie's house. You say you're his friend—I don't doubt you—but—"

"What can I tell you—"

"Nothing. *You* can't fucking tell me. You've already said more than I want to hear." His narrow features contorted for an instant setting his face even more at odds with his shock of curls.

I put a hand on his arm. "I get it. Maybe there's nothing in Guthrie's house that you'll care about going public. Nothing about you, nothing about any of your other clients. I don't know . . ." But I do know when to stop talking.

He opened a drawer and flipped a ring with two keys across the desk. "Get it back to me when you're done there."

Where is there? I, his girlfriend, could hardly admit I didn't know.

The phone rang.

"Don't answer that," I said as I shut the door. In the waiting room, I gave the receptionist a smile worthy of an old friend and flashed the keys. "I'm on my way to Guthrie's. D'you have any mail you want me to take? You've probably got a ton of junk waiting to forward." *Please, Guthrie, have used this as a mail drop.*

"He was in a couple days ago, so I doubt it."

"Take a look anyway, huh?" *Surely, if there's one thing an American can count on, it's junk mail. Surely.*

"Here. Just this."

"Thanks." I waited till I was outside to read the address.

I've spent time in L.A., but not enough to know shortcuts or light hours on the freeways, if such exist. One thing you can say for it, though, is there's no dawdling on the roads. You merge onto the 405 doing 70 miles per hour and never go that slow again. So, it didn't take me long to get to the canyon where Guthrie lived. Lucky for me, since the last thing

I wanted was the local cops, whom Higgins would have notified by now, finding me here. Not after she'd leaned on me to stay out of it and I'd huffed about her having no leads. Then the next thing she knows, I leave town and show up at Guthrie's house. She would have gotten hold of Rex Redmon by now, and there was no percentage in him sticking his neck out for me. All I had going for me was speed and the fact that for the LAPD, any local call would bump an out-of-town request.

Why was I so surprised Guthrie had a house down here? A bed and coffee setup do not a home make. The address on his driver's license was the truck yard. Had I just wanted to believe that bed in the trailer was for nightly use rather than recreation up and down the state? Whatever. As I drove up the winding canyon road, whipping around the curves, I could see why he'd chosen this spot, and why he'd found a sea-level spot to stash the eighteen-wheeler.

A patrol car pulled around me on a short straightaway, but it wouldn't be headed for Guthrie's, not at that speed. Indeed, when I found the address it was nowhere around. Still, I parked a ways down the hill and walked back up thinking about the cottage.

Zen masters talk a lot about illusion: we create illusion after illusion, taking what we eyeball of a situation and filling in the empty spaces the way you look at a painting and automatically brush in the garden behind a picket fence. In the time since I'd seen this address on Guthrie's mail, I'd created a picture of where he lived—in a modern box of a house, sort of like the truck on a foundation, with windows. His real house, here before me, was a white cottage set on the downslope behind a street-level garage. Boisterous red-flowered bushes pushed out under blue jacaranda trees by a steep curve of stone steps leading precariously to the covered porch. It was the last place I would have pictured for the king of the trailer gag and the antithesis of his sister's miserable shuttered-up affair.

The stone steps were irregular slabs salvaged from a torn-out sidewalk; the descent would have been daunting to anyone not in great condition. Behind the garage was a pulley with a car engine dangling. I smiled, picturing him hauling it up and lowering it into a spiffed-up ride like that black convertible he'd been driving across the bridge.

The one, I remembered with a shock, that had covered his body.

Brakes screeched above. I jerked back, listening as the vehicle whipped down the hill. Patrol car, or a thrill-seeker? The winding two-lane had to be a speed-freak's wet dream.

The house was small, with a peaked roof and a two-step porch. The window shades were drawn. I had the feeling they'd fluttered; I leaned closer, checking for an aftershock, but they hung straight down. Something crackled behind me. I jerked around, but saw only leaves. *Enough drama! Just do it!* I stepped up on the porch, stuck the key in the lock, and pushed open the door.

"What the hell are you doing?" The woman was blonde, tan, and pointing a huge pistol at my heart.

"Hey, I've got the key. I just let myself in with Guthrie's key. What are *you* doing in his house?" I was shouting, to cover my shaking. *Who was she?* Her fingers tightened on the gun.

"Put your hands up!"

"What've you got in here that you need to come to the door with a gun?"

Wrong approach! She clicked off the safety. "Turn around and put your hands—"

On the road, brakes squealed again. "You hear that? It's a police car. Don't believe me? Take a look."

She took a step toward the window.

I lunged. She hit the floor with me on top. The gun skidded across the hardwood.

My head was crammed into her shoulder. Her eyes were blue, wide, and scared. I eased myself up till I was glaring inches from her face. "Who are you? What are you doing in Guthrie's house? Tell me!"

"What?"

Another set of brakes squealed. I didn't have time for this. "Who are you?"

"Melissa Guthrie."

"Guthrie's—?"

"Guthrie's wife."

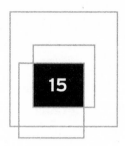

15

IN AN INSTANT everything fell into place—Guthrie's comfort with secrets, his long absences, and the rolling bedroom for the quick and intimate, all the things I'd taken as corresponding to my own need not to share. My face went scalding hot; my eyes blurred. I was ashamed, humiliated, and disgusted. I wanted to bury myself two miles deep. I was nauseated and clammy all over. And then I was furious.

I pushed myself up, grabbed the gun, and pointed it at her. "Guthrie's wife? Prove it."

"Hey, you're in my house."

"Prove you're his wife. Show me your marriage license, your tax return, his will or yours, for chrissakes."

"I'm gonna call the police."

"They're already on their way and they're going to be asking you the same question. Show me the proof! Now!" I was yelling to keep her off-balance. It was dawning on me how untenable a position I'd gotten myself into. I just wanted to find something and get out before I ended up in a cell.

"In the bedroom." Her voice was breaking. She was shaking all over.

When this was over I was going to feel bad about her, but now I was just scared. "Walk! I'm right behind you."

She moved, flat-footed, like she was dizzy. Maybe she was.

With every step I realized more what a mess I was in. She'd be okay once I was gone—shaken, but okay. I was facing a breaking and entering charge and I had her gun in my hand. Jesus, kidnap! That's serious time! My only chance was to really find something here.

If there was something here. If Guthrie wasn't just your standard jerk getting some on the side. If he hadn't been fooling this woman more than he had me.

She moved through a hallway with doors leading off in all directions—to the bathroom, a closet, the bedroom. There, abruptly, she stopped.

"Where is it? Get it!"

She didn't move, except to hunch her shoulders. Was she blanking from fear or—

"There is no proof, is there?"

She spun, arms out, hands clasped, and knocked me back into the hall. By the time I got my balance, she was out the front door.

I raced after her, but tires were screeching before I cleared the porch. I walked back into the house. I'd been worried about running into the police here when I arrived. That seemed lifetimes ago. Once Guthrie's wife—*wife!*—called 911, patrol cars would be lining up outside. I needed to get out fast. I wasn't crazy about taking the gun, but I damned well wasn't about to leave it lying around here. I pocketed it.

But why did she have it? What kind of woman comes to the door with a gun? What was she hiding? Who was she afraid of? What the hell was going on with this guy I so obviously had not known? I'd come here to get a sense of the life he lived beyond me, before the police rooted through it. Now I was twice as much in the dark.

I didn't expect local cops who'd picked up Higgins's request to warn me with a siren, but if Guthrie's wife called about a burglar, they might. I unlocked the back door and eyed the terrain for fast exits.

The cottage was three rooms and a bath. It was the kind of place a guy with a bed in his truck would live: rattan love seat with print cushions, a couple of folding chairs, and a plastic milk crate in between as a poor man's coffee table. The bedroom was practically an ode to cardboard: an open packing carton displaying socks and underwear and another with T-shirts. Laptop on square box. Hard, uninviting double bed. Plus still-sealed boxes. It looked like he was moving in. Or out. Or like his wife was.

His *wife*!

I paused, listening for a car, then booted up the computer.

It demanded a password.

Guthrie? Stuntman? Stuntgag? Truckjockey? Much as it galled me, I tried Melissa, but it didn't work either.

Why a password anyway? That didn't seem like him. I could hear Guthrie laughing and saying, "Who'd give a shit what I wrote?"

In the closet were more clothes—*his* clothes—slacks and shirts on hangers, jeans on hooks, and on the shelf some sweaters stuffed up there. The one in front was a green heather number that looked familiar. Had he worn that last year? Or the year before? Or was it just a green sweater like thousands of others? I pulled it down to sniff the neck. The others fell with it.

Behind them was an Oscar.

A gold-plated statuette. The real thing.

What was that doing here? Stuntmen don't get Oscars. Even stunt coordinators don't. The hoity-toity Academy of Motion Picture Arts voted against an award for best stunt coordination twice. No way would an Oscar come into Guthrie's possession, much less be hidden on his closet shelf.

I reached, stretching high. Not high enough.

Dents be damned. I jumped up, swiped, and knocked the statuette to the floor.

Outside brakes squealed. And again.

Jesus!

I grabbed Oscar and ran for the kitchen door.

I leapt from the steps down to the canyon side, doing a controlled slide down the dry grass. Too much noise. Too obvious. Catching a branch, I swung sideways. The gun smacked my thigh. Her gun. Could I be more red-handed? But I didn't dare toss it, not till I knew who was running toward me.

The front door slammed against a wall. "In here!" a man yelled.

Yelled. So, at least two people. I had to get back to the car and out of here. But the little house nearly filled the lot. A hedge, eight feet high and full of brambles, ran beside it. There was no way out but in the gauntlet between it and the building, right under the bedroom window where they were.

"Just find the goddamn keys! Okay, so look in the kitchen. Use your brain!" one of them yelled.

Keys? I had Guthrie's key. But of course they wouldn't be looking for the house key when they were already inside. Safe deposit box? What?

I couldn't go downhill. This was fire country, the underbrush already dead dry. My every step would crunch.

From inside I could hear movement, voices, but no more words. Sweat ran down my face, pasted my hair to my neck, my shirt to my back. My breath sounded like a locomotive. Who were they? Police? Friends of Guthrie's wife? Who?

An interior door slammed. Bathroom? Kitchen?

My foot slipped on the brush. The breaking brush crackled like the Fourth of July. I rammed my knees together to keep from sliding. The

men were six feet away from me. They could be out the back door in
ten seconds.

"What was that?"

"Hey, that's a car out there. We gotta move!"

These guys weren't the police! Who were they?

"They're coming down the steps. Move it, kitchen door!"

I jerked back. Both my feet slipped. The brush beneath them thun-
dered. I didn't dare budge. But I couldn't stay here.

The door sprang open.

Nowhere to hide! I had to divert them. With one look down at the
recipient's name, I grabbed at a branch, jumped hard to dig in my feet,
lobbed Casimir Goldfarb's shiny gold Oscar toward the brush at the far
side of the door. Then I ran.

"Hey, over here!"

I barely saw them as I raced up alongside the house. I started around
the front and caught myself just in time. Midway up the stone steps to the
street was a uniformed cop. Behind me men skidding, shouting. I could
wait and hope. Nope, last resort.

I eyed the cop. Was he here for Higgins or responding to Guthrie's
wife? I still could barely even *think* that word. Odds were he wouldn't
know her. I could trot out from my hiding place, trembling—boy, that'd
be easy—and say I was she, I was Guthrie's wife. It'd be the smart move.
A lot better than jail.

But I couldn't. I just couldn't. Even if I got six to ten to regret it.

The cop was beyond the end of the garage. He could see the house, but
not the rope hanging from the garage roof to the car engine on what must
once have been lawn. At least it wouldn't crackle under my feet. I shot him
one more look, but he was facing the other way, toward the shouts of the
chase downhill. Moving oh so carefully I crossed the dirt, took hold of the

rope, and pulled. It held. I grabbed it tight and climbed hand over hand. *Thank you, gym sweat!*

Eight hands up I swung into the garage exactly as the engine was meant to. I just caught myself before slamming into a cover stretched over a car. I caught my foot under the bumper and eased myself down to the floor, quietly but not silently. I barely dared breathe, straining to make sense of the thrashing around outside. I was safe—for the moment. But no way could I let the rope loose to swing back like a hand signaling, *Over here! Over here!* The bumper would do. I pulled up a corner of the cover and the whole front came loose, revealing a green Mustang GT fastback from the late sixties. Despite everything, I almost whistled. This was one great old car. It had dents but otherwise was so well preserved the paint had barely faded. A *Bullitt* car. Poor Guthrie! He must have spent ages on it. For an instant I pictured him squealing around a San Francisco corner like he was Bud Ekins or Steve McQueen.

With his fucking wife!

Could it be the real *Bullitt* car? No license plate—that meant nothing.

No time for fantasies! Still, I couldn't let it go. I checked the VIN on the dashboard, willing myself to remember it, as I pulled the cover back on.

The garage was crammed. Outside the shouts were coming closer. Had the cop nabbed the other guys? I eased back, closer to the hole I'd come in through. I still couldn't make out what they were saying. But my impression was that not much in the way of criminal apprehension was taking place.

Whatever. It wouldn't be long till someone was peering in here.

I eased next to the car. At the door, I stopped and tried to catalog sounds. No brakes were grinding or tires squealing now. I peered under the door, trying to get a fix on the action. And then, dammit, another patrol car pulled up.

The last thing I wanted, after getting myself out of Guthrie's house and avoiding the two guys inside, was to wait here, cringing in this dusty, dirty garage until someone opened the door. But that's what I was going to have to do.

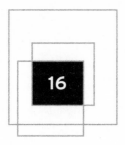

16

GUTHRIE'S GARAGE WAS not only filthy and filled with spiders, it was hot. The sun had been searing outside, but in here, under a dark roof, with no air circulation, it was a sauna. I swabbed my face and neck with a paper towel, but I was dripping before I wadded it up.

The sensible thing to do—if *sensible* could be used in relation to anything about this mess I'd gotten myself into—would be to find a perch above the garage doors so when they opened, I'd be ready to swing down and run. But I'd be damned if I'd gone through all this just to come up empty. I crept to the far end and stood next to the hole I'd climbed through. The front door of the house was visible, but no one was going in or out.

There were so many questions. Nothing made sense. For one thing, why were all these cops still here? They'd lost the guys who'd routed me. And they didn't seem to be searching for me, not that that was much comfort. Were they going over the house? Who'd called them? Guthrie's wife? Or had they caught the call from Higgins and arrived to find the burglars? Were they waiting for backups . . . and her? Lots of options, none good.

"Move it! Kitchen door!" Those weren't the instructions of a guy comfortable with the police. It wasn't likely that Rex Redmon would have given me the key and then called the goon squad. Which left, as I'd assumed all along, the woman with the gun.

Crap! How long had the miserable bastard been married? *Damn you! If you were here this minute I'd smack you black and blue. How long had you been lying to me, a year? Five years? The whole time? But you weren't satisfied with that, were you? You had to up the ante and say you—say you were as close to loving me as you'd ever managed. Why! Dammit, why? And what was it that put Leo in the picture? Why talk to him? About two-timing me?*

But then there was John. He was next on Guthrie's agenda and that conversation sure wasn't going to be about stringing me along.

Wait a minute! Melissa had answered the door with a pistol in her hand. There was nothing threatening about me. So, who was she expecting or avoiding? Or what was she hiding?

What the hell was going on here?

A cop in uniform trudged out the door of the house. Poor guy looked worse than I felt. He looked like he'd been in the shower, like he'd done chin-ups there, a thousand of them.

Go to your car, turn on your air conditioner. Drive away!

He was motioning to his buddy on the steps.

Oh, damn, they were settling in to guard the scene.

I leaned closer to the window, straining to make out their words.

"—switch off. You on this here porch, me in the car to start. Every twenty minutes."

"All fucking day?"

"Like I make the rules? Yeah."

"Hey, I didn't sign on to—"

"Write a note to the brass. Put it on pink paper, while you're at it."

The second guy muttered something, but the one on his way out was already headed for the steps and his car.

A car that would have the engine running and the air conditioning blasting loudly. Finally, my opportunity. I crept back, beside the Mustang, stepping over the mess of stuff on the floor. The place looked like Guthrie was using it for storage, not rebuilding that engine. I'd seen him work on his truck. Afterwards he always cleaned his tools and put them away. I'd watched him clean and replace them in the same order each time. He wasn't a guy to leave his garage a mess.

But he had.

Much as I wanted to, there wasn't time to think about this. What I needed to focus on was the cop. His air conditioner might cover the sound of me opening the garage door, but it wasn't going to keep him from seeing the action. It would, though, keep him from hearing me make a call and setting up a scene that just could work.

I had an ace in the hole. Blink Jones, long-time stuntman and now, according to Guthrie, an all-too-fearless driver. Also, all-too-loud. Guthrie had bitched about being woken out of a dead sleep by him gearing down into the switchbacks.

I had my own connection to Blink Jones.

I called. *Pick up! Come on! Bingo!* "Blink? Darcy Lott. I need a favor. It's dangerous and involves a fast car," I added, before he'd said more than "Hello."

"Where are you?"

I gave him the address.

"Guthrie's?"

"Yep." A spot well-known to everyone but me.

"So, what d'ya need?"

I told him. "It could get you in serious—"

"Honey, I'm sixty years old, got bones broken in every extremity, plus ribs and pelvis. I'm on six kinds of meds. The state's not going to jail me— can't afford my upkeep."

"Okay, just don't get caught."

"Hey, I'm not called Blink for nothing. And you're on the hook for dinner. I'll be there in ten minutes. I'll call you from the top."

I put the phone on vibrate and prepared to do what I hated most—wait.

Blink Jones was a legend. Many legends. I had no idea which ones were real, nor did I care. The stories were far too good to bother worrying about facts. But the one I happened to know was true was a few years back and ended up with him lighting out minutes ahead of the authorities and me ending up with his—now my—dog, Duffy, plus a bag of burglar tools. His contact information had been on Duffy's tag.

I started to grin, remembering . . .

Outside, a car door slammed. I listened for the slap-pause-slap of a cop heading down the wide cement slab steps. But there was no sound.

"—garage?" he yelled.

I started toward the back window. No! Too chancy. This was bad!

"Yeah," the cop said, "while I'm still cool."

The hell with escaping. Just where to stash the gun? Hell, where to stash *me*? Under the car? Too obvious. Out the window and down the rope? Too iffy. If the other cop spotted me I'd be cooked.

Which left a garbage bag. I unrolled the black plastic, lifted myself up on an old metal filing cabinet, squatted head down, pulled the bag over my head, and poked the smallest eye hole in history. As a hiding place this was so dicey. The old, rusty cabinet threatened to buckle. The flimsy bag stuck to my sweaty skin and crackled every time I breathed. And I was scrunched up so tight my feet were about to go numb.

And I still had the gun!

How much time had passed? What about that ten minutes? Worse yet, if the cop was in the garage with me, my deal with Blink wouldn't matter.

The garage door opened. My head was on my knees, arms around them, like a fat little amphora.

"Look at this mess. He could hide a tank in here."

The other cop yelled something I couldn't make out.

"Yeah, I don't know either. I'll poke—"

My legs quivered. The bag was rattling like tin in the wind.

"Hey, look at this! Guy's got a *Bullitt* car. Good shape, too. Man, if I—"

Please don't be a car nut!

My phone vibrated. I squeezed every muscle in my body to keep from reacting. The cop was out of my sightline. Did he hear it? They could have heard it in Vegas!

His footsteps stopped. He was listening. My hand was on the phone. Desperately, I pushed the toggle. *Please catch before the next ring! Please go silent!*

It sounded like he was treading carefully among the clutter, moving toward me. I could jump him— *No, idiot! Then what would you do, after you assaulted a police officer?*

Outside, brakes screamed. There was the unmistakable noise of wheels jamming hard to the side.

"Jesus! What's that asshole—"

Metal crunched.

"He hit my car! He hit my fucking car!" He ran.

I jumped and whipped around the side of the garage.

Blink kept on going down the hill.

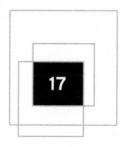

17

"THE COP DIDN'T get close enough to see your rear plate?" I asked.

"He couldn't even make out the color of the car. Honey-love, I'm the best."

"You sure are in my book. You saved my hide on this one. I had—"

Blink Jones made a "stop" sign with his hand. "Don't tell me! I make it a point not to know what I shouldn't. I make sure everyone's aware of that. That's how I've survived as long on the outside as I have."

I could believe that. The first time I'd come across him, he'd beat it off a set a hair's breadth before the sheriff pulled up.

He hoisted his glass and drank. "Like I told you, better to not know what you don't know."

I shrugged. The nondescript wooden booth in this easy-to-miss tavern east of Santa Barbara was the architectural equivalent of Blink himself, who'd made being unmemorable his life's work. He was a short, muscular guy in loose chinos and an oversized T-shirt that hid his physique. Brown stubble covered his head above his round face. I was holding my own with him, but inside I was shaking, and the more so the farther I got from my crazy afternoon. I was desperate for someone with whom to talk it out, sorry it wouldn't be him.

Logically, that was just as well. Regardless of his protestations, Blink Jones lived too close to the edge to be a secure receptacle for anyone's secrets. I didn't know a lot about him, but that much I did. I was drinking Scotch. I hate Scotch, so it's the only safe liquor when I don't dare drink as much as I need. And rattled as I was tonight, I needed to upend the bottle. "Sidescraping the patrol car was brilliant. And that 360 you did? How'd you know where the road could take it?"

"You askin' how well I know Guthrie?"

"How well do you?"

"Like I say, I steer clear of secrets."

"And he had some. Which one, in particular, are we talking about?"

"Like I say—"

"Blink, to a woman trying to find out about a guy she cared about, discretion isn't a virtue, it's a pain in the butt. Guthrie's dead. Murdered. I've known him for years and I'd've sworn he wasn't a guy to bring down murder on himself. And yet . . ." I looked over at him, waiting till I caught his eye. "And yet he ended up with the back of his head bashed in. He's not asking you to keep secrets now. You know where he lived. What else?"

If he hadn't had nearly a full glass, he would have been waving the waitress over and chatting her up while he decided how to handle me. As it was, he sipped his drink, washed it down with a swallow of water, and sipped again. "I don't like knowing things, even—especially—about a guy who gets murdered. I half wish I hadn't caught your call. Only half, and that's a compliment. But, okay, Guthrie. Hard not to like the guy, right? Great trucker, the best! He loved that truck, would spend days tweaking the systems, getting that baby to slap left like a hand after a mosquito. And other gags, high falls, bike work, tube climbs. I'd see him out at Zahra's hole in the desert—"

"Blink, he had some strange things at that house. There's a green Mustang that's a ringer for the car in *Bullitt*. And, even odder, he had an Oscar."

"Stuntmen don't get Oscars."

"Exactly. But"—I didn't want to say I'd been rooting through his closet—"he had one. In his possession."

"Whose?"

I hesitated. I liked Blink; I owed him; but trust him? I was on the fence.

"Damn. You can't sell them. You get one and hit hard times, tough; statue has to go back to the Academy. That's the contract." Now he did signal the waitress and pointed to his empty glass. "You can't sell them, *legitimately.* 'Course private collectors'll buy anything. They say there's a guy in Vegas who's got one from every year. There was a spurt of movie memorabilia burglaries a while back—you wouldn't believe what Mary Pickford's headdress or Silver's harness sold for. The real Oscar winners panicked. They started putting copies on the mantel and the real ones in the vault. There're always stories about statues going missing. One ended up on the edge of the La Brea tar pits. And it wasn't for *Jurassic Park*."

I laughed. God, it felt good to laugh again. In that spirit, I jumped off the fence on his side. "Casimir Goldfarb."

He actually whistled. "Guthrie had Old Oscarless's Oscar? Damn."

"Come on, tell me!"

"Goldfarb was a director and a prize asshole, though that's not what he got the award for. He pissed off a kid. Kid slashed his tires and snatched his most prized possession."

"And?"

"Kid vanished. Goldfarb never came near winning again. Thus the ep-ithet 'Old Oscarless.'"

"Didn't he—"

The door to the bar opened to let in an appalling sight. Two uniformed officers. One was bald.

"Yikes, cops!"

"Stay cool."

I clutched my glass, my hands just about melting the ice cubes. *They aren't the same guys. There are thousands of cops in Southern California. Probably thousands with shaved heads. Relax.* Relax—was there ever a more useless order?

The hairless cop took a bar stool. The other headed for the john.

"I'm too visible," I said. "I should have shaved my head, too. Look at this, it's—"

"A red flag?"

"Right." The time for chitchat was over. "I have to get out of here. I'll owe you that fancy dinner."

"Hang on. They'll be leaving."

"How do I know they aren't reconnaissance?"

"Like ants?" He was laughing.

Maybe he was right. But the arrival of cops was a bad omen. I leaned forward and lowered my voice. "Listen, I know you keep secrets 'cause it's healthy. My mom's that way; it's how she survived raising the seven of us. But Guthrie's dead and you know more than you're telling me. So spill it."

"Or?" He was still grinning.

"Just cut the crap. If he's so crazy about his truck, how come he's living up in the canyon where he can't drive it? If he's so straightforward"—shit! I hated to sound like such an utter patsy—"how come he's coming on to me while he's got a wife down here he's living with?"

"Whoa! A wife?"

132

"Well, a woman who *says* she's his wife."

"News to me."

"Opens the door of his house, gun in hand, and says she's his wife."

Blink shook his head. "Doesn't that gun bit send off a few flares? Sure doesn't sound like 'the little woman' to me."

"Okay, then, live-in?"

"Not as I saw."

"Then who the hell is she? She called herself Melissa Guthrie."

"Good question."

A wave of emotion—relief, guilt, the whole mix—swept through me. *I am so sorry, Guthrie!* I felt like shit. I wanted to take this new info and run with it. But this time caution prevailed. "Okay. If she wasn't his wife and wasn't his girlfriend, just how'd she get into his house? The door wasn't forced."

He glanced at his glass that was, once again, too full to provide an excuse to call the waitress over. "You know Guthrie. He's a loose guy. Gone a lot. Work's tight, we all know. So you give someone a hand—"

"That woman wasn't bunking in there till she could find work."

"Hey, we all take Acting 1A."

I had one more question. I could have asked him, but I was sick of Blink's loop of not-knowing. Besides, I could find out a lot more easily without him.

I had come up empty on Guthrie's house. Going back there was not merely tempting fate; it was poking it in the eye. Guthrie's house was the last place I ought to be. The last place I wanted to be.

To Blink, I said, "You drive up the road again and let me know if anyone's watching his house."

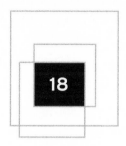

18

I PICKED THE darkest spot at the bottom of Guthrie's canyon and waited
for Blink's call. It would take him a good fifteen minutes to get to the
house, which would be all the time I would need to do a little research.

It was almost midnight, but I wasn't exhausted, or apprehensive, or
anything else. Blink had, after all, insisted on having his promised dinner.
We'd talked about the decline in live stunt work, the rise in electronics,
the shift in emphasis to acrobatics that left old guys like Blink focusing
on car gags and praying that they wouldn't be digitalized. I'd been lucky,
he'd said. It was true, though not flattering. *He'd* been unlucky. But we
all make choices.

Guthrie's choice may have been to let friends use his house. An Oscar
was stashed there. I hauled out the new everything-phone that my brother
Gary had given me (so I could figure it out for him), pulled up Google, and
typed in "Casimir Goldfarb + Oscar theft." The first hits were trade rag
stories on the theft that told me no more than Blink had. I tried the name
of the movie and scrolled through the cast and crew on three sites before
I found one that named personnel down to the gaffers and grips who as-
sisted the lighting techs.

Omigod!

One of the grips was Ryan Hammond. *Ryan Hammond,* Guthrie's friend from the Union Street bars.

The Oscar theft was in July, two and a half months before the Loma Prieta earthquake. Now, twenty years later, there's the statuette in Guthrie's closet. What did that mean?

My phone vibrated. "Yes?"

"It's clear."

"Thanks."

"You want me to help?"

"Yeah, answer me this about Casimir Goldfarb's Oscar, was Ryan Hammond the kid who stole it?"

It was a moment before he said, "That's the story. But there's no proof."

"Circumstantial evidence?"

"One day that kid and the statuette are there; next day both are gone. That's all I can tell you. But listen, you find anything tonight, let me know." Before I could protest, he clicked off.

Blink might be trying to figure out how the Oscar got from Ryan Hammond to Guthrie, but he didn't know about their San Francisco connection. Had they been friends all along? Or not-friends? Whichever, Ryan Hammond was my best bet to find out about Guthrie. But where was Hammond?

That was one of the things I was hoping Guthrie's house would tell me. It took me twice as long as I expected just to get up the winding road in the dark. In daylight, finding Guthrie's place had been easy, but now picking out the house was a whole lot harder. I parked a hundred yards farther down and walked back, eyeing cars that might be there for surveillance. Carefully, silently, I crossed the uneven slab steps, tossed a pebble down against the house, and stood dead still. But there was no sound, no reaction. I had to believe no one was there.

The police had closed up the house. But, of course, I had the key.

There is no way to search a house in the dark, on a moonless night, except with a flashlight. You can keep the light low to the ground, shield it with your hand, and turn it on only at strategic moments, but if anyone's watching, you're busted.

I unlocked the door and walked into the living room where Guthrie's not-wife had greeted me with a pistol nine hours ago. I crossed the tiny hallway where she'd tossed me aside. At the bedroom door, I switched on the flashlight and laid it on the floor, whipped back into the kitchen, and waited. If anyone showed, I'd be out of here in a snap.

As my eyes adjusted to the dark, I thought again how much this place resembled a college guy's apartment, with its easy-to-move furniture, makeshift coffee table, and the predictable candles on the mantel.

After five minutes, I began to worry more about the batteries running out than being discovered. I'd known so little about Guthrie, I'd automatically made up the rest. Whatever I'd assumed was like a dream, and with the same staying power. Leo kept reminding me I was looking through my own eyes, but this was way worse. It wasn't that I'd so much *believed* he lived in his truck as that I'd never really thought about him living elsewhere, certainly not a place like this. Had he actually lived here with the hostile Melissa? Surely, Blink would have known. Surely, Blink would *not* have told me, either. I wanted to trust Guthrie the way I had the day before he died when he was so tormented, when I was ready to overlook anything. But now, he was making it damned hard.

Now, something didn't feel right about this place. Something niggled—what was it?

It suddenly occurred to me what was missing. There were no newspapers, magazines, mail, glasses, plates, napkins, tissues—not a scrap of the detritus of people living here.

Outside, a car engine strained coming up the hill.

No time to stand around and ponder. I headed back to the bedroom. The sweaters were in a heap, the underwear scattered over the floor, and the laptop gone. I lifted the bedspread.

It wasn't a bed at all. I yanked the spread off and stared at the cardboard boxes underneath. Big boxes that held brown paper, bubble wrap, tape. I picked up one and tore it open. It held two framed pictures, wrapped professionally. I pulled out one and stared, dumbstruck, at a poster from the original *Stagecoach*—not the remake—the one with John Wayne, Claire Trevor, and Yakima Canutt doing his famous gag. For an instant I imagined standing in the back of a dark theater in 1939, watching him work his way back between the pounding hooves and under the stagecoach.

I checked the back, but any key to the provenance was covered beneath the frame backing. I pulled the wrapping off the other: *The Grapes of Wrath*. There was Henry Fonda under the orange title, above the credits. The colors weren't even faded. The corners were worn, but otherwise it was perfect—no rips. It barely looked handled.

I cut open the boxes that had been the bed and unwrapped masks— elaborate painted numbers with curved feathers two feet long. Obviously costume artifacts. Likewise a red damask robe. None of it was priceless, but none would sell for less than three figures, and none, I was willing to bet, was here legally.

I couldn't believe Guthrie was a thief. A smuggler? A fence?

I wanted to give him the benefit of the doubt, but the truth was I didn't know what to believe any more. Guthrie'd been so distraught, then so relieved after he'd talked to Leo. If I could call Leo— But Leo was off at the monastery, far out of phone range.

If I could find Ryan Hammond, I was guessing there'd be plenty he could tell me—about this house, the Oscar, and what Guthrie had been up to. I shone the light around, but there were no papers at all here—no sheets, business cards, receipts, nothing that could give me even a hint where he was. Whoever had been here last hadn't missed a scrap.

But what about that ranch Guthrie'd talked about, the one where he'd tried to deal with whatever it was he'd done?

A ranch in a hole in the desert, he'd said.

Hole in the desert. Blink had used that very phrase. About Zahra Raintree's place. He'd seen Guthrie there.

I'd heard about Zahra Raintree's secret stunt ranch ever since I started in the business. The place was almost myth, located in the high desert somewhere around the old oasis of 29 Palms where Hollywood stars of the talkies went to get soaked or dry out. Or both, maybe. When Guthrie and I had been on location out there, I'd heard tales of Zahra Raintree's secret place, Rancho Desperado. But no one knew quite where it was, and when pressed, no one really knew anyone who'd been there. As if it were a mirage.

Guthrie'd had a Jeep that week and we were sure we'd find Zahra's no matter how well concealed or how forbidding the terrain. We were, after all, stunt drivers. But things heated up on the set, and when my bit was done, I had a message from my agent to hightail it back to Burbank for a gag on a TV show that was sure to turn into steady work, but didn't.

Guthrie, though, had no need to rush away. I'd left him as I always did, with a kiss and the certainty that there'd be a next time even if I didn't know when. Almost a year had passed before I saw him again. If I'd thought about Rancho Desperado at all, I might have assumed he'd tell me if he'd unearthed it. I didn't think to ask. And now it struck me that he might have found the place and, like the rest before him, kept it to himself.

I didn't expect Zahra Raintree to answer all my questions—not by a long shot. If Guthrie'd been out there trying to get his head straight, she might not know a lot, but she was the best hope I had.

I climbed back up the cement steps to the road. The gun in my fanny pack slapped my back. A gun that could have been involved in theft or who knew what. I'd skated too close to the edge to have it found on me. Time to wipe it down and get rid of it. If I left it under the clutter in the garage it could be there for years unnoted.

I pulled open the garage door and looked . . . looked at the empty space. The car was gone. The green Mustang like Steve McQueen's in *Bullitt.*

Like? I remembered one of the cops, this afternoon, carrying on about how well preserved it was, scrapes and dents and all.

One way to tell. I called my brother, John. Luck was with me—the call went to voicemail and I asked him to see if he could come up with the vehicle identification number for the *Bullitt* car and check it against the VIN I remembered.

The car hadn't been heard of in years. I couldn't begin to guess what it would bring from a collector. Maybe the memorabilia trade here was a lot pricier than a couple posters.

I checked the garage door again. If there had been crime scene tape, it had been ripped off.

There might be other possibilities, but one thing I knew was that "Blink Jones" and "playing loose with the law" went together. I hadn't mentioned the Mustang to him. But there's a time and place for everything. This was the wrong place to be hanging around making phone calls; the hour was way too late. I punched in his number anyway.

19

"Blink?" I said to his machine. "Blink? Pick up. I'm not calling from jail. Hey, I just want to ask you a question." Still no response. I peered out at the steep, narrow street, thinking about Guthrie's tale of Blink burning rubber on this residential street. Odd, for a guy who valued keeping a low profile. Why take the chance? Why here? But he'd recognized Guthrie's address right off. Odd, too. You know where acquaintances live, but how often do you remember the house number?

Just what *was* going on here? Was Blink involved with the memorabilia stash in Guthrie's house? Was the stuff hot? And the Mustang, was it hot, and more to the point, *where* was it?

Calling him now was not the safest move, but it was nothing to my next plan. "Hey, Blink, how long's the message memory on your phone? I'm ready to use it all."

That got him. "What?"

"I need to ask a question. I don't expect you'll know the answer, but—"

That smallest of grunts I heard now wouldn't mean anything to someone who hadn't just spent a couple of hours with the man. I recognized offense taken.

"Rancho Desperado. How can I get there?"

"You can't." *Big surprise!*

"Because?"

"Well, obviously, because you don't know where it is."

"And you do?"

"I didn't say—"

"So you don't know, right?"

No reply. Silence with Blink was a bad sign. "That's okay. From everything I've heard, Zahra Raintree's very picky about who she lets in. Guthrie went there in—"

"Guthrie?"

"Yeah." I was fishing and he knew it.

Another grunt was all I heard.

"Yeah, well, I get that no one goes around talking about it, but I'll bet she hasn't heard about Guthrie. I'll bet, too, she's the kind of woman who'll be pissed if she sits out there ignorant." I was holding my breath. Maybe Zahra never got angry; maybe I'd trotted too far out on this frail little limb. He stayed mum and this time I didn't break in. If he didn't bite now . . .

"She's probably already heard," I said, as if backtracking.

"Maybe so."

Enough of this! "Listen, I'm headed out there. Are you going to help me or not?"

"I didn't say—"

"What *are* you saying?"

"Come to my house and let's talk."

If it seemed like I'd landed my fish, I actually wasn't fooling myself. I knew he figured his best bet was keeping an eye on me.

□ □ □

Barcum Lane was dark, too rustic for street lights. The wind fingered my hair and iced my neck and back, reminding me anew that even in August, it's cold near the coast. I grew up a couple of blocks from the Pacific; how could I have forgotten even for a moment? Despite the attempts to land-scape it otherwise, Southern California is desert; after sunset the heat evaporates fast. I got out and double-checked Blink's address. If he'd had me come to a trailer park I wouldn't have been surprised, but this hacienda was on a full lot with old trees. There was no outside light on, but even so I could tell the house was in good shape. I was halfway to the door when he appeared, shutting it behind him.

"Shhh. We'll take my truck."

"It's 3:00 A.M."

"We'll get there with the sun."

"Let me use your bathroom first."

"I need to get gas and pick up coffee. You can—"

"I've done this before. I can be quick."

"Do it at the gas station."

I patted his arm. "Is there a reason you're keeping me out of the house?"

"Damn right. Like you already admitted knowing, it's three o'clock in the morning. My wife has to get up at six to get to work."

Your wife! Knock me over! Wife, and a house on a tree-lined street! He'd sure landed on his feet! "Gas station's fine. But one request."

"What's that?" He opened the door of a tan pickup.

"The coffee. Is there some better place to get it?"

"Like you said, it's three in the morning. Even in Frisco you'd be drink-ing swill."

"Maybe on the way? It won't be three o'clock forever." *Coffee shop or any other place I could use as a landmark?*

"Just get in, honey-love."

143

"I'll follow you."

He glanced at the rental. "Not in that. We're not talking pavement out there."

I climbed into his truck. Most of the time when I'm in the death seat, I'm alert for every danger a nonprofessional driver's going to miss—the belch of pavement that can flip a fast-moving car, the hidden slicks on the road, the kids and bikes shooting out from between cars, idiots chatting away on cell phones and pulling into traffic without a glance. But Blink was making rent doing car gags. The truck was dark and warm, the suspension good. And it had been how long since I'd slept? I was so tempted. But not enough to be riding into the dark and not map the route as we drove. If things went bad, I needed to know if the nearest town was San Bernardino or Calexico. "Okay, you're right. Coffee first. No matter how bad, it'll be better than nothing."

That was untrue, as I realized when I woke in a panic hours later at sunrise in the high desert.

How could I have let myself sleep?

Now I had no idea what direction we'd come or where we were. Blink could have driven in circles for all I knew. Now—oh, shit! My eyes were crusted shut and I had a headache, maybe from sleeping funny, or could it have been something added to that revolting coffee? Was I really safe with this guy? "Where are we?" I said, trying to keep the panic from my voice.

"Almost there."

"What're we near?"

"Nothing."

That was the truth. Flat and tan in all directions. "What's the last—"

We shot over a hill and off into air. I grabbed for the door moments before the wheels hit road. We weren't going straight down, but close to it. I braced my feet. Ahead was scrub brush. The "road" was a path with sharp turns. "No wonder no one comes here on their own."

"Getting out's worse."

"Great."

Dust blasted through the window, but I wasn't about to let go to press the button to raise it. On one side was the hill, on the other a drop. The truck hit a rock and bounced so close to the edge there was only sky out my window. "Slow down!"

"Don't dare."

I knew what he meant. On runs like this you've got to focus on things as they are. A change—*any* change—will throw you. Literally.

The truck bounced against the hillside, slammed into the track, skidded right. The front wheel was off the track. It was spinning in air. *Ease left! Don't pull hard. Just ease it!* I kept quiet. Any change . . . I was desperate to slide to the window, stare out, find a spot out there to jump to, to start my tumble down into nothingness.

Instead, I did the smart thing and slid tight against Blink, shifting the balance in the truck. The wheels grabbed. Neither of us sighed, not yet.

Ahead was air. Blink pulled hard left around an outcropping.

"Goat trail," I muttered.

He made a sound that could have been anything.

The air was hotter; the bright morning sun glinted off the hood ornament. *Hood ornament! What a stupid—*

He hit the hillside, using it to slow the truck. Then I saw why. The path shot straight down. The hillside gave way. The wheels were on the edge on both sides. It was like driving on a rope. I eased back midway to the window, my hand braced as close to the handle as I dared. If the truck went off, it would go where Blink couldn't see the edge, on my side.

There'd be no time to aim, only to slam the door open, leap, and try for a controlled slide.

Something scraped the sides. Cactus. I risked a glance out the window. Barrel cactus was growing up over the edge. The truck was slowing.

"Look ahead, Darcy."

"Omigod!" Under an awning of anorexic desert trees were cabins, alongside what looked like an adobe lodge and a barn. A hundred yards to the side were three tall cylinders. Bud vases for prehistoric flowers? But straight ahead, out in the open, was the thing that caught my eye. "That's what I heard about this place."

It looked like a thin jumble of wires. Like a high-wire setup gone mad. Wires curved and turned, like the scariest of roller-coaster tracks. But there were no comforting support beams; only the air seemed to be holding them up. It took me a minute to spot the platform forty feet in the air and make out a girl standing on the edge, one hand reaching behind to what had to be a carabiner attaching her to the wires, the other hand over her heart as if she were praying.

"Look, she's going to shoot the wires! Wow, this really is a great place!"

"Yeah," Blink agreed. His tone reminded me he was a car guy, not someone who did high falls or leaps. He wasn't looking with envy as I was.

The girl was dead still, like she was doing a run-through in her mind, picturing herself pushing off hard enough to take the first loop. She reached around her hips to check the lower carabiner behind her sacrum.

The truck was barely moving now, and Blink was watching her, too. I realized he'd shut off the motor lest he spook her. People like us are trained to deal with sudden noise, but a distraction's a distraction. He eased to a halt.

When I looked up, she was rechecking her shoulder harness. I followed her gaze down to the safety net, a thick, wide cocoon that could haul in a rhino. There was no wind at all. My arm out the window already felt hot from the sun. Perfect conditions. "She's not going to get buffeted."

"Nope," Blink whispered.

Now she double-checked her butt harness. She had blonde hair, long and tied in a knot in back to keep it from cutting into her field of vision. For a moment I thought she was naked but quickly made out her beige unitard. "That's the fourth time she's checked the harness. Must be her first try on this."

"There she goes!"

She pushed off. Hands out, feet together, she looked like she was flying straight out, picking up speed, holding form. I forgot the harness and went with the illusion. The wire curved left and she sailed around it, now straight again, faster. She shot up a loop, momentum carrying her over the wire now and around. Suddenly her feet dropped, her momentum died, and she skidded back to a low point on the wire, suspended there like a sack. It was a moment before she managed to rock back and forth enough to reach the wire with her hands and then her feet and to start inching back toward the platform.

"Bad form break."

Blink nodded noncommittally.

"Bitch to get back. Still, not bad for a first try."

He said nothing and I had the sense that he was waiting for me to make a move. I eyed the wire one last time. This trek was taking way more time than I had. Still I couldn't resist. "I've got to try that!"

"Big surprise! But don't count on Zahra letting you. This isn't Disneyland."

"I can ask." I opened the door and eyed the lodge, beyond the aerial setup. There were no other vehicles around. Did Zahra Raintree take a mule train out of here to get groceries? Driving the path we'd come in on would get old fast. During rainy season folks would be eating roots and tubers.

I could have asked Blink. Instead, I tried for surprise. "Where'll I find Ryan Hammond?"

"Hammond? What makes you think he'd be here, with Zahra?"

"Have you seen him here?"

"How many times do I have to tell you, I don't know the guy. Don't know where he is, where he's been. He could be dead for all I know."

"It's Guthrie who's dead. And could be Ryan Hammond's been using his house to store his Oscar. Guthrie's idea, or Hammond taking advantage of his absence?"

He jumped down from the cab and slammed the door so hard the glove compartment door sprang open. I leapt out and got in his face. "So what's the deal with Hammond?"

"Jesus, I can't tell you how sorry I am I answered the phone. I do you one favor after another and this is—"

"Oh, please! I like you, Blink, I really do. But I don't fool myself that you're any altruist. You didn't survive this long without watching your ass. You drove me here because you knew I'd hunt this place down. And if I did, you wanted to be here for . . ." *For what?* "Cut to the chase and just tell me where to find Hammond here."

"Hey, I'm the one with the wheels. I can leave you—"

"Not likely. Because, Blink, you know I will spread the word—"

"I don't think so."

"Think again."

He rested a hand on my shoulder, and not in a friendly way. "Stunt guys have come and gone from this place and no one has ever sold it out.

Including Guthrie, your boyfriend. He didn't even let on to you. Make you wonder? Trust me, you're not going to rat it out either. And so," he released my shoulder, "you got nothing to pressure me with. Better do what you're going to do and get back here before it's too hot to breathe."

"So why'd you bring me?"

"I'm an altruist."

Shit! What was it the man did not want me to find? It was still not quite 7:00, but the place seemed oddly empty. No one was out watching the girl on the wire. Beyond the final support pole for the wires was the barn. What went on in there?

A screen door opened in the lodge across the dirt parking area. Before I could make out a figure, it shut. "Hello?" I called, running toward it.

The metal door was sturdy and new, at odds with the sod building. "Hello?"

I knocked. No response. I waited, then tried the door. Locked. "Hello!" I peered in around the edge of a drawn shade. The room was dark and looked empty by now.

Where were all the people this place was set up to serve? I ran across the hard ground to the big aluminum barn. Not the best for a desert that's baking in summer and bone-chilling in winter. If you were inside in the rain, it'd be akin to an artillery attack.

The narrow end had a roll-up garage door and a small door with a window. Both locked. I went through the knock and holler routine again, to the same end. Blink sauntered up but offered no help. I couldn't tell whether he was just waiting me out or what.

"Does that girl on the wire live here alone?" I asked in exasperation.

"She's not Zahra."

"I can see that. Zahra Raintree must be sixty. She was doubling before I was born. But where's everyone else?"

Blink shrugged.

"Who was here the last time you were?"

"I never said—"

"Oh, come on! You found a road a vulture would have missed."

"I've seen the road, not the ranch."

"Who took you?"

He looked up, but not as if he was expecting the answer from the wire or the sky. He was concocting.

Goddamn you! "Never mind."

I strode back to the lodge door and pounded. "I know you're there. Save us both time."

Nothing. I pounded harder.

"Go away!" It was a female voice.

"Zahra?" I said.

"Leave!"

"Or what? You'll call the sheriff to come bouncing down your road? Look, I'm just here to ask about Damon Guthrie."

"I don't know any Damon Guthrie."

"Sure you do. Stunt guy. Little older than me. Balding, ponytail. Genius with truck gags."

She hesitated just the way Blink had. "Nope." She was standing a couple feet behind the screen door, backlit in the dark room. Her hair was cropped and I could see the outline of muscles in her lean body. She looked like she could still handle any stunt I could. She looked like she could handle *me*. I wished I could see her face, to read her and get a clue how to play this.

I went with the truth, sort of. "Damon Guthrie was my guy. We're both in the business and we weren't together much—really not much—but suddenly things popped for us, you know? And then he died. And I realized I know nothing about him, except that once when we were doing a truck-and-drop sequence near 29 Palms, we'd talked about finding you after. That was ten years ago." I paused, trying to assess the sound of her breathing.

Was she wary, suspicious, or, like Blink, concocting?

"Back then he had hair on top. Short, then. He did high falls—you've got to have seen him. The long slide down the cliff in *Red Rock*? The leap over the ravine in *Cayenne Bramble*? Now he's got this eighteen-wheeler he modified so it slices left and right. I'm sure you've seen it, I mean in gags, not coming down your road here. He did the gags in *Drag Shot*, both the truck one and the high fall."

I thought I heard her murmur appreciatively but wasn't sure.

"Now he's dead. And I don't even know who he was."

"Well, honey-love, ain't that always the way?"

Honey-love! The term had a sweetness when Blink used it, but it was all acid coming from her. I'd never, ever heard it from anyone other than these two, who Blink insisted had never met. Yeah, right! "Zahra, I—"

She stepped out of my line of vision and walked away.

She could simply stay inside there. But I'd be damned if she was going to scoot out the rear. I ran to the end of the lodge, around the side to the back. No sign of her. Blink was nowhere in sight. If he was smart, he'd be sitting back in the truck with the air conditioning on.

What held my attention, however, was the trio of junk cars at the bottom of a narrow dirt path. Three of them, all so rusted it would take forensics to figure out their original color. They could have been parked there yesterday or in 1977.

The only person visible still was the girl on the wire. *Still* on the wire, inching back from her failed try. I swiped my arm across my forehead, hoping my T-shirt arm would mop the sweat. Then I pulled up the shirt and used the front. Even with that, the effect was momentary. How bad was it up there, hanging from the wire in the direct sun?

I eyed the truck to make sure that's where Blink was. Then I strode over to the upright that anchored the wires, a wooden utility pole with metal rungs sticking out on both sides. Above, the blonde was a yard from the platform. She was in no danger of anything greater than frustration. I could sure share that one with her. I moved quickly up the pole, the metal hot on my hands.

Spotting me, she stared; her face tightened with fear. Her hands went slack. She dropped and slid. If she hadn't been hooked on, she'd have fallen to the ground.

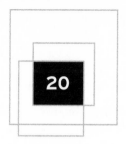

20

"You okay?" I double-timed it up the pole, onto the ledge. "Swing your legs up so I can grab them and reel you in."

She didn't move.

"You're not going to fall. You're harnessed on in two spots. Swing your legs over here." Still no shift. This was fear. Logic was useless. But there was one sure way to cut through and get action. "Guess your glutes are so out of shape you can't lift those tree trunks of legs."

Her legs shot up. I grabbed an ankle and guided her onto the platform beside me. She shifted into a squat, head on knees, panting.

A crack came from below. I just about dived for the net. But it wasn't a gunshot, only the lodge door opening. No one came out, but the door had been opened for a reason, probably not to bring me lemonade. Blink must have seen it, too; he turned on the truck's engine. Ready to cut and run? Him, maybe; me, no. I had too many questions. This place was like stunt camp. But why the secrecy? With one ad or even word of mouth, Zahra'd be turning people away. Stars would be paying big-time; studios would underwrite a pool, sauna, and masseuse, whatever Zahra wanted.

The blonde lifted her head. "You didn't do me any favor."

"Wasn't my intent. I'm here about Guthrie."

"Who?"

"Damon Guthrie. The best truck wrangler in the business. About fifty, balding, ponytail."

"What was he in?"

I reeled off a couple of chase flicks in which he had truck gags and the high falls I'd mentioned to Zahra.

"Never heard of 'em."

"Ah, stunt work. The industry's way to maintain our anonymity."

Her eyes twitched, suggesting she'd heard that line before.

So you are *in the business.* "How'd you wind up here?"

She shook her head stiffly.

"Just curious."

She grabbed the pole looking uncertain. "Who *are* you?"

"Darcy Lott. Just did a power slide on a set in the Port of Oakland—bike under truck. You?"

For the first time she really looked at me, looked me over. "Wow! How'd it go?"

"There was a minor timing problem. Nothing, really. I saved it. Just minor burns on my hands." I held one out to show its recovery.

"So why are *you* here now?"

"Like I said, I'm looking for Damon Guthrie. Do you want me to describe him again?"

"What was his problem?"

I was beginning to get the picture. "Don't know. But it's an unusual name."

"We don't use names here."

Below, metal scraped. She jolted, clasping the pole tighter. I shot a glance at the lodge. Had a door opened and shut again?

"You say you've done gags," she said. "Prove it."

"You're on." I wrapped my arms around her ribs, clasped my elbows, and pushed off. Still harnessed to the wire, she shot off the platform with me on her back. We hit the first turn fast, flipped up and over the loop and down—me hanging below. My legs were taut, my feet outside hers, forcing her into position. We swung left, halfway up a loop, but there was no way to work the wire from my position. Our weight was too much. We slowed to a stop around the same spot she had before.

"Here's your proof." I let go and dropped into the net, stretching wide to spread my weight and deaden the bounce. The air felt good in the second it took to hit the net. I bounced up, ran to the edge, and climbed back up the pole. When I reached the platform, she was hauling herself back along the wire. I might have convinced her I was a stunt double, but I sure didn't make a friend.

No one was coming toward us. Were we alone out here in the middle of the desert, just us, the woman behind the screen door in the lodge, and Blink in his climate-controlled truck?

When she was near enough, I hauled her in again. Her leotard was soaked.

"Big joke, huh, Marcy?"

"*Darcy.* I'm sorry about stranding you. But, look, I'm just asking a simple question. Have you seen my guy? I know he was here," I lied, "but I don't know when."

She stood hanging into the pole, looking down.

I couldn't tell whether she was avoiding my question or merely exhausted. "How long have you been up here?"

"Since light."

Hours. Hours on a platform in the sun, on a wire that she couldn't handle.

"How's this for a deal? Tell me about Guthrie and I'll show you how to do the loops."

"You think you can do them on the first try?"

"I know it." *Yeah, right.*

"Then do it."

"Tell!" *What's the big secret?*

Her neck and shoulders were red. Her blonde hair was matted to her head.

"You've been here for hours, not doing the loops. You could be here for days, weeks. This is a big gift I'm offering you, for a very small and easy bit of information. Guthrie, what did he do here?"

She scanned the ground. "He's the chimney builder."

"Chimney builder?"

She pointed to the three cylinders I'd thought of as giant bud vases, a yard wide and each one larger than the next. The smallest was maybe ten feet high, the largest between two and three stories. "He built chimneys."

"Are those picnic areas? Ovens leading to those chimneys?"

"No. Just the chimneys. That's all I know."

Chimneys not attached to anything. Chimneys in the desert. "Why?" Boy, did this make no sense at all. "You must have asked why."

"No, I mustn't. I'm here because I panicked on a set, doing something just like this. I hung over a ravine for an hour while the crew battled a wire pulling off its mooring and I tried not to move a muscle. After that I could barely make myself look down to tie my shoes. I lie awake every night, dreading morning when I have to come back here. It took me over a week to step off this platform and even hang from the wire holding onto the edge. I don't have time to worry about what other people are doing."

I wanted to wrap an arm around her and press the panic out. I'd had a friend, a newbie, stranded like that. I'd heard her screams. She was okay, no thanks to me. I still couldn't bring myself to talk about that incident. "Listen, I know what panic is. I had a tree phobia for years. I couldn't be in the woods, even in a city park. And I sure couldn't tell anyone. I was a stunt double living in an apartment on a street in Manhattan where I never had to see a tree. If you're going to make it in the business, you're not turning down location shots for fear you'll see an oak. Trust me, I know."

She just stared. And I felt as stupid as the first day I'd admitted my fear. "It's like having a wart on the end of your nose. With hairs growing out of it. Give me the harness."

She unclasped.

I would have guessed the vest in a place like this would be a clunky one-size-fits-all affair, but this number was made of a sturdy open mesh, weighing in at under a pound and looking like it was tailored for her slight figure. I got it fastened, but it wasn't an item I'd want to wear all afternoon. When I turned back to her, her hands hung by her sides. She was standing on the platform like it was a sidewalk. Like she'd never felt fear.

"So . . . ?"

But she didn't offer a name.

"Okay, so we've got three loops to get around. Momentum'll carry you through the first one, right? That's why you ended up hanging on the far side of it. But momentum gives out halfway up that side loop. What you need to do is thrust your head down the instant you hit the top of the curve."

"Yeah. And the last one?"

I laughed. "We'll see." I exhaled and pushed off hard. I shot around the first loop, weightless compared to my last ride hanging on to her. The second loop veered to the left. I bent into the curve, feet together, arms tight to my sides. I was losing momentum fast, barely moving at the top of that curve. I threw my head down, shimmied like a swimmer, and coasted

157

over the top back around the horizontal curve, picking up speed and onto the final loop. I flung my hands over my head, shimmied, caught the wire between my heels, and pushed off.

It was a cheat, but close enough. I didn't exactly sail to the end, but I had enough energy to swing myself onto the platform.

"Ta da!" I called across to the start platform.

The girl was gone.

You spent hours pushing off, failing, and dragging yourself back. Now someone shows you how it's done and suddenly there's something more important?

Apparently there was. I scanned the grounds and caught sight of her blonde ponytail disappearing into the barn. The door slammed afterwards.

Not an answer, but the next best thing! I tore off the vest and flung it to the ground. I eyed the pole—too slow—and jumped into the net. No spreading arms and legs this time. I hit feet first, taking the bounce and leaning toward the edge of the net. When I hit net again, I bent, grabbed the edge, flipped over, dropped to the ground, and ran full out for the barn.

The metal door was locked. I banged. "Open up! What the hell is going on here? What are you all afraid of? Let me in or I'm coming back with the cops." I stood panting, straining to hear footsteps, peering through the small dark window at what looked like green paint. Could that be the Mustang just beyond? "This is your last chance! Open up or I make that call."

The room inside burst into noise—feet slapping the wooden floor, doors slamming at the far end. Then metal clicked on my door. The door swung back. I stepped inside and stared.

Not a garage. No car in sight. But still, I stood and stared. The place was better than the best professional workout space, the kind I'd been to only once when I had to learn a lift, heave, and toss for a high-budget movie with a tight schedule. That space had been outside Burbank and frequented by lead actors with specific needs and excess cash. But this was its equal.

The far end held a diving pool with three platforms and two boards. Along one side they'd built a ski jump that tossed the skier into a catcher net that looked like something on an aircraft carrier. But the side of the jump didn't have regular scaffolding. It was deliberately irregular, the type of thing that would challenge a climber and be great practice for an escape bit. The wall beyond it *was* a climbing wall, one that went to the roof, forty feet above. In the middle of the floor, like something abandoned by a giant toddler, was a rubber ball half as tall as I was. And from that ceiling hung an array of ropes, swings, and rings, a mouse run suspended in air. The place was part uber-gym and part pure fantasy—what any stunt double dreams of should a million-dollar inheritance be in the offing.

The only thing missing was people. It was the Flying Dutchman of gyms—free weights abandoned on the floor, massage table with towel in a heap, while above, ropes still swayed uselessly. Doors had slammed, but the people who'd been working out here weren't standing outside in the heat. They were in here somewhere. The blonde I'd followed hadn't raced in here only to race out.

I was just about to yell out another threat, when what I had taken for a wall quivered and revealed itself as curtain. Behind it I could see Zahra Raintree's outline. I reached for the cloth.

She grabbed my hand, pressing the rough fabric into my skin.

I let my hand go slack. "This is insane. What's— Why did people scatter like ants?" As frustrated as I was, I wanted to accuse her, but no accusation made sense. You don't keep drugs or contraband in a place you can barely get to. You may hide illegals, but you don't build them a fantasy gym. "Why are you keeping all this secret?"

"If my reason meets your approval, will you promise to hold silence?"

"If *I* think it's good enough?"

"Yes."

Why not? "Okay."

Zahra Raintree pushed aside the curtain and stepped into the light.

Half her face had been destroyed.

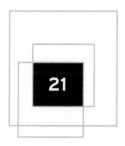

21

HALF HER FACE was the normally weathered visage of someone who lived in the desert. But the other half looked like it had been strafed. Deep, ugly, irregular red crevasses had been seared between patches of skin. The gouges cut at an angle from above her ear to the edge of her nose. It looked like something had clawed her, dragging the skin with it, leaving raw edges to heal or not. Between the scars even the skin that had survived was gray, blotchy, and dry, and the hard scars had pulled it unevenly so it had developed its own lines, shadowy reflections going in opposite directions. It looked stiff, painful, and horrifying, and I couldn't stop staring. When I realized my appalling insensitivity I froze, unable to find an escape.

"That's why this place exists," she said, with only a fraction of the disgust she might have.

"I'm sorry," I muttered, looking at the floor.

"Sorry! Now there's a useless word. What you mean is, get me out of here!"

She'd read me. I didn't know what to say.

"And now you're waiting to be forgiven for your rudeness because like all good children, you were taught never to stare at freaks in the street."

The air conditioning that had been so welcome a minute ago was freezing.

"You stare like you're at the zoo, then you steal my time with your stupid apologies. You demand *I* feel sorry for *you*. Out there—up the road—in L.A., San Diego, there are hundreds of you every day. A trip to the grocery is running the gauntlet. It never changes. New people, new freak-outs."

I felt like the kids who point, the drivers who slow down next to an accident to see the bodies, the boys who pull the legs off centipedes. "So you built this place?"

"Oh, so now you think I built this escape to protect my vanity! A playground without mirrors all for me."

"I didn't say—"

"Because I'm afraid to look?"

What do you want me to say? I can't be any sorrier than I already am.

"Look around you. Do you think this is what I would choose?"

"Hell, yes!" I said. "You were legendary in the stunt world. Yeah, I think this is exactly what you'd choose, and by now you can swing from one side of the ceiling to the other and walk across the floor on top of that giant ball. And each time you get bored, I think you build something impossible and conquer it." I looked around the gym anew, suddenly aching to try the rope swings, to practice the trickiest high fall from the diving platform, to see what I could do with that giant orb.

But she was glaring at me. "To what end?"

"Oh."

"Right. What's the point of being the best if you can never do it when it counts? If the cameras never roll for you?"

I nodded. There's more to being a stunt double than doing the stunts. The camaraderie with the crew, the excitement, the focus of performing when the director says, "We need this in one take."

"Like being the backup quarterback."

"But he, at least, has the hope of playing."

I nodded again. It was too awful to consider, to never again— I looked at her more closely, not at her face, but her body. "You're in great shape. You must work out as much as you ever did. And you've got whatever equipment you want. You can still do gags with the best of them, right? So why not? I mean, the last thing directors want in a shot is our faces. They need the star's face. So what difference—"

"You even have to ask what difference a face like this makes? What director wants to see this on his set? What stunt double wants a reminder that she could screw up, or worse yet, not screw up and still come out of it looking like Halloween?"

I nodded yet again, hoping that would pass for words I couldn't force out. She was right. No one's going to add that extra pressure on a set. Stunt doubles double- and triple-check every piece of equipment. Our careful-ness is our Saint Christopher's medal and we count on it to protect us. We don't even want to think that it could fail us, much less that it could fail someone as legendary as Zahra Raintree. My voice was almost inaudible even to me as I admitted, "None of us wants to see our worst nightmare suiting up next to us."

"Exactly."

I was desperate to look away, to gain time to regroup. But I didn't dare. I said, "But if you can afford all this, you could have your own pro-duction company. You could—"

"I could have made bleu cheese. I didn't choose to. What I did was create this place, which you have barged into. I have security men; I chose not to call them."

"Why not?"

She lifted one eyebrow. I wondered if that ironic expression was her intent or merely the best she could do with half a mobile face. It made it impossible to read what she might have assumed was her response. Leaning in toward me, she said, "Ask your question and don't ever attempt to come back."

"If this place is not a one-woman amusement park, then what is it?"

"Don't condescend to me!"

I laughed. I don't know whether she was stunned or merely appreciative of the acting skill that laugh had required, but she took a step back and when she spoke a bit of the edge was gone from her voice. "You could have come here two years ago. You could have stayed and no one would have bothered you. When you were ready, I'd have planted you a forest."

I almost gasped. The blonde could have blurted out what I'd told her about my phobia as she raced in here. But I hadn't let on it was as recent as two years ago. Still, Zahra knew. If freaked me out. It was all I could do to control my voice as I asked, "You do therapy?"

"You had therapy, right? It didn't work, right?"

"Because I couldn't take the chance of anyone knowing—"

"Exactly."

"So I could have come here, sat in my little forest day after day, and no one in the business would have known?"

"If that's what you wanted."

"Do you have only one person at a time?"

"Sometimes. Sometimes not."

"Then how can you be sure secrets stay secret?"

Again she raised that eyebrow. "Because there's only one reason to be here, so no one's going to admit they were here. Even you. If you do, people in the business will ask why and that phobia of yours will come to light and they'll question whether you're really over it. They'll come to the logical conclusion that you don't go to the hassle of finding a place most people think is a fairy tale and checking it out if you don't have a very serious problem. And the next time a gig comes up, they're going to decide to take the safe route and hire someone else."

"But I'm only here . . ."

"Right. You're only here to ask about Guthrie. Maybe people will believe that. Maybe word about your tree phobia won't get out. Why would you take that chance?"

"But—"

"Have you missed the point entirely? I'm here to protect secrets, not dispense them. Guthrie, is he really dead?"

"Murdered."

"How?"

Not when, but how. "Blunt force trauma to the head and then run over."

An unmistakable look of relief flashed on her face. It was a moment before she said, "Why both?"

"I don't know. The truth is I probably know as much about you as I do about Guthrie, and I thought I knew him better than anyone."

"For instance?"

"He and I were hot to find you. But he never told me he did. He came more than once. He built those cylinders. How come?"

"I don't talk about—"

"Was he claustrophobic? Could that possibly . . . Is that why you asked how he died? Was he afraid of— How could I not know he had a fear like that? I told him about the tree thing. I *told* him. And he kept this—"

She put a hand on my shoulder. "You came to terms with your phobia. He never did. He'd try and try. He built that low cylinder, the eight-foot one, but it was too easy to get out of. He'd panic and be out before he knew what happened. He built the second one, twice as tall. The first time he climbed out he was sweating so hard I was surprised he could get any purchase at all. He couldn't make himself go back for days. When he did, he was out again in thirty seconds."

"Stunt man all the way. He must have been mapping the escape route in his dreams." I ached for him. How could I, of all people, have overlooked the signs? I missed him, grieved for him and for me, but now I was overwhelmed by the need to hold him tight to me for every moment of anguish I hadn't seen. I could barely make myself ask, "What about the third cylinder?"

"The first two are just brick. But that one has a metal tube inside. It's slick. In the first the sun shone on his head midday. In the second he could see the light. But that third one, it's like a tomb."

"Did he—"

"He spent weeks building it, taking it apart, and rebuilding. But he never could climb in."

"That's crazy! The whole thing's crazy! Anyone would be panicked at the bottom of a chute like that with no way out. What was he thinking, that he'd become Superman? Why didn't you tell him he was crazy?"

"That's the one thing I never ever say. I offer the place; I don't give advice." Her hand was still on my shoulder. She gave it a pat and released. "Now I've answered your question and—"

"No, wait. I need to find Ryan Hammond."

"Another missing boyfriend?" She'd meant a stab of sarcasm, but she'd hesitated too long and her voice quavered a tad.

"So you know him."

"No."

"But you know of him, right? I don't know how he's connected with Guthrie, but he knew him in San Francisco and his prize possession was in Guthrie's house in L.A. And now Guthrie's dead and no one knows where to find Hammond." Again she hesitated. "Zahra, we were being straight with each other. You're right in saying I never will admit I've been here. So, what've you got to lose?"

As if to reiterate that she didn't have to tell me anything, she walked over to a three-foot-high ball lying on the floor and jumped up on it, balancing with apparent ease.

"I could smack you off."

"You could try."

"Playing for Ryan Hammond?"

She shifted her hips, keeping balance on the ball. It was akin to my lawyer-brother's balancing on two chair legs. I'd watched him distract people so completely they forgot what it was they were asking. The ball was dead still and Zahra atop it appeared the same until, abruptly, she bent right, sending it left. It took exquisite control for me not to thrust out my hands to catch her as she twisted, leapt, and landed lightly on top once more. "I'm not surprised," I said, "but I'm definitely impressed."

She straightened up and smiled.

Then I shoved her off. "So, how is it you know him?"

Her shoulders tightened and I was sure she was going to stonewall, but she said, "Truth, I don't know Hammond. Only know the story of him."

"Which is?"

"I'll walk you back to the truck."

And make sure I leave. I followed her outside. The dry heat was searing. It was hard to breathe. But Zahra Raintree moved effortlessly and so fast it was all I could do not to pant. "Hey, slow down, unless you want to tell this tale to Blink Jones. Is Ryan Hammond a stuntman?"

She eased off infinitesimally. "He was a kid on his first location, a gofer there."

I'd heard Blink's version. I was anxious to get hers. "Where?"

"Don't know. Doesn't matter. Here's his claim to fame. He's a kid—twenty-one, twenty-two—and so excited about being on the set that he brings his girlfriend. Well, you can imagine how well received that was. Second unit director tells Hammond to pack up and take the girlfriend with him. Hammond's humiliated. And he's new, so he trots over to the director—"

"*The* director."

"Mr. Big. In this case, Casimir Goldfarb."

"Mr. Big indeed."

"Right. Mr. Big Ego, Mr. Big Womanizer. You can tell where this is going."

"Goldfarb tells Hammond they can stay and then he makes a play for the girlfriend?"

"You got it. No one's surprised except Hammond. Girlfriend blows off Hammond before he can open his mouth to whine. She's moved into Goldfarb's trailer by day's end. Hammond, of course, is a mess. I mean, you got to feel for the kid. Here's this famous director in his trailer showing the girlfriend his Oscar and much much more."

"And then?"

"There was a predawn call. Goldfarb leaves his trailer. Normally, it's locked, but of course this morning the girlfriend's inside. She lets Hammond in. He takes Goldfarb's Oscar and leaves."

I couldn't help laughing.

"That was everyone's reaction. Goldfarb, as you probably know, was a royal pain and a priss. And, boy, did he value that Oscar. I mean, he carted it with him to a location set! How crazy is that! Locked his trailer religiously. And then, well, it's perfection."

"But what about Hammond?"

"No one's heard of him since. No surprise. It's not as if he could get on with some other company. Goldfarb was on a tear about him. He was blackballed on every set in this country, this *continent*, and if they'd been making pictures on Mars he wouldn't have gotten a job there."

"Damn. Isn't there anyone who can track him down? What about the girlfriend? What became of her?"

She turned to face me, and for the first time she looked pleased. "This story's made the rounds for a decade. Everybody's got opinions. But you are the first person who asked about her. Lots of offhand speculation, none of it flattering. None of it accurate."

"You know anything?"

"Oh, yes."

We were twenty yards from Blink's truck. She stopped.

"The story is that a pissed-off young guy steals Oscar while airhead girlfriend fucks Goldfarb. Truth is, Ryan Hammond stalked off. She took the Oscar, let the blame fall on him."

"*She* took it? How do you know that?"

"Because"—she was enjoying this—"she told me."

"The girlfriend came here? How did she even know you existed?"

"She turned up here. Wanted to know what the statuette would go for. When I told her no one can sell the things, she went wild. I thought she was going to bash me over the head with it, she was that out of control. Then she charged off and did the one thing she was apparently quite good at."

"What?"

"She hot-wired my car."

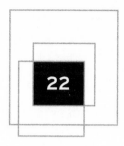

22

I HAD A hundred more questions for Zahra, but she had no more answers for me. She never broke into a run, but she strode toward her house at a pace that had me trotting to keep up, firing questions futilely until she shut the door behind her. Amazing woman. You couldn't exactly call her a role model, but she'd created a world most aging stunt doubles could only dream of.

As put out as Blink had been on this whole trip, I expected he'd be revving up the engine and swinging open the door for me. Instead he rolled down the window and said, as if reading my mind: "You probably want to see those chimneys before you leave, huh?"

"I won't be long."

"Check 'em out good; we're not coming back." As he spoke, he hoisted himself down from the truck and began to keep pace with me.

I started to wonder just what it was he hoped or feared I'd discover. Of course, he was holding something back; I never expected otherwise. "Now that I've met Zahra, I understand about her, just like you said. You'd never have brought me here without her okay, right? So, what's your connection?"

He didn't respond for a bit, then surprised me with what sounded like the truth. "I'm a gofer. It's not easy to get someone who'll run in groceries, mail, you name it. I respect her, and she pays good. Can't beat that."

It was an oddly domestic arrangement for a guy like Blink. And hardly convenient for someone who lived hours away. "How'd you come into this little sinecure?"

I waited for an answer, but he only sighed.

"People have written screenplays in less time than you're taking to create an answer."

"Are you suggesting—"

"No, I'm saying definitely, what I want is the truth. How'd you meet Zahra? How come she picked you to be her errand boy?"

"Why does it matter?"

"I'm going to find out what was going on with Guthrie and how that connects to the ranch. You're going to want to know before word gets out, right?"

He could have protested, but he just nodded.

"So, either we're in this together or we're not. Your choice."

He seemed to be considering.

"All I need is the short version."

"Shortest one is this: I hit a rough patch a few years back. Landed me in the middle of nowhere headed the wrong way, toward more serious nowhere. I needed a place to crash. Stuff was bad with me, real bad. But then I remembered two things, the first was Zahra Raintree. She'd been on a set five years before that, bitching up a storm about her divorce—that her ex ended up with the stock and she got some miserable hole in the desert outside a town that used to be a resort and wasn't even that anymore. 'A hole outside a has-been,' she called it."

"29 Palms isn't going to be including her in their brochures."

"Later, I heard rumors she'd had a bad screwup and got a gonzo settlement. It was a real long shot she'd be at the ranch, much as she'd bad-mouthed it. But, either way, it'd work for me, or so I thought. If I'd known how remote it was, I'd have thought twice, believe me."

What I'd viewed as the "small" chimney now thrust up in front of me a couple of feet above my head. Had it had a broiler, it could have been on a patio in Encinitas. The whole thing was brick—bricks Zahra had to have hauled in. This entire business—the chimneys, Guthrie's connection to them, the place itself—was hard to get my mind around.

Climbing the brick sides was a snap. I peered into the chute. I could have lowered myself down and had enough room to bend over—not easily or comfortably, but still I could do it. But there was no need to. The sun was high enough now to show it empty. Here in the desert, not even a couple of leaves had blown in. How could Guthrie have been unnerved by it? But fear is fear; the object's secondary. Who was I to judge? I just felt bad for him.

I jumped back down next to Blink. The guy was a caricature of disinterest. It made me wonder just what he suspected—or feared—might be hidden in one of these chutes. I let him talk on about finding the ranch as we headed to the middle one.

"So, I'd had a real spate of bad luck and I was due. The first guy I caught a ride with bought my story about heading to a job to help me get on the wagon. I must've looked totally wasted, quick as he was to believe that. He dropped me at the top of the road down."

"What was the second thing?"

"That almost anyone will be glad to see you if you're willing to pull your own weight."

"So, what happened then?"

"My luck turned. Okay, I was stuck back of beyond, but I'd come at just the right time. The only guys here were deadbeats. There'd been good people before—I learned that later—but right then there were just three lowlifes living off her. She'd built the barn, but there was nothing in it. The road for car gags was mud. She was too down to deal with it. She'd had this great, decent idea to help out people who needed it and the whole thing had come to nothing but a rest stop for hangers-on. If I hadn't come, she'd have died. Literally. She was that depressed."

"Blink to the rescue! Nick of time and all that?"

The man actually flushed. Thick-skinned as he was, I'd never have guessed a bit of sarcasm could turn him pink. "Hey, the loafers *did* pack up and I *did* impress upon them that it would not be to their benefit to come back or publicize the location. Then I dynamited the road and spent weeks creating the one that's there now. Not long after that I headed back to town, but I made a deal with Zahra to keep helping from the outside."

That deal, just what was in it for you? I couldn't decide how much of his tale was true.

Being around these weird remnants of Guthrie was distracting. It was hard to switch my focus away from them. There couldn't be anything worthwhile inside these chimneys. They'd sat here, open to the weather and the curiosity of stunt double after stunt double dealing with fears other than claustrophobia. Surely they'd all peered down, and some had climbed in. Hang a rope over the top, it'd be no problem. Only torture for Guthrie—Guthrie, whom I couldn't remember ever being afraid. Wary, careful, yes. But never afraid. Why this?

"What would you say it is? Twelve feet?"

"'Bout."

"You got a flashlight?"

The one he pulled from a pocket could have been in a spy catalog. It looked like a pen but had a light worthy of a tow truck. As I climbed up the bricks I considered the "coincidence" of his having that handy right now.

I leaned over the edge and peered down into the chute, aware of just how easy it would be for him to climb up, lift my legs, and send me head-first to the bottom.

I shot the light down. Brick outside, brick inside. But this one was nar-rower than the shorter version. I could have braced my arms and legs and lowered myself down and inched back up without problem, even if there weren't handholds, which there always were with weathered brick. Still, it had a murky feel to it. Poor Guthrie! But it also stood on bare ground. With a crane, it could have been lifted up and whatever in it exposed, be that Guthrie or . . . something hidden.

The tallest of the smokestacks was twenty yards away. I started to run, but Blink trailed behind. Why was he so interested in what I was doing? Did he suspect something was down in them, or was he just happy to waste my time? To keep me from poking into anything else back in town?

I hurried to the tall stack and climbed up. The outer bricks were every bit as easy to scale as the others. But the inside was a different story. The inner cylinder was metal, slick and just wide enough across for a stuntman to slide down. It was nowhere near broad enough to allow him to bend his elbows or knees and get purchase coming back up, assuming his shoes would stick on this slick surface. Bare feet? Not likely unless he went down in sandals. No way anyone could manage to untie laces. I didn't need a phobia to be unnerved by this baby. What had Guthrie been thinking?

Despite the desert sun, I was shivering. I clicked on the flashlight and stared down. The tube was two stories high. The light bounced off the bright metal and I had to squint to make out even the disk that formed the bottom, to see how it was unlike the others. The bottom was actually a foundation. So, even with a crane there'd be no lifting the chimney up and freeing a prisoner at the bottom. I stuck my head in. "Omigod!"

"What?"

175

"It's really hard to see down there."

"What? What do you see?"

"I don't know. It's . . . hard . . ."

"Is it shiny?"

I stuck my head back into the tube, peering down. The dead air shrouded my head and neck. I was ridiculously relieved to come up for air and see Blink watching eagerly. "Really hard to see that far down. What could he have dropped?"

He didn't answer.

"Forget it," I said and snapped off the flashlight. "If something's there, it's not going anywhere. I'll tell Zahra and—"

He came whipping up the bricks, sunglasses falling to the ground, keyring still in his hand. "Where do you see it?"

"The edge. It's tricky, but you have to get the beam right to the edge down there." I held out the light. "This whole thing is freaking me out. I'm sweating all over. I'll wait in the truck."

"Fine."

"Give me the keys." I took the ring, lowered myself down the stack, forced myself to walk, not run, to the truck, got in, fastened the seatbelt, and started the engine as one would to turn on the air conditioning.

I'd be halfway up the exit road before he realized I was gone.

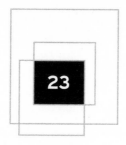

23

BLINK'S TRUCK WASN'T a junker. But in the family of vehicles it was a ne'er-do-well uncle dragging home after an all-night bender. The steering was loose, the brakes were stiff, and everything rattled. I eased out the clutch. The engine pulled, straining the low gear, but I wasn't about to try shifting here where failure meant disaster—not and have to shift back the instant I started up the exit road. Coming down that road, peering out across the hood ornament into nothingness, I'd told myself that despite Blink's warning, going uphill would be easier by far. It always is.

Or almost always. That miserable road Blink had built was all pebbly sand, no wider than the truck, with only a few low cacti to mark the drop-offs. An inch too far to either side and I'd roll the truck all the way back to the desert floor. Tires had worn ruts in the sand and I steered so the hood ornament stayed halfway between them. Now I understood why Blink had that odd addition! I just hoped—had to trust—that the ruts remained even and the rise between them reliable. There was no way to check. Even if I stuck my head out the window and looked down, I wouldn't have been able to see anything but air.

"Hey, stop!"

I hit the gas. For an instant the wheels spun and then caught, jerking the truck to the right. I could feel the right tire grabbing air. It was all I could do not to snap the wheel back. I edged it slightly to the left, listening for the deeper sound of sand under the full width of tire, feeling for the evenness of the grip.

"Darcy!"

Blink sounded closer, but I didn't dare adjust the speed or take my eyes off the road even to check the rearview mirror. All I could hope was that the heat, the run across the desert floor, and the steep road would slow him.

Ryan Hammond's girlfriend, Melissa, stole the Oscar. She foisted blame on him. Any hope he had of work in the business was gone.

Something scraped the fender. Blink? Could he— But no way. It had to be the cacti.

A "Melissa" claiming to be Guthrie's wife was in the house with the Oscar. But it was only after I mentioned his name that she said she was his wife. If I'd asked for my brother John, or Gary, or Arnold Schwarzenegger, would she have annexed herself to them?

Still, she was there, with the Oscar.

Omigod! She *brought the Oscar there. There was no reason to believe Ryan Hammond ever crossed the threshold.*

The path was steeper. The wheels slipped. I had to slow down—I hated to—to check behind me for Blink. I forced myself to ease my foot up, feeling for the solid sound of traction. "Ah."

He had to be somewhere behind me, on the path. If only I could go faster, but I didn't dare.

Hammond and Melissa had once been involved. Maybe they got together again and Oscar made three. Maybe. I was in serious speculation land here. The only thing I was sure of was whenever there was a question these days, the answer was likely to involve Ryan Hammond.

Him, I couldn't find. But her! There she was, just yesterday, in the house of his friend, Guthrie. How did she go from showing up at Zahra's ranch with her stolen statuette to answering the door at Guthrie's house with it and a gun? There might be connections other than via Blink Jones, but none so obvious.

The bumper hit rock—the cliff wall on the left. The truck bounced sharp right. I pulled left, held steady, and slowed. The bumper scraped the wall again, but it didn't jerk the truck. My shoulders were near my ears. How much longer was this damned road, anyway? I kept moving a gnat's breadth from the wall, very slowly easing the gas in. After a hundred yards or so, I checked the mirror. No Blink in sight. Had he given up and gone back down to co-opt one of those rusty rattletraps? Did they even have plates?

Something buzzed. I jumped, almost lost contact with the pedal. It was a moment before I realized the sound was my phone. It was vibrating. I was near enough to the top to get the signal! The truck crested the rise out of the basin where Zahra's rancho hid, off the miserable goat track of a road Blink had built, and onto a superbly flat, graded, two lane. I turned west and stepped on the gas.

My phone nearly vibrated off my hip. I flipped it open. Missed messages were lined up, looming, like clouds out of the Gulf of Alaska in January. John. John again. Gracie. Gary. Mom. Gary again. Janice. *Janice, the nice one!* She'd called me maybe three times in my entire life and one of those was when I got married. We were as close to acquaintances as biological sisters can get. Her message tempted me, but I went for John's latest. "A couple of digits off? You had reversed two pair!" *Leave it to John to lead with complaint!* "But it's the VIN for the Mustang GT used in the movie. Car was sold four times and then reported stolen end of last year. Where is it! Call me."

179

Good work, John! I was sure he could run down the info, but not that fast. Computer-wary as he was, he must have called in a favor from the tech guys. I could have called back and asked. Instead I reconsidered what had happened yesterday. First I surprised Melissa in the house with the stolen Oscar. Then I called Blink with the news the cops were outside. He pulled that snazzy maneuver, sideswiping the patrol car, giving the cops a lure they couldn't refuse. I'd assumed it was to get me out of the garage free. But what if it had been to allow *her* to get the *Mustang* out of there? I had to give the guy credit for panache.

I almost wished she'd pulled it off alone, but, no, she had to be in it with Blink. No way she'd leave her own car near Guthrie's house when she drove off in the Mustang. Damn Blink! The guy gave her a lift there. Had to be that!

She wasn't Guthrie's wife—

Was she—"Oh, shit!"—Blink's wife?

No wonder he wouldn't let me in the house!

No wonder, so I wouldn't see her? Or the Mustang? I was piling suppositions upon suppositions, but if, indeed, she was in this with Blink, where else would she hide a hot car fast? These might be suppositions, but they were going to be easy to test.

Things were about to come together. For the first time since Guthrie died I felt hopeful.

I hit the gas, coming as close to speeding as possible in this old vehicle. And I started through the rest of my phone messages.

John: "I'm at SFO. I'll be south of Matamoros by morning. I got word from my guy in Brownsville across the border there. They've discovered another one of those unmarked gravesites, could be ten years old. There are reasons to believe some are Anglos, kept separate, much better preserved. Looks like they were buried with possessions, so maybe . . ." His breath hit the phone, slow, thick, as if he were putting off something he couldn't bring himself to say. "Amazing, but . . . one of them still has some red hairs . . . curly."

Curly red hair, like Mike's. Like my own.

I couldn't move, couldn't breathe. I stared at the phone, not seeing it. It couldn't come to this; it just couldn't. Mike could not be dead. He couldn't have been dead all this time. No! It wasn't true. I would have known if he died; I would have felt it.

Wind slapped my face. The body in Mexico, it didn't mean anything. There are two hundred million Americans, not to mention Canadians, Brits, Australians, and Europeans, who could be called Anglos. Hundreds of thousands with red hair. Thousands with wavy—not wiry—dark red hair. It wouldn't be Mike.

John would have thought that. And still he was on his way there.

I clicked on the next message.

Gary: "John's going to Mexico. I'm checking international law. I can't believe . . . God, I hope this is nothing. Call me."

Gracie: "I know you heard from John. Odds are— But, look, Mike could take care of himself . . . bottom line, he'd survive."

Mom in tears. I couldn't make out a word.

No! I couldn't bear to think of Mom like that. Suddenly my face was wet; I could barely see to drive.

Gary: "I've got the best guy in the state on international law. Whatever we have to do, we'll do pronto. This whole thing sounds crazy, but you know, Darce, ragged as Mike was that fall— He hated working for Dad. It's my fault. I should never have goaded him. When he didn't go back to school that semester, I was on him all the time about freeloading. If he wasn't going to school, get a job. I just kept at it. And Katy, too—I know she feels terrible—she shamed Dad into taking him. Still, though—"

The message had run out. He called again with the oft-uttered mantra of us Lotts. "Mike would never hurt the family."

Janice: "Mom called me about Mike and the bodies outside Matamoros. I guess John left for there yesterday. No one ever tells me anything. Sometimes, I think they forget I even exist. It's like Berkeley's on the other side of the country instead of the Bay. I mean, except Mom. But I'm not calling you to complain about that; that's not your . . . Never mind. I mean, the thing is, I don't want you to worry. Drugs and voodoo and murders in Mexico: it's common knowledge. Mike's not a fool. You may not have realized it because you were a kid, but Mike and I . . . I know him. Anyway, what I'm saying is, don't worry, I mean, despite—"

Don't worry, indeed! I couldn't even stop shaking. I couldn't remember the last time I cried. I knuckled the tears from my eyes, but it was useless. I kept thinking: one day I don't think about Mike and I let him die.

Why did guys just assume they could do any asshole thing and survive? Mike, and, dammit, Guthrie.

I was desperate to put off the question none of my siblings had raised. When would we see the possessions that'd been buried with the bodies? When would each one of us have to go through them, desperately hoping to recognize nothing? I couldn't leave the family hanging again. I needed to get home and be ready.

I focused on the road, and by dusk I was on Blink's street. I gritted my teeth and pulled the old pickup into his driveway.

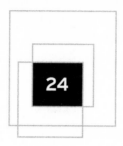

24

I WAS READY for Blink's wife to come running out at the sight of his ride. But not all wives are homecoming cheerleaders. It was dark enough to have lights on, but she didn't. Which didn't necessarily mean she wasn't home.

The lot was protected on one side by a creek, on the other by a stand of trees. The backyard was large, wooded, overgrown, more of an East Coast yard than the normal manicured and fenced California plot. No place to hide anything.

But the house was a two-story affair, as if it had been raised to allow for an above-ground basement. Home improvement for thieves? An entry door led from the driveway. A circuit of the house showed that every window was curtained off or covered with thick shades. To keep the light out or the curious from peeking in?

I actually laughed! Thank goodness the place was empty; I was too light-headed to confront anyone. I'd grabbed some junk food at a gas station, but otherwise I couldn't remember when I'd last eaten. But I had to stay, to watch, to be ready. I'd forgotten about Mike all day and look what had happened.

Oh, shit, I really was losing it.

I considered my options. I needed to sort, to plan, to call one of my siblings. I needed to charge my phone. Needed to eat. Needed coffee, really needed coffee. I climbed into my own little rental car and headed toward the ocean.

Luck was with me. I found a Peet's Coffee in a mall minutes before it was closing and left with two triple espressos. I stashed one in the car for an emergency, and took the other to a burger place and ordered the cholesterol special minus the roll. Bread'll put you to sleep faster than you can chew. But the bacon cheeseburger with fried mushrooms, I was counting on that to keep me going. I slipped the counter kids ten bucks to plug in my phone and took my meat and coffee as far as the cord would stretch.

I was calling my sister Janice before I realized I'd chosen her as my least-close sibling. "Janice, it's me. Listen, I've got two minutes. Anything new?"

"No, I mean, not that I've heard, but that doesn't signify anything really. It's not like they'd tell me any—"

No wonder no one ever called her! "Will you phone Mom— No wait, make that Gracie."

"I really hate calling Gracie. She doesn't say anything directly, but just her tone—"

"Okay, Mom then. Surely Mom likes you." I could hear Gracie in my own voice! "Tell her I'm in L.A., trying to find out about Guthrie's—"

"I'm so sorry about him. You've had a hard time with guys. When I heard about this one I really hoped it'd work for you. He sounded so right. It's just awful. I'm really sorry."

"Yeah, thanks. But the point is his friend—"

"The one with the Mustang from *Bullitt?* Do you need any more background on the car? I can do an advanced search and—"

"John called *you* for that?"

"Hey, I know the Net. How do you—"

"Sorry. I just figured he'd heavy-handed some rookie." I also figured Janice would carry on with her gripe.

But she surprised me with: "Do you remember Mike?"

"What? Hey, there's not a day—"

"I'm not asking about your emotional hangover, Darcy. Or the pictures of what might be. Do you remember him as he was?"

Whew! "Of course I do. Better than anyone."

"That's exactly what everyone in the family says."

"No way! They're into self-deception, then. None of them was anywhere near as close as I was."

"Close isn't knowing. It can be just the opposite."

What was with my sister? "Whatever. I gotta go."

"I'm just saying, remember Mike, the guy who planned that big birthday bash for you in Golden Gate Park. The guy who knew the secret paths in Sutro Baths—which, incidentally, he learned from me. Does that sound like someone who'd stumble into a seedy bar in Matamoros and swallow whatever he was offered?"

"Listen, you want to do something useful? You're the family geek, right? I'm looking for this guy named Ryan Hammond. Normal spelling. Go online and get me anything you can, okay?"

"Sure, but—"

"Thanks. I gotta go!" I hung up with the same mix of frustration and guilt that ended every conversation with her. The woman was infuriating. Did all her phone calls end with people slamming down the phone? Who the hell was she to think she knew Mike better than I did? Me, who did my homework on the floor of his room. Me, whose room he used to make secret phone calls. Me who took the heat for those calls past my bedtime.

185

Me, whom he taught to drive and to dance when Gracie and know-it-all Janice couldn't be bothered. Me!

I wrapped the rest of my food, unplugged my barely charged phone, and made for the car.

When I pulled up outside Blink's, the only thing that'd changed was the clock. An hour and a quarter had passed. If the woman was behind the curtains in the dark, she could wait me out forever. I'd killed enough time here. She might be tops at theft and hot-wiring, but she'd be no match for me. I climbed the six steps to the porch and rang the doorbell. And when no one answered, I rang again and kept my finger on it. "Come on, dammit! I know you're there! If you don't answer the door, I'll have every cop—"

Hands grabbed me from behind, one over my mouth. I elbowed back hard. A woman gasped but didn't ease up. She slammed me into the wall. I kicked back into her shin, switched quick and kicked the other leg, thrust my weight full toward the stairs, and sent us both toppling down. She let go midway and I rolled, caught the side of the staircase, and flipped myself so I landed in a squat. She was on her back, winded. I yanked her up, pulled her arm behind her. "Where's Ryan Hammond?"

"What?"

"Ryan Hammond? Take me to him."

"How would I know—"

"That's your problem. My—"

But *my* problem was behind me. Then it was over my mouth and around my arms. And this time I couldn't get loose.

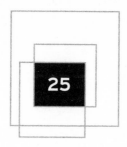

25

"SO YOU'RE BLINK'S wife, never Guthrie's wife, and no longer Ryan Hammond's girlfriend? Which is it?" I wasn't in the best position to be shooting demands—on the sofa, hands and feet tied. Blink shrugged me off, like one more thing in a day that had forced him to drive one of Zahra's clunkers back here and was now stretching to eternity.

Not so Melissa, the same not-so-small blonde who'd tossed me like bag of groceries twice in two days. Whatever had made me take her for a fearful young wife yesterday was sure gone now. She was in jeans, a work shirt, now ripped and dirt-streaked, and hard-toed boots. She had the look of one of those pointer dogs focused only on its own goal. "Who did you tell about our house?"

No one. "My brother's a police inspector, do you think I would be crazy enough to come over here alone, at night, without a call?"

"Yeah, right."

"Check my phone, my last couple of outgoing messages. Feel free to call. Name's John. That's *Inspector* John Lott."

Doubt flickered on her face, then disappeared. Her hand shot out and my phone vanished in it. "There's a Frisco number."

"Your local cops'll never get so good a chance to ingratiate themselves with a big shot in a big cop shop."

That got her attention. She gave a crisp nod toward the hallway and Blink followed her out.

The living room could have been any upper-middle-class setup not inhabited by Blink or intended for a hog-tied victim. It had the look of a parlor entered only for dusting, the kind displayed by people with family rooms filled with dogs, clutter, and giant TVs.

In the kitchen her voice rose: "Your fault . . . rid of her . . . in the whole fucking desert." How "rid" did she mean? His grumble was too low to make out.

Again, her: "Dumpster."

Dumpster!

He was disagreeing.

Her: "Okay, okay. You're right. Too close . . . *your* stupid fault for letting her come here. What's the matter with you? This was the perfect property—*perfect*. When are we ever going to find another basement like this? Damn you, Blink. Now we're going to have to clean out, clean it out *good,* and—"

He muttered something.

She: "Okay, yeah, too close. They'd be on us before we got out of the county, before we could boost new plates. But . . . container . . ."

Him: "not breathe."

"All the better," she said as she slammed back into the living room.

I heard her footsteps, felt the air on my sweat-coated shoulders. I inhaled and exhaled and inhaled again. "So, are you going to wipe down Guthrie's house, too? They'll trace me there, find your fingerprints all over. You can never clean them all up. You're tied to me. No way you can change that now."

She swung her arm and slammed her fist into the side of my face. My eyes went blurry. "Stop that!" I yelled. "Look, we've got the same problem here. So stop with this 'getting rid of her' business and focus on our mutual problem."

"Which is?" She had stopped in front of me.

"Ryan Hammond. Lookit, Guthrie was killed in San Francisco. Who was Guthrie's partner in crime back there? Ryan Hammond. Who knew the other missing member of that gang? Him. Guthrie's got a house here. Whose contraband was in it? Ryan Hammond's." I was going with the story of Ryan Hammond as the Oscar thief, trusting she wouldn't guess Zahra Raintree had incriminated her. "Where is Ryan Hammond?"

She was about to hit me again, for the pleasure of it. She caught herself. "Ryan? How would I know where he is?"

"Tell me and I'm gone."

She looked at me a moment, then she laughed.

I hadn't expected her to buy that, but it was worth a try.

Blink dropped into a padded chair behind her.

I sat up as straight as my bound hands would allow. "Okay, we're all pros here. You're burglars and fences. No way are you going to let me walk out of here. I heard you talking 'container' back there."

"But?" she said, still looking amused.

But what? What chip did I have? "Those cops who came flying up to Guthrie's house, did you call them?"

She didn't answer.

"Right. So let me tell you how come they were there. My brother, the San Francisco detective, knew I was there. No, wait, I'm not saying he sent them. You've got a bigger problem than that. One of his colleagues, in charge of Guthrie's murder investigation, told me not to leave town— San Francisco. When I bolted, she called Guthrie's agent and he gave her the address."

"You're saying she's concerned about you?"

I forced a laugh. "Not hardly. The woman's got a bug up her butt about me. If she had her way, I'd be arrested every time I ran an amber. If you"—I didn't want to say "kill," on the off chance that wasn't really their plan—"If I don't come home, my brother will trail you for the rest of your lives. But if she—Inspector Higgins—thinks I'm mocking her and her order, she'll be a pit bull at your throat. She'll use every reciprocity, call in every debt SFPD has. She'll do it now. She won't eat or sleep till she shows me who's boss. And if that means tracking you down and sending you to Corcoran, that'll be an extra gold star on her chest."

Melissa stared down at me. "We'll take our chances."

Which will be better without dragging me with you. Damn, what could I trade? What?

She gave me a snort of disgust—the woman was Higgins's soulmate!— and headed through the hallway. "Blink, get off your ass. We gotta move!"

He shifted in his chair but didn't stand. His eyes were half-closed.

"Hey, we don't have time for this!"

He dragged himself up and came back through the living room, lugging a box that might once have held a television. "Honey-love, I've exited more venues than you ever staged."

"Oh, for chrissakes," I blurted out. "Can't you even call your wife by name?"

He started, then kept going. But I'd hit a nerve with Melissa. She shot through the living room, cut him off at the stairs, and kept going. Doors banged, and the couch shook, bouncing me forward and back against my tied wrists.

They didn't want to hands-on kill me; they just wanted me dead. Nervous crooks with problems, John always said, were the worst adversaries. Melissa would snap and shoot before she realized she had a gun in her hand. Or, more likely, she'd stuff me in a container, toss in more stuff, and let me smother before the top was sealed.

What could I trade? What did I possess, connect, know? What could they want?

Did they kill Guthrie, or was it Ryan Hammond? Why go all the way to San Francisco and bludgeon him across the street from his sister's house? Just to throw suspicion on Gabriella? It didn't make sense. Didn't even look right. As aggrieved as any sister might be about Guthrie's long absence, it wasn't likely she'd take a mallet to his head—to the *back* of his head.

Melissa raced through the hallway. Her hair stuck to her neck. She was panting, but she didn't break stride. Oddly, since they were so physically different, she reminded me of Gabriella, or Gabriella as she might have been years ago before she turned into a caged animal. Melissa had that same tight-eyed, quivery-mouthed look of a woman about to spin out.

What was it about Guthrie and these women of his? How could this be the same sweet, tormented guy I'd known? The best truck jockey—

Wait! That day he hadn't been the best at all. He'd muffed the gag. Because he'd been late. Because he'd been held up by . . . something. What was his lame excuse, a truck overturned on the freeway? An incident that never made the news? That he'd admitted to fabricating. What *had* held him up?

Blink chugged through toward the basement, carting what might have been a boxed painting.

What did Melissa and Blink need?

A guy with a truck is involved with thieves selling collectibles. A normally reliable guy is delayed. *Hmm.* When Melissa rounded the door from the basement, I said, "Guthrie's truck."

"What about it?"

"Guthrie got delayed on the way to the movie set doing business for you, right?" I didn't dare be more specific. "That truck of his, aren't you worried about it?"

She balanced her load on a chair arm. "Where is it?"

"The cops probably impounded it. But maybe not. I'll have to check."

"What, you're going to call the police chief and ask?"

"I told you my brother's a detec—"

She looked so shocked at that being true I almost laughed. Her eyes went blank as if she was trying to remember all I'd threatened in connection with that brother, trying to factor it into her plans for me.

"I'll find out about the truck in return for—"

"I'm not negotiating—"

"Of course you'll deal. You're a fence; that's what you do, for chrissakes. I just want to find Ryan Hammond. Easy swap. I'll find the truck; you take me to Hammond."

"We don't have time—"

"I'm not asking you to drive me to him. Just tell me where he is."

"I'm not—"

"There's a murder investigation. If the police haven't impounded the truck by now, they certainly will. If you don't care what they find in it . . ." I made to shrug, but my trussed hands just shoved my shoulders forward. Melissa wasn't looking at me anyway. She was thinking; then she was gone.

In less than a minute it was Blink standing in front of me and Melissa was back to carting boxes. I had to give her a silent thumbs up for realizing she'd lost and snapping into the next move. Blink looked like he'd noted the same thing, though his reaction was less positive. I was betting he'd been dragged along to the next thing more than once with her.

He slumped heavily on the couch, sending me bouncing.

"Hey, I'm tied up here."

"What if the cops don't have Guthrie's truck?" he said.

She's the moving force, but you're the one who knows the ropes. Does she get that? I couldn't afford to underestimate either of them. If I'd been dealing with anyone less exhausted than I was, I'd have been mincemeat. But Blink looked happy for any excuse to sit. Happy to discuss "what if." He looked so worn out he couldn't be bothered being angry about my abandoning him in the desert. I said, "Why are you so concerned about Guthrie's truck?"

"Why d'you think?"

"You used it to move your stuff. Guthrie was late—uncharacteristically late—getting to the set. Was he making a pickup?"

His face flickered and he caught himself just before he laughed. Okay, no pickup. That made sense. You don't pick up valuable contraband, then wag your trailer all over the set. So, he was making a delivery.

"Ah, but when you make a delivery you get a payment, and you're hoping it's in the truck, right? And you don't know what else is there, good or bad."

"You going to speculate till we leave? Or you going to answer me: If the cops don't have the truck, where the hell is it?"

"Where we left it."

His face lit up a bit. "By the location set."

"Not so easy. There was a fire. We had to move it. If you had infinite time you could cover all of the Port of Oakland hunting it down, finding it among all the other nondescript trucks there. You could come every day and try to remember what was where the day before."

"Ports have records—"

I laughed. "You're going to call the Port and ask for the records on a truck carting illegal goods, owned by the subject of a murder investigation. God, you really are tired."

He didn't even summon up a reply.

"Or you can give me Hammond."

"Done." He made to stand up.

"Hey, not so fast. Where is he?"

He looked down at me and gave an odd laugh, as if he'd just realized something ironic, something he liked a whole lot more than I would. "San Francisco."

"San Francisco's a big city."

"Oakland's a big port."

He sprawled back, head draped over the sofa cushion, baseball cap sliding down over his eyes. He was way too pleased with himself and his insight. It was as if he'd been waiting to get even with me for his long drive back in Zahra's rust bucket, and just discovered how—and then some.

Of course I didn't trust him. But I did believe him that Ryan Hammond was in San Francisco. "Okay, Blink, take me to him."

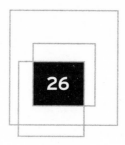

26

IT WAS NOT quite dawn, already hot and clammy. My feet were bound, my hands were tied behind me, and I'd been plunked in the cab of a truck the size of Guthrie's, between two people eager to have me dead.

At least I wasn't in the back of the truck stuffed in next to the Mustang. Now a forest's worth of packing boxes were crammed around it. Getting it all in had taken hours and hadn't improved anyone's mood. I'd hoped they would overlook my rental car, but they didn't. Between dealing with that, Blink's truck, and whatever Melissa had been driving, it was five in the morning before the rig pulled away from the house. She was at the wheel, I was in the middle trussed like a basting chicken, and Blink was snoring into the window, which rattled and slipped as if in response.

I figured I might as well try a little conversation. "What did Ryan do after the Oscar theft?" I said, as if we'd just resumed a pleasant chat and one of us wasn't tied up.

"Stayed clear of me."

"How'd you get back in business together?"

She arced left on the two-lane road. Her shoulders were hunched; her nose was nearly to the wheel. But tense as she was, she had enough control not to admit partnership with Hammond. Yet.

"Ryan?" I went on. "How long has he been in San Francisco?" *Long enough to kill Guthrie?*

"I don't know."

"Of course you do."

"Just shut up!" She reached over and turned on the radio. Beethoven burst forth. Who'd've imagined it? She poked the volume and turned it down.

We hit the flats and turned right and right again, me bouncing against my bound hands. I caught the end of the rope and climbed my fingers up to the knot. The truck jolted; I hung onto the knot, willing it to loosen. Sun was slicing in through the windshield. It coated Blink's eyelids but didn't wake him. Even the window slipping down didn't get to him. The only rest he'd had in the last twenty-four hours was sitting in the truck at Zahra's waiting for me and those few moments of shut-eye on the sofa.

We were still on city streets, but that wouldn't last long. It never does in L.A. The roadway was wide, and early-morning empty. The traffic light turned yellow. Melissa hit the gas. Clearly, the signals were timed, and although she'd gotten through this one, the next would be close. It was still green. A car waited to cross. The light turned yellow. She accelerated.

I stamped on her feet. The engine roared. We shot left. A horn blared. She shoved me back into Blink. I kicked up through her arms, hit her chin. The truck was headed into the center divider. Blink pulled me across him. Melissa hugged the wheel. Sweat covered her face; she was panting. But she got control.

And then there was silence. No sirens, no one running up to check what was going on in here, no one even racing up to scream at us. Nothing. Just a truck rumbling down the street.

"Do something with her! You—"

"I'm trying!"

"I can't handle this huge thing and—"

"Okay, okay, let me drive."

Good plan, except it was a fantasy. It took me less than ten minutes to exasperate him as much as I had her.

"If you can't keep her still, Melissa, stick her next to the window. Smack her around as much as you want."

She wanted to a lot. She smashed my shoulder into the door and my head against the roof and managed to bang my knees twice before giving up any effort to belt me in. Every bump we hit smacked me into the windshield. I was going to have a duck's egg on my forehead. The window jiggled and slipped; wind smacked my face. The knot binding my wrists was infinitesimally looser, but it was going to take more than mere bounce to free me. The truck was nowhere near new and the door handle a four-inch metal arm parallel to the floor, the kind you grab and rotate down. If I could just create a little give in the knot, maybe, just maybe, I could hook it over the handle. But catch the knot wrong and it would pull so tight my hands would go numb. Still, I had time to be careful; I had the whole five-hour drive to Oakland.

Unless they got rid of me before that. Well before. Where could they take me? To some secluded garage? A storage unit? Or—*oh, shit*—there was national forest just to the north. A whole big empty forest where bodies get eaten long before bones are found.

No matter what, I was *not* leaving this truck without a solid lead to exactly where in San Francisco Ryan Hammond might be! Ostensibly, we'd had a deal. But we all knew better. They were in the driver's seat, literally and figuratively, and I was fooling myself to believe I would provoke answers to my questions. There were a dozen reasons for them to stonewall me. After that one smug pronouncement of his, Blink had steered clear of even a mention of San Francisco. They weren't likely to spend hours satisfying my curiosity even when we turned onto Route 5 and there was nothing to do on the hot, boring freeway north.

The truck chugged up over Tejon Pass and then down, away from the national forest. I was just about to allow myself a small sigh of relief when I spotted the sign for the fork to Route 99.

"Hey," I said, "this is the lane for 99! 5's that way!"

"99's safer."

"Safe from who? Who's looking for us?"

He grunted and Melissa took the opportunity to give me another hard jab in the ribs. I jolted up against the roof. The movement seemed to have loosened the binding on my wrists a tad, but at this rate I'd have a concussion before I got loose. I needed to think while I still could. There was no reason why a panel truck with a man and two women in the cab should draw the attention of anyone, even with me bouncing around. Therefore, there was no reason to avoid taking Route 5, the fast road, in favor of 99, the old four-lane that skirted every town in the San Joaquin Valley. No reason except dumping me in some storage unit outside Hanford or Fresno.

"You're not giving me Ryan's address, not because you're bargaining. You don't want me to find him. You should never have said San Francisco, right?"

I looked across Melissa at Blink. He was making a show of focusing on the road, too great a show. "You blew it, Blink. You know I've got the resources to run him down a lot faster than you can find that truck."

He hit the gas, a virtual admission I was right. That was his only response, and I had to assume he was concluding it'd be easier to hunt the truck on his own than deal with me.

"Look, if you—"

"Shut her up, will you?"

Melissa obliged with a hit. And I had to admit to myself that all I was going to get from these two now was bruises. What I needed was to figure a way out of here, and relay word of Hammond's whereabouts.

The window had slipped a quarter of the way down. At this rate I'd be in Oakland before it was open enough for me to slide out. I shifted, giving Melissa a kick for good measure. She smacked back. I managed a bounce and came down facing the window. I could see the handle and how to land the next time to work the knot against it. I was braced to spring up again, when I spotted something that changed everything.

The door'd been left unlocked.

For the first time in this miserable ride, something was going my way. Still, exiting a truck going 60 miles per hour, with my hands and feet bound? Even for a stunt double that'd lead straight to the morgue.

I peered at the gas gauge. Almost full. Damn. I was already creating all the distraction and havoc I could and changing nothing. How could I—

Then, suddenly, I thought of Leo. *Be aware!* Leo was always telling me. He meant be part of the whole gestalt of things, alert to them all. I leaned back against the door and watched as Melissa edged away from me, nervously checking both side mirrors, glancing at me, and back to the road. Blink was resting an arm on the window, his eyes at half mast.

I'd been handling this situation exactly wrong. In order to be alert, I needed to appear asleep. I let my eyelids close, or almost. I had had a bit of sleep; they had had none. The day was already hot, the sun bright. The radio was loud, but on that classical station it wasn't likely to jolt anyone awake.

His eyes closed and snapped open twice before he was sleepy enough to forget the gas pedal. The truck slowed. I shot a glance out the window at the shoulder and reached for the handle.

"Blink! Dammit, wake up!"

"Huh?"

"You were asleep!" Melissa insisted.

"No, I wasn't." But he straightened up. In seconds the truck was moving faster again.

I released the handle.

Traffic was getting heavier.

A car cut in front. He jammed on the brakes.

I shoved the handle down, flung my weight against the door, feet out onto the step. Melissa grabbed my shoulders. Horns blew. The truck was moving again. I braced my feet against the side. Then I shoved off hard.

And landed hard on my back. It was all I could do to protect my head. My shoulder screamed. I pushed and rolled onto the soft shoulder. Brakes squealed. I pulled my hands loose. My head throbbed.

I wanted to curl up in a ball, but I had to move. Up ahead the truck was pulling over. I had to get out of here, had to avoid "help." No ER, and definitely no police. Used as I was to bouncing up after a bad landing, I didn't bounce now. I slid back into the weeds and just about sheared the skin off my ankle getting a foot free.

Melissa was jumping down from the truck, Blink coming at a run. No one else had stopped. Dammit, not one other vehicle!

I shoved up, and wobbly as I was, I ran. The shoulder was short weeds—no cover. I made for the access road. Holding out a hand, I cut in front of a car, skidded to avoid one in the other lane. Brakes squealed; horns blared. I could hear drivers yelling at me.

Ahead was a gas station. I ran all out and flung myself into the minimart. "Phone! Emergency!"

The guy behind the counter hesitated, then handed me a big black cordless.

Moving in front of the window, I held it to my ear and pretended to talk. I couldn't spot either of my assailants, but if they were still after me, I wanted them to see me making a call.

It wasn't till the clerk said, "You done?" that I did the last thing I wanted, called the last person I wanted to speak to.

"Higgins."

"This is Darcy Lott. I'll make you a deal."

"We don't—"

"There're two suspects in Guthrie's murder driving north on 99 near Bakersfield. In a big white truck. No markings. California plates. They've got a van load of stolen goods, including a vintage Mustang. They say they know where Ryan Hammond is—in San Francisco." Before she could reply, I hung up.

At that moment all I wanted was just to sit down and melt into the ground. My head throbbed, my shoulders ached, my eyes were puffy and so dry it hurt to blink. I'd assumed this trip would show me the man I loved between the times I'd loved him. But all I knew for sure was that I didn't know anything for sure. Everything I'd discovered about Guthrie was something I didn't want to know.

If I was counting on Higgins, I was really grasping at straws.

I needed to find Hammond myself.

Maybe my sister Janice had come up with something on the Internet about him.

If I was reduced to counting on Janice, I was beyond grasping at straws.

Wan stalks of dead weeds poked up hopelessly from the hardened ground I'd just crossed. I was somewhere around Bakersfield, and for the first time it struck me how aptly named that town was in August. It had to be over 80 degrees and it wasn't even time for breakfast. Between the dust and the heat, it was a struggle even to breathe. Or maybe I needed to check my ribs for cracks.

Getting a cab was one possibility. I could have him drive me to the airport, but Bakersfield is a two-flight-a-day town. I was tired, sweaty, bruised, and sinking into immaturity. Without a second thought, I did what I'd done in adolescent crises. I called Janice.

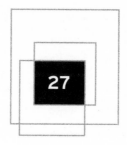

27

"I'M SURPRISED YOU called me," Janice said a couple of hours later when I got into her car.

In a way, I was, too. "It just seemed right."

She handed me a bottle of water.

She wanted to ask why, I could tell, but instead she kept her mouth shut and just pulled into traffic. I flipped open her phone, reconsidered, and snapped it shut.

"Mind if I check myself in the rearview mirror?"

"Go ahead."

It wasn't an attractive picture. My clothes looked like a diary of my last three days, smeared with dust from Guthrie's garage two days ago and coated with dirt from Zahra's yesterday and blood from my fall. I glanced over at my sister and regretted every exasperated thought I'd had about her. "Janice, you were the one person who'd come and wouldn't ask questions, force advice, make demands. I'm wiped; I've got to think. But I just want you to know I'm so grateful to you." Janice, the odd sister out. "I know you hate being called 'the nice one.' You talk about how successful the rest of us are, but kindness—paying enough attention to know what kindness will entail—it's not nothing."

"Maybe."

"And keeping your mouth shut, that's really not nothing."

I didn't have to explain that one, not in our family. She laughed, then turned toward me. "Thanks."

In that moment she seemed like the big sister I remembered from childhood, the calm one amid all the bigger personalities. She was twelve years older than me. When I was starting grade school, she was a college freshman. Yet she'd stopped and listened when I babbled about finger painting or soccer practice. Not quite one of the "black Irish" of our family, she'd never stood out like Gary and Gracie with their chiseled features and startling blue eyes.

But now, her not-quite-black hair had gone gray and she'd pulled it back off her face in a way that classified it as a nuisance rather than an enhancement. Her bare and slightly fleshy arms had a tan line a couple of inches below the shoulder that said gardening was as close to exercise as she came. Her pale blue eyes seemed watery. *Pay no attention to me!* her whole being said. I drank some of the water she'd brought me. It would have been so easy to picture her in a house in the Berkeley hills, with a husband who appreciated her and a bunch of kids. But we all knew too well that the Lott family wasn't good at marriage, at least not since Mike disappeared. I didn't want to think about that. "Hey, what did you come up with on Ryan Hammond?"

"Nothing at all, really. Nothing useful."

I sighed.

She glanced over at me. "Sorry. I couldn't find anything else. I wasn't expecting a website or Facebook page, but if I Googled *your* name, I would at least get your political contributions."

"Let me tell you how surprised I'd be to find Ryan Hammond had sent a hundred bucks to the DNC." I'd had one iffy lead to the guy, via one of the most unreliable people on earth, and now even that was gone. Even if he was in the city, I'd never find him. I didn't even know what he looked like. I sighed. "What about Mike, any new word?"

"No. Well, nothing good. John's found a body that could be a match—"

"No!"

"It doesn't mean it is. He's somewhere south of the border. In the kind of place where they don't have their own forensic team. It's probably nothing, but . . ."

"I'm sure you're right," I forced out, and my words hung there with neither of us believing them. I couldn't deal with this possibility at all. Instead I focused my attention back on Guthrie and Hammond and their friend Kilmurray whom I'd been so desperate to get ahold of a couple days ago. Now I couldn't bear to call him. I forced myself to say, "I've got a possible lead to Hammond in Thailand; guy's a friend of his and Guthrie's. He's my last hope for some insight into Guthrie. I'm going to call—"

"Too early."

I looked at my sister gratefully.

She intuited what I was thinking. "I know the family thinks I'm not good for anything but digging in loam and sitting on soft chairs. But I can tell time."

"And you're the one who checks the missing persons' sites." I swallowed, remembering the pictures of unclaimed dead and the descriptions of how they'd died. I'd looked once and never been able to make myself go back lest without warning I discover what I couldn't bear to find. "That's sure not nothing, either. Do you check out ones all over the world?"

"This is going to sound strange. But it's like they're friends now, the dead. I'm rooting for them. If I go to one of the coroners' sites and a body's been claimed, I'm happy for them."

"And their family, huh?"

"Of course. But anyway," she said awkwardly, "I got to know time zones and you don't want to call yet. Do it from my house; I've got a serious phone. Not a satellite, but serious."

I could hardly believe this was the infuriating babbler I'd all but hung up on yesterday. How many sides did my sister have? Family legend portrayed her as being so endlessly accommodating and so overwhelmed that she'd ended up hiding behind the washing machine, and when Gary found her she'd come at him with a knife. Now I wondered how much that particular tale had gotten inflated with years of retelling.

I didn't call Thailand till we got to Janice's place. Meanwhile, I slept.

It was a bit after nine by then, which meant seven in the morning there. I punched in the number.

A woman answered but didn't sound like the one I'd spoken to before. She seemed annoyed at being disturbed, and less than eager to go and haul Kilmurray out of wherever he was. I kept Janice's phone by my ear as if his voice might come on any second, but minutes passed with only odd clicks. My own breathing sounded thunderous. But Janice, I noted, seemed unperturbed.

"It was about the same time Mike disappeared," I said softly, as if the woman in Thailand who was nowhere near the phone might be listening. "Kilmurray was involved with Guthrie, Ryan Hammond, and Tancarro right before the earthquake. It's not as if he's connected to Mike. Just stuff happened . . . back then." Suddenly, I was thinking of Mike and the body in Mexico and I was choking back tears. "Sorry, sorry. After all these years you'd think . . ." But Janice had turned away. She extracted a couple of tissues from a box and held out one to me without ever turning back.

"Hello?"

"Luke Kilmurray?"

"Who's that? Who'm I talking to?"

206

"Darcy Lott. I'm calling from San Francisco, about Damon Guthrie."
The line crackled.

"I'm calling about Guthrie!" I said, louder.

There was no response. I hesitated, then added, "I'm Guthrie's girlfriend."

Still Kilmurray said nothing. I could hear background noises, but if the line was this clear on his end, his silence made no sense.

"Guthrie!" I said, "He's dead!"

"It wasn't my fault. I kept telling myself that. Not my fault."

Of course it wasn't his fault. He was thousands of miles away.

"But I always knew," he went on. "The monks, they know what fault is. In the *wats* they talk about the wheel of dharma. You set it in motion, it turns and turns, and there's no stopping it. And whatever you pretend, here's the truth: your hand was on the wheel."

"Karma," I said. Actions have consequences.

"Yeah . . . karma. But . . . why now? Why'd you call me now?"

"Because Guthrie's dead and I need to know about him when you knew him. You were buddies with him before the earthquake, right?"

"Who are you? Why should I talk to you?" He sounded so not-American-any-more. Like he'd put my question in a pipe to see what the smoke told him.

"Karma," I said. "There isn't only one turn of the wheel. You turn the wheel every day, every moment, with everything you do. You can turn the wheel again—now—and send it in a different direction." When he didn't answer, I said, "Chances come. Not taking them is turning the wheel, too. But I'm not telling you anything you don't know, right?" I added. Then I waited. I could hear his breathing, thick, as if he was hauling in each individual breath. I thought he repeated "karma" as if mulling the possibilities, but I couldn't be sure.

Finally, I said, "You and Pernell Tancarro—"

"That jerk."

Whew! "Why do you say—"

"He was such a wuss. 'You go first. You take the risk.' Couldn't decide if he was going to be a judge and needed to keep his ass clean or if he was a goddamned poet and needed to sulk in iambic pentameter."

"What risk, specifically?"

The line went fuzzy and I couldn't tell whether he'd changed position or if it was static. "Huh?" Kilmurray was sounding more like the line itself.

I'd worry about Tancarro later. "You remember Ryan Hammond?"

"Oh yeah. Opposite of that ass Tancarro. Ryan was a bundle of enthusiasm, like a big puppy. Try anything."

"He was Guthrie's friend?"

"Dunno. Met him in a bar. Think Guthrie met him there, too. Ryan was so perfect. That's what Guthrie saw. Went right up to him. He was just what he needed."

"Needed for the burglaries?"

"Yeah, the roof job. Not like Tancarro was going up there first, you can believe that. But Ryan, boy, that kid was strong. S'not easy climbing a yew tree. You gotta be strong to press those flimsy branches in before they break. I know. I tried. No way."

Climbing a yew tree? Was this guy delusional? Only squirrels climb yews. Maybe not even squirrels. Tancarro had said Guthrie'd picked Ryan for the burglaries, so at least Kilmurray was good with that. "So it was Hammond who climbed up?"

"He went first, up the tree. Fuckin' amazing. Him not hanging on but pressing in with his arms, and all the time he's got the rope looped around his neck. He was like Tarzan. Guthrie couldn't wait to get up after him. He was high." Kilmurray giggled. "High on the ground, you know."

"High-before-he-climbed high?"

"Yeah. Well, I was, too."

Big surprise. "And Ryan?"

"No. He was all business, like he had to prove himself. He and Guthrie'd been carrying on about stunts in the movies that night in the bar, what a cool job, and on and on and on. He'd had some kind of problem that was keeping him out of the business. So, for him, this was a great job. Guthrie'd paid him enough. He was a monkey, flying up that tree, bending the top of it over, leaping onto the roof. Me, I waited too long, had too long to think. I went, but I'll tell you I was shaking. I can still see the two of them up there. They looked like demons around a fire."

"This was a burglary—"

"I still see them, still see Guthrie on the roof," he said in the voice of somebody recounting a dream. I had to wonder if that's what it was.

"But, Luke, you were committing a robbery, right? Why the roof?" *Oh, shit! The chimney! Guthrie's chimneys!* "Were you going down the chimney? Did you go down?"

"No. Like I said, Guthrie and I were high. We made a lot of noise. He was talking about Santa and how some uncle or something of his had done the chimney bit there when he was a kid. Bag and all. Like a backpack, he said. He kept saying Hammond would have no problem going down because he wasn't as fat as Santa. We were high; I guess I told you that, huh? Anyway, suddenly there were sirens all over. We could see the red lights coming. Ryan freaked; I think he had something on his record already. Guthrie grabbed him and dragged him to the chimney. He kept yelling, 'Go! Just go!' He meant the chimney. But Ryan was freaked and shook him off and, man, he was gone. I slid down the rope so fast both my hands were bleeding."

"And then?"

"I ran. It was every idiot for himself."

"You just ran?"

"Well, yeah. I mean, we were talking felony. It was Guthrie's family house where he grew up, but his sister was the one who'd inherited it—that's why he was so pissed, so hot to get in there and steal some bonds or something. They didn't get along. She'd have pressed charges, no question. We could've gotten real time. Tancarro kept telling us that."

"Tancarro? Where was he?"

"Him? Keeping away from the edge. Taking care of number one. But yelling at Guthrie, 'Just fucking do it! This is what you were so hot to do; just do it!'"

"What did Guthrie do?"

"He went down the chimney. It was crazy, but he was so furious at Ryan and at his sister and all. He just went for it, you know, like the uncle he kept on about."

"And then?"

The line sounded fuzzier, or maybe it was Kilmurray catching his breath. "The next day," he said, "that was the earthquake."

"Was the house damaged?"

"Guthrie's sister's house? Hell, I don't know. The whole garage level of *my* apartment collapsed. Place was a total loss. I was watching the World Series and I went sliding into the wall. TV crashed. I had to go out the window. My neighbor's leg was broken and the woman across the hall ended up with her ribs crushed."

"What'd you do?"

"Got out of the city before things got worse."

"So you and Ryan and Guthrie drove—"

"No, just me and Ryan."

"Where was Guthrie?"

"I wasn't thinking about him. After the roof bit, I'd had enough of him and his stupid vendetta. But if I had been, I'd've figured he probably stepped out of the fireplace into the hands of the cops that night and after the earthquake they'd've let him out. Much as he was always griping about his sister getting everything, still, you know, it was the family house in the earthquake. But Ryan was like me; he had no reason to stay. The Bay Bridge had collapsed, phones were dead, we didn't know what was happening. We aimed to get out of the city before the whole place shut down. We lit out across the Golden Gate and drove north."

"When did you talk to Guthrie again?"

"What?"

I repeated the question.

"No," he said, as if explaining to an idiot.

"But—"

"Only in my dreams."

His voice was fading.

He was fading.

"Wait! What about Ryan? What happened to him?"

"We got pulled over for speeding. How crazy is that, with the city in fucking chaos on the other side of the bridge, and there in Marin County you got the Highway Patrol riled up about ten miles over the limit. It freaked us out—we thought they knew about the burglary. Ryan had Guthrie's license—"

"Ryan had Guthrie's ID? How come?"

"Guthrie'd emptied his pockets on the roof, like he was going to slide down the chimney faster without ballast. Ryan could've waited for him to give it back, but when we heard the sirens, he split fast. So did I. And then, later, when we got stopped, he didn't want to give the cops his own license. He handed the guy Guthrie's—"

"What about the picture?"

"Close enough."

"That's a big chance."

"Yeah, you know, I thought that." There was a different tone to his voice, speculative, and I had the sense it was the first time some other feeling had crept in along with his guilt. "I don't know whether Ryan planned to give the cop Guthrie's license or if he just had it and that's the one he pulled out. He was lucky, real lucky it was close enough. But, you know, once he had it in his hand, it wasn't like he could say, 'I just happened to have someone else's license here.' Whatever, the whole thing was the last straw, and when the cop pulled off I told him to drop me at the next exit. And that's the last I saw of him."

You have to know more than that! "Where was he from? Did he mention family? What did he say?"

"I knew he wanted to get into the movies, to be a stuntman, but something happened. One time he said he'd been framed, but then he said he'd just been stupid, that he blew his chance."

"What about parents? Other friends? Where'd he come from?"

"Dunno. He was like a little kid who wants to be a pirate. All he talked about was movies and stunts. It's why Guthrie figured he was perfect for the job. Guthrie paid him, sure, but he flattered the kid so much that Hammond would have done it just for the thrill."

"And you never heard from him again? Or even heard *about* him?"

His breath against the phone sounded like a storm. For a moment I thought he wouldn't be able to speak at all. When he did, his voice was barely audible over the crackling on the line. "I've spent most of my fucking life away. I don't hear from anyone. Why do you think I took your call? Just to talk about friends, about the city . . . I've been gone so long it's like I don't exist anymore."

"Gone so long . . . like you don't exist anymore." I realized I was speaking out loud.

It sounded like he was clicking his tongue, like he was thinking. Maybe that was just the line. I glanced at Janice, or where Janice had been, but she'd left the room.

Gone so long, like you don't exist anymore. "I'm so sorry," I said to him. But I was thinking of Mike. Tears poured down my cheeks. "I'm sorry."

The phone made a gulping noise. Then I realized the phone had gone dead.

My sister had walked back into the room. She didn't come to me, didn't put her arms around me as she'd done when I was a child. She, "the nice one," didn't offer me a tissue or comfort. She looked like she was about to speak but couldn't. She didn't look devastated; she looked scared.

I stared at her, taking this all in. For a moment I couldn't believe it, and then it all made sense. "What was it you said about Mike yesterday? 'Does he sound like someone who'd stumble into a seedy bar in Matamoros and swallow whatever he was offered?' Janice, you know what happened, don't you? You've always known."

She looked like the world had crumbled around her.

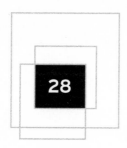

28

"Janice?"

Her face had gone ashen. She was looking at me, but she wasn't seeing me, wasn't seeing anything.

"Janice?" I repeated, in a softer tone. I was afraid to move toward her. She looked like she'd crumble to dust at one touch. I sat, still holding the turned-off phone. It was night, but outside I could hear street noises, a bus accelerating, a car alarm whirring. For an instant she seemed to snap out of it. She looked at me, *saw* me, and recoiled.

Before she could move I was up and reaching for her. She pulled away, started toward the outside door, froze, and then sank down against the wall.

"Mike came here, didn't he? Back then?" *When he 'disappeared,' he came here, sat here, when we were waiting in Mom's living room, terrified that he'd been in an accident, injured, dead!* "He came here because . . . For the same reason I called you to come get me today. He came because he knew he could trust you."

She was sobbing too hard to speak, but I knew I was right. All these years she'd let us wonder—I could have strangled her. *Stop! Focus!* I couldn't go there, not now. I had to stay with what happened, only that. "He needed someone he could talk to, someone who would listen without interrupting every third sentence to tell him why he shouldn't have done what he did or what to do about it, like Gary or Gracie would."

Her lips quivered. At a better time she would have smiled at that.

"But he knew you'd be there for him, that you'd take care of him like you did when he was little and—"

She mumbled something and it took me a moment to make it out: "All along." She looked at me pleadingly. "Both of you."

"Like you did all along," I said. How had I never realized that? I'd never thought of Janice being anything special to Mike, or to me. I'd never thought of Janice . . . period. Like the rest of the family. "He came here and . . ."

"He . . . he said he just needed to get away a little while. I thought he'd be gone a week. I never dreamed . . ."

"Of course you didn't. How could you have imagined he'd disappear forever? Of course you didn't." *But he didn't come back. Why didn't you tell us you'd seen him? How could you not have told us! Told Mom!* I sank down beside her and pressed in close. *Because we'd have squeezed you dry, every one of us, year after year, one of us after another after another.* My head was spinning. I took a breath, willing myself to stay focused. *Even so, how could you watch Mom year after year after year—* "Where'd he go?"

"I had friends . . . in Mendocino . . . logging protesters, you know. He left in the morning. I"—she swallowed—"I packed him a lunch and gave him forty-five dollars. It was all I had in the house. I wanted to go to the bank, but he was in a hurry. He just needed to get away, he said. But I never imagined . . ."

"Of course. But didn't you start to wonder?"

"Yes!" she snapped.

Whatever I did, I knew I had to stay still and not lose contact with her.

"I called and called, but one of my friends had gotten arrested and the others were protesting that and no one was home with their phone. No cell phones then. And then Gary called me, and Gracie—you know what Gracie thinks of me—and John, and then Gary again because he was sure he could find out something when John couldn't. I kept saying I didn't know anything. Finally I took the bus to the closest town up there and spent a week hunting up my friends and, of course, they had no idea where Mike was. He hadn't meant much to what they were into. I had to really poke before they remembered he was there. They just weren't paying attention. They had their own stuff to worry about."

"That's it? He walked away and vanished?" Why was that such a slap in the face? We'd always hoped that was what he did when he ambled out of the house that Thursday after the earthquake. It was the best possible outcome. But now . . . I felt—but I didn't dare let myself feel at all. "What'd they say?" *Didn't you fucking ask?*

"There was a tree sit farther north that needed a support crew. He'd gone with them." She was shaking.

As gently as I could, I said, "How'd you discover that?"

"It took me weeks, finding out who-all was there. You don't give out that data when you're doing stuff that could land you in jail. I had to prove myself to each person, explain about Mike, about me, go to protests that weren't my thing at all. I got arrested twice. That was good. Lots of time to talk in the lockup. People are happy to talk."

"Holy crap!" I looked at this sister whom I didn't know at all. "You were in *jail* and none of us ever knew about it?"

She nodded.

"And then what?"

"I went farther north and did it all over again. Only then I had some cred because, see, I'd been arrested."

"He was gone?"

"And they were glad. One guy'd figured him for a company spy and they were all freaked. They were really relieved when I vouched for him."

"And then?" I could have cut to the chase, but I was afraid.

"He'd headed south. There was a hot springs sort of hostel in Mexico. Turns out he'd cooked there. Who knew, eh? But it did a winter business, and by the time I tracked it down it was already May. He'd been there all winter."

It was too much! She'd been gone looking for him all that time and none of us even wondered about her! What did *that* say about the Lott family? "What'd they say about him?"

"They liked him."

"Of course."

Janice almost smiled. People always liked Mike. "But that place didn't work for him, long-term. Nothing did. They said . . . How they put it was, 'He stayed alone in his soul.'"

I pressed my arm tighter against hers and we sat like that a moment.

Then she said, "And one day at the end of the season he hitched a ride north and that was that. It took me another year to get word of him."

"How'd you do that, Janice? I mean, get yourself to the off-the-grid place? Coming back here only to get some new lead and drop everything to go off?"

Now she did smile. "It made me what I am today. The family thinks I'm a flake. Don't bother trying to deny it. To John I'm irresponsible. Gracie thinks I'm lazy. Gary—he'd never say this straight out—but he wonders if I've got brain damage from too many drugs. And Katy keeps saying, 'You have a master's degree; you could get a teaching job. Why are you sitting around, doing gardening jobs, running errands, doing all this half-assed stuff?'"

"Because you had to, right?"

Her eyes widened. It was a moment before she said, "Yes. Because I had to go to meetings, to marches, spend hours on the Net, call sources in India or Nepal in the middle of our night. I couldn't keep any job with regular hours."

I nodded. "For years I'd spot guys on the street I thought were Mike. I'd go racing out of cafés without my coat, forgetting my purse, totally abandoning whomever I was with. I'd only have to chase for a block or two. But you did it big time."

Her mouth quivered. For a moment I thought she'd cry, but she didn't.

I couldn't put off asking any longer. "And now? Where is he now?"

"I don't know."

No!

"He was in Maine two years ago, working on a lobster boat out of the Stonington Co-op. But lobster fishing's way down. And now I don't know. It's funny, it's as if he and I have walked through these last twenty years hand in hand, but separated by a year or so and by geography. As if we're not going anywhere, but together."

"But you think he's still alive. Still in good shape?"

"Oh yeah. I mean, why wouldn't he be?"

Why wouldn't he be? She could have been talking about okra! Okra's in the store, why wouldn't it be? *Why wouldn't he be?* My hands were knotting into fists. *Focus! Damn it, focus!* I exhaled slowly, then said, "Okay. It's got to end. You have to tell John and get him on it. It won't take him a year; it'll take him a week. It'll—"

"I can't."

"You can't *not.*"

"I promised Mike."

"He'll get over it."

"John wouldn't take me seriously."

"Surely—"

"That big family meeting you set up, the last-ditch effort? No one even called me."

"Oh."

"I'm not complaining. I'm not this distant from the family by accident. I can't see them. I'd have to be lying all the time. I don't care much anymore, except about Mom, but most of all I can't see her."

"Oh, God." Now I did wrap my arm around her. "All this time. I'm so sorry. Listen, I'll do it. I'll get John on this."

"No! Not John! Mike would—"

I lost it. "Janice, what the fuck is going on with Mike? What is it that is such a big deal that he's put his family through this for twenty years?"

"He didn't want to hurt the family."

I snorted.

"No, really. He was in such a bind—"

"Why? I can't imagine any scenario that's worse than letting all your brothers and sisters put their lives on hold and leaving your mother to think you're dead. Look at us: Katy's the only one with a decent marriage. It's like the rest of us froze in time when Mike walked out. I just thought I was in love with a guy because our connection was that we didn't ask any questions. So, what's this thing that's so important to Mike that he could let it paralyze us all these years?"

She took a deep breath and then another, and then shifted so she wouldn't be looking at me. "The summer before he left—"

"The summer before the earthquake.'

"He worked with Dad."

"On a job he hated," I said.

"Right. He tried to avoid it, but we all forced it on him. John kept at Dad, reminding him that he'd made a job for him and would have for Gary, so why not Mike? Dad was in charge; he could hire. Gary chided Mike about being lazy. Even I thought Dad was being unfair to Mike and said so. Everyone had an opinion. So, in the end Mike went to work for Dad, doing foundation work in the Marina."

"Omigod! The foundations that failed in the earthquake!"

"Right." She inhaled and let out her breath very slowly. "Dad . . . this is what Mike discovered. Money was tight. Mike was in college, Katy's husband had gotten laid off, and Dad had cosigned the note on their house, I'd—I'd borrowed money for grad school and hadn't paid it back. Mom and Dad had gone on that big anniversary trip to Australia. It was all coming due. So Dad cut corners on the materials. If the earthquake had been smaller . . . if he'd been working in another part of town where the ground didn't turn to mush . . . But, Darcy, people died."

I was sitting with my head in my hands. My hands were nearly over my ears. I didn't want to hear. Dad? "There's got to be some mistake—"

"There isn't. Trust me. Trust Mike. If there had been a mistake, he'd be sitting right here. But there is no mistake. And Mike never would have hurt the family. But he couldn't stay here, knowing about Dad. He couldn't bear to face Dad, because, of course, Dad knew. Why do you think he had another heart attack? The one that killed him."

"But then, after he was dead—"

"I'm not certain he ever heard that Dad died. But even if he did, what was he going to do, come back and tell the family he left because Dad was a chiseler who killed people? How could he do that to Mom?"

"Are you saying he's alive, but he will never be able to come back? No! That's not going to happen. I don't care what comes out. You find him. I'll deal with John. I'll smooth this over with everyone. I'll lie for you; I'll lie for him. I will do whatever I have to, but I can't stand knowing he's out there and I can't see him!" Now it was me who was sobbing.

And it was a few minutes more before I said, "Do it now. Okay?"

She nodded. She looked empty.

As I sat there, in the swamp of our emotion, I thought of Gabriella. Our entire family had devoted our adult lives to finding our brother. Her long-lost brother had done something really stupid before he left, but he came back, he rang her bell, and she didn't even open the door.

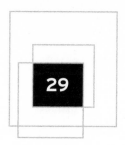

29

JANICE WANTED A week to work her networks, a week before I told the family. I talked her down to a day, with a check-in before I'd say anything to anyone. To her it was no time at all, to me an eternity.

In the meantime, I needed to get Tancarro to at least describe Hammond, or the Hammond of twenty years ago. It wouldn't be much to go on—well, next to nothing unless he had a birthmark on his forehead or three ears—but at least I wouldn't be sitting on a trolley next to the guy and not know.

As for Gabriella, I had to get in her face and let her know what an ass she'd been. I'd tell her what I'd learned about her brother during his long absence. Him helping out Zahra. How he struggled against his own fear year after year. I wouldn't mention the smuggling or other things she wouldn't want to hear—that's what police were for. Maybe my information would be a gift, the way Guthrie had viewed what he was returning to her. Maybe it would just make her feel lousy. That would be okay, too. I wouldn't be doing it for her. It'd be for him, likely, the last thing I'd ever do for him.

What I did not want, however, was to piss off Higgins. Or distract her from however much effort she was making to find Hammond. Or, worse yet, run into her there.

Nor—God forbid—did I want to run into my family. Not before I figured out how to pass on Janice's information without setting them at her throat. I wanted to do the right thing.

□ □ □

"I want to do the right thing, Leo."

"One might say that would be returning one of Inspector Higgins's phone messages."

"How many?"

"Three."

"When?"

"Right after you absconded through Mr. Tancarro's rear door. That's pretty much a quote."

"Nothing since then?" *Nothing useful to me.*

"Nope."

"Did she sound threatening?"

He hesitated. "Threatening? No. 'A competent police department never lowers itself to threats.'"

I laughed. "Now even you're quoting my brother, John."

"He called, too."

"What did you tell them?"

"I said I'd pass on the messages. I know you worry I'll give away secrets or be pushed to push you. I'm truthful; I'm not obedient. Still . . ."

"Right. I'll check in with them before they all end up here."

Leo and I were sitting in his room, him cross-legged on his futon, me on a zafu on his carpet. It was midday, and warm for San Francisco. He was wearing a black T-shirt and drawstring pants. He looked like he was melting down into his futon. I'd made tea. Making him tea had been one of his first requirements of me when I became his *jisha*, his assistant, and now the simple, focused actions had pulled me from the turmoil of my worries into the calm of the room. I'd poured the tea and we each held a small handleless cup gingerly, waiting for it to cool enough for us to drink.

As if reading my thoughts, Leo said, "Such a simple process. So many actions all coming to one point."

He was asking, "What's your point?" When I didn't—couldn't—answer, he began recounting once again the story of Seijo, the Chinese girl whose father promised her to her cousin but suddenly announced he was giving her to another man. He paused and nodded at me to pick up the thread.

"Her lover stalked off because he was offended." *Like Mike, sort of.* "She followed him because she loved him." *Like me, like Janice, like all of us.* "And when they came back home to her father, it was because they missed him. They missed the decent person he had been before he did that terrible thing. Her lover-husband was still caught up in the broken promise, but she wasn't and so she could walk back in the house without hesitation." *Oh.* "If her father had been an evil man, the story wouldn't exist. They wouldn't have been shocked by his betrayal; they wouldn't have wanted to come home." *Oh.*

"I need to talk to John."

He nodded in response to my certainty. "But?"

"But? Well, unless Janice works a lot faster than I'm thinking she will, John can wait till tomorrow."

Leo had to be baffled, but he chose not to show it. He raised his cup, took the smallest of sips of the still-too-hot tea, and set the cup on the napkin on the floor.

"But Guthrie? If Guthrie was Seijo and he was aggrieved that his parents left control of his inheritance to his sister . . . but that's more like

Seijo's lover, the guy who's indignant. So if Guthrie's like the lover . . . but that doesn't make sense."

"Koans are like dreams. All the characters are you. And the story varies depending on the translation." He paused. "Things change."

I smiled. Things change: Suzuki-roshi's answer to the question, What is Zen? I'd heard it condensed to just "change," since "things" have no permanent being. "Well, Guthrie sure changed. The guy I knew had done a world of changing from the pain in the ass his sister knew."

"Why did Seijo come back?" he insisted. "The story says it was because she missed her father. But what did she really miss? What really drew her back?"

"Oh, of course. Herself. The story says that when she and her husband came back to her father's house, the husband went to apologize to her father and her father said, 'What are you talking about? Seijo's been here, in a coma, the whole time.' Seijo came back because of her 'self' in the coma. And when her self in the bed saw her, the two came together and she was whole. When the halves come together it's the first time she stands up and takes an action on her own. Up till then she's just been reacting. Ah . . . she came back to be real."

I sipped the tea. It had cooled now. "Guthrie wanted to return something to his sister. Maybe something that would make things right."

"And that would be . . . ?"

"Okay, so I still don't know what he wanted to return. But, Leo, you remember you said I was stuck, like Seijo in the bed, paralyzed by my need to find Mike. My whole family is."

"Bed's crowded."

"Mmm. But Gabriella sure got stuck when Guthrie left. From what Guthrie's friend Pernell Tancarro said, she was fine and as up-and-coming as he was back then."

"Tancarro didn't rise?"

"Not poetically. He isn't in a coma like she is, but he didn't run away with his love, either. He just stopped writing. That night seems to have changed all their lives. Look, there were four guys involved in the burglary plan—to send one of them down the chimney. They make such a racket, someone calls the cops. They panic and the rest of them run, but Guthrie's so obsessed he goes down the chimney. That was twenty years ago and since then he's been obsessed, climbing down ever-taller chimneys and trying to make himself stay there more than a few seconds. Makes my family seem downright normal."

"Odd."

"Odder yet, because after that Santa move, he wasn't freaked. Au contraire, he got himself together and became an A-1 stuntman. So that's Guthrie and Tancarro. A third guy's taken himself into exile in Thailand, and who knows about Ryan Hammond, the guy Guthrie wanted to go down the chimney. Blink said he was here, in the city, but unless the police pick him up, that means nothing. And none of this suggests why Guthrie should be bludgeoned and left under his car in the park. What I have to do is see that room and find out what happened when Guthrie walked out of that fireplace."

"You're going down the chimney?"

"No. That'd be the easy way. I'm—"

But it didn't matter what I intended to do. At the moment I had to go deal with my brother, John, who was standing in the downstairs hall calling my name.

30

"You look awful, John."

"Yeah, well, I was up all night trying to get a flight out of Houston."

"Have you had coffee?"

"Do I look like it?"

"You look like you've been in Guantanamo." I steered him through the courtyard onto the sidewalk and toward a family in Bermuda shorts. Tourists. They were comfortable now, but if they stayed out past five they'd understand why they hadn't seen shorts on San Franciscans. "Do you know if Higgins—"

"No. Haven't even checked in, and if I had, I still wouldn't know if Higgins— Anything."

"What are you doing here? I thought you were still in Matamoros."

"Janice called."

"I thought she just told you I was okay."

"That's what she thought." He was holding open the door to Renzo's. We took one of the tables and ordered.

"You still haven't said how come you raced back," I said warily. "Janice just told you I was okay, right? Not to worry—"

"She called me. That's one red flag. She steers clear unless it's dire. You called her rather than Gracie or Gary. Another. And you were spending the night with her when she could have detoured over here and left you on your own mat. Or, more decently, taken you to Mom's."

"She called Mom."

"Hmm."

"Okay, so I didn't want to be pressed. But what about the body in Mexico?"

"What about the body in Mexico? Doesn't that say it all? No question about whether it was Mike. That's exactly the way Janice asked. She said what she had to and then, as if she remembered her manners, she inquired about my trip. You don't need to be a detective to catch on that there's a big lead on Mike and that it's coming from you, you who have been incommunicado for days."

Renzo set down the cups and came back with a porcini and chanterelle mushroom focaccia. I took a large bite. It was still too hot, but I didn't care. "I've got a lead. I can't tell you more yet. But you're key to making it work."

"There's nothing I won't do."

Nothing, but what I have to ask you. "It can't have been cheap to fly to Brownsville and back at the last moment."

"Couple thou," he said, as if it was a couple of trolley fares. How much had he spent searching for Mike all these years? More than I wanted to know about, definitely.

I sipped the espresso. The café was the wrong place for what I had to say. I was the wrong one to tell John. He'd changed a lot, or my perception of him had since I'd come back to the city, but expecting him to understand about Dad was just unreasonable. If I could find someone else to talk to him, someone who was not his baby sister . . . If, if, if. Hesitantly, I said, "Mike worked for Dad the summer before he disappeared."

"Great job. Y'know I did that before the academy," he said, wrapping himself in the safety of happy family reminiscence. This was going to be harder than I'd thought. He was gazing out the window as if seeing the city circa 1989. "I was good, but Mike, he was a natural. I remember Dad saying that by the time he'd been there a couple of months he knew every job, plus how to do payroll and keep the books. Dad said to me once, if it'd been another era, he'd've been walking out proud knowing he had a son like that to take over the business. And Mike, he didn't want to do foundation work at first, but he loved working with Dad, hanging around like one of the regular guys, listening to them talk about the old days. I did, too. Do you remember Preston O'Malley and Jerry Larsen? Did you ever meet—"

I had to stop him! "It was so perfect for you at that age." *Not for Mike.* "But like you said, Mike was into every part of the operation. And he found a, well, a discrepancy—"

"You mean Dad's accountant—Mr. Weller?—was cooking the books?"

"No. Nothing to do with him." I lifted my cup, but now I couldn't even bring myself to drink. "Okay, here's the thing. Dad cut corners on materials—"

"Dad would never—"

"He did!"

"How can you say that about Dad? How *dare* you say that?"

"Because I hate to tell you as much as you hate to hear it." I put my hand on his arm. "John, think how hard this is for me. I loved Dad, too. Not like you did—no one was as close to Dad as you—but he was my father, too. He was the one who was okay with me taking chances, who believed I could make the leap, balance on the fence, do three backflips in a row. He was the one—" My eyes were filling, my voice catching. "I can't begin to tell you how much I do not want to say this . . . but for some reason Mike believed Dad was using bad materials."

"Mike was a kid. He made a mistake."

I plowed on. "Mike loved Dad, too."

He nodded. "Mike would never hurt the family."

God! The irony! "So, then, you know Mike believed Dad was using substandard materials. He . . . would never, ever make an accusation like that if he didn't"—I almost said "know"—"assume it was true."

John's fingers were arched back, his hands tense as claws.

"Just accept that, that Mike *believed* it."

"Mmm."

"Then the earthquake hit and people in those buildings were injured. People died. Because the buildings crumbled. Put yourself in Mike's place. He worked on those buildings; he knew about the materials. He knew about the materials, John, and he did nothing. Think how he felt."

"If he was so depressed—and I'm not saying I'm buying into this story—how come not one of us noticed?"

"It was after the earthquake! You were working double shifts; Gracie was interning in the ER. We didn't hear from her for days. The phones were down, and getting anywhere was a hassle. Everyone was panicky. It would have taken a lot more than depression to get our attention then."

"Still—"

"The only one who was around a lot was Gary. You remember what a hotshot he was then. There was nothing he didn't see as cause for damages. That week after the quake he was driving everyone crazy. Even Mom told him to can it with the talk of injuries, damages, jury trials, and gonzo settlements. And on the criminal side, jail time for the people responsible. That's what Mike kept hearing."

"Gary wouldn't—"

"So—and this is the point—if Mike stayed here, what would he have faced?"

"He wouldn't've been jailed. No one went to jail. It's crazy to—"

"You're looking at it with hindsight. At the time he *believed* Dad was responsible—legally liable—for those people in those buildings. I'm guessing now, because I never talked to Mike about this, but he was a witness to Dad's operation. He knew what was purchased and how it was used. If Dad had been indicted, Mike would have been called as a witness—against Dad. Mike would have been responsible for Dad going to jail."

"No one went to jail!"

"We didn't know that then! Then, we didn't even know how many people died. You're forgetting what it was like. The roadway on the Bay Bridge fell down; the 980 freeway collapsed. We had no idea how bad it was. Mike loved Dad. Of course he'd worry about the worst-case scenario. If not jail, then disgrace. The whole family would have been shamed, and responsible. Mom and Dad would have lost everything, not that there was much. You and Gary, all of us, would have felt responsible, financially, and so we should have."

"But—"

"Look at this from the point of view of a nineteen-year-old boy. Even if none of that happened, how could he face Dad again? How could he explain to Mom or any of us why he was avoiding Dad? So he left in order to figure out what to do."

"Dad drove all over the city looking for Mike, driving, driving. He'd call, leave messages at the station, as if I'd get a lead and not tell him! The man was beside himself with worry."

I lifted my cup, holding it in both hands, sipping slowly.

John sat unmoving. He was facing the window, not to look out now, but to avoid contact with me, his coffee and focaccia untouched. After a while he lifted the cup and drank it in one swallow, like medicine. "It's lucky for Mike he never told me that crap."

There was a roteness about his delivery. He couldn't face this accusation, but he couldn't dismiss it either.

It was as much as I could hope for.

"Okay, even if Mike believed that garbage, even if he *thought* he was leaving town to nobly save the family, what about after Dad died? That was only a few years later, a few years of grief over Mike."

"Then he really couldn't come back. Would he pretend nothing happened? He certainly couldn't admit anything was wrong with Dad's business practices then, after he died. He definitely couldn't tell the family then. And Mike still had his own guilt. Every time he'd walk through the Marina he'd feel it. Every time there was a news story about the quake. Hell, every time he drove over the Bay Bridge, which they're still rebuilding now, all these years later."

"He could have sucked it up and kept quiet."

"*You* could have, John, but Mike isn't you. He's the guy everyone felt they had a special connection with. If he'd come back then, he'd have changed; he'd have to have. We'd all have noticed. Every one of us would have taken him aside and demanded an explanation. We're nothing if not persistent. We'd have worn him down or driven him crazy. Look, it's not as if I've talked to him. I heard about the first part, about Dad, but why he didn't come back later, I'm just guessing. For all I know, he doesn't know Dad is dead. But my point is, the only way he can come home is if he isn't in the position of condemning Dad—"

"Let him—"

"The facts are the facts. So, the only way he can *not* be responsible for destroying our memory of Dad is if we can deal with what Dad did. If we can accept that he did that one wretched thing and remember the rest of who he was."

"Skip the psych crap!" He slammed his chair back.

"Don't you leave! This is the most important talk you'll ever have. You've spent twenty years hunting Mike. Don't get up! Look, we all thought Dad worried himself sick about Mike. But Dad knew the whole story, what he'd done, why Mike was gone, how much that hurt Mom and the rest of us, and why he couldn't afford to own up. I think that's what ate away at him. I think . . . I think there is no way anyone could condemn him more than he did himself."

John looked so gray and drained, I longed to help him. But there was nothing I could do except leave him alone.

"We all make mistakes. If Dad were alive, he'd have done what had to be done. We'd have dealt with the consequences. That would have been just one part of his life, not the central thing. We'd have forgiven him for not being what we thought. That's what we have to do now."

For an minute, John said nothing. He was sitting, but he wasn't still. He was like an old car, clutch held in, engine racing.

I struggled not to get pulled into his vortex. *You don't have to choose between Dad and Mike!* "I have to know what you decide. Not today, but soon. Sooner than it's fair to ask of you."

"If not?"

"Maybe it'll be too late."

"Now or never, that's his ultimatum? Fuck 'im!" He shoved up. The metal chair careened into the next table and John would have strode out the door had that door not been blocked by Inspector Higgins.

She leapt back. He shot by her as if she were a lamppost. And when she pulled herself together and came in to my table, she looked as outraged as he had.

31

"YOU'VE ARRESTED BLINK Jones and his wife?"

"The alleged thieves driving a plain white truck somewhere in California or points east? Surprisingly, no." Higgins loomed over the small table, standing in the spot vacated by the chair John had kicked over. If I thought the atmosphere would lighten up with John's departure, her expression disabused me. She was one testy-looking lady.

"Ms. Lott, I need answers from you. Now!"

"Sit."

It was too much to ask. "Downtown."

I know my rights. "The courtyard." As I was about to ask for another coffee, I saw Renzo already had the paper cup on the table for me and a bag for the rest of my focaccia.

She held open the door, tacitly moving me along. "I told you to keep me informed."

"What you *said* was not to go see Guthrie's sister."

"Which you did."

"Which I informed you I'd do and which your surveillance guy saw. That was two days ago. How come you're just getting—"

"I told you not to interfere."

"Do you want to know what she told me?"

"What?"

"Exactly what you expected. Zip."

"And Tancarro?"

"Twenty years ago, Guthrie, a friend who's now in Thailand, and a guy they met in a bar—Ryan Hammond—planned a burglary of Guthrie's sister house, the house where she's all but entombed herself now. That's what I learned from Tancarro. Ryan Hammond may be in the city right this very moment. You could be closing in on him, if you found Blink Jones."

She'd pulled out her pad but hadn't put pen to paper.

"You seem so disinterested it's almost insulting."

Another woman might have noted that I hadn't given her anything worth a raised eyebrow. Higgins, however, strode after me into the court-yard, planted herself on the bench, and continued without missing a beat. "After you skipped out from Tancarro's—"

"You never—"

"What were you doing in L.A.?"

Conspiring with thieves, eluding the police. It would have been a bit obvious to drag out the focaccia and buy time eating it. The thing was I had no legal and non-incriminating explanation. I was reduced to offering the truth. I hate that; it leaves no fallback position. "Like I told you, I knew so little about Guthrie, I went down there hoping to find out more."

"And?"

"I checked with his agent. You remember I gave you the name."

"They're not great on phones."

Boy, they'd really taken my warning to heart. How long had they kept up not answering Higgins's calls? "Agents! Never get back to you fast enough!"

Higgins, of course, missed the humor in that. But she wasn't snarling; she was waiting with unexpected patience. It made me uneasy.

"He gave me the key to Guthrie's house."

"What did you find there?"

Oh, shit! I was going to be thinking that with every other question now. "An Oscar. Not a copy, a real, engraved, numbered Oscar. That was weird because the Academy doesn't give Oscars for stunt work or direction. So—"

"It came via Ryan Hammond."

I dropped the bag. "How do you know about Ryan Hammond?" *Why didn't you let on when I was just talking about him. Oh wait. We're the cops: we ask, you answer.*

"Tell me about Hammond."

You're the police; find out. "His moment of fame was the theft of that Oscar from Casimir Goldfarb."

"The director."

Uh-oh. "It's like a morality tale. He was desperate to do stunt work, but he was blackballed. And he can't get rid of the damned Oscar."

"You're saying that theft—"

"I'm saying what everyone in the business says. Goldfarb was a bully who got his comeuppance."

"Do you think Mr. Goldfarb carried a grudge?"

Despite everything, I laughed. "Think Atlas."

"After all these years?"

"Hey, I'm not even sure Hammond stole it. There's another version that has his girlfriend, now Blink's wife, making off with it. But why are you focusing on this part of Hammond's life?"

She looked down at her pad—unblemished by notes—as if it would give her the right answer. "Ryan Hammond is dead."

"Ryan Hammond is dead? How? How long ago? Where?"

"Murdered."

239

"Omigod!"

"I'm asking you. Who, besides Goldfarb, who now, by the way, is directing commercials—"

"Directing commercials? Good money, no glory."

"Hammond?" She prodded.

"Like I said a couple of days ago, we're on the same side here. You must be thinking Hammond's death is connected with Guthrie's. How could it not be? I want to help you to zero in on his killer. But I need to know why you think so. Deal?"

Surprisingly, she nodded.

It made me very uneasy. "Okay, here's what I know," I said. "Hammond's Oscar was in a house either he and Guthrie shared, one of them used, or neither of them did and it was only kept as a drop for a burglary ring run by the same woman who actually stole it."

"And?"

"Guthrie hired Hammond to break into his sister's house, to go down through the fireplace."

"And?'

"That's it. Now you?"

She put down her pad and looked directly at me. "The body you found in the park by the Palace of Fine Arts was Ryan Hammond."

"What?"

"The body is Ryan Hammond."

I couldn't take it in. It was all I could do to mutter, "Not Guthrie?"

Guthrie's body is Ryan Hammond? How could that be? Guthrie, my Guthrie, the guy who made love to me a week ago, was someone I don't even know? I've never known? He didn't even tell me his fucking right name!

Guthrie is Ryan Hammond. He was the kid with Melissa when she stole the Oscar!

"What do you make of that?"

How the hell do I know, bitch! You drop this bomb on me, then you sit and watch me smolder in the ruins! I could poke your eyes out with my thumbs.

"Ms. Lott?"

Do not give her the satisfaction.

"Now the issue is who killed Ryan Hammond. Who would have done that?"

I "saw" Ryan Hammond, the stranger, lying under Guthrie's car, pretending he was Guthrie as I held his hand and felt him die. That was convoluted crazy, but the whole thing—Guthrie, Ryan Hammond—was like a jigsaw with the pieces all mixed up. I couldn't make sense of it, not now, not with Higgins staring at my face.

With everything I'd ever learned about acting, I made myself focus on a pleasant scene, on walking into Renzo's first thing in the morning and him handing me a white porcelain cup of espresso. I smelled the coffee. I saw him smiling. I felt the back of a metal chair as I sat down to sip.

I may have had the smallest of smiles on my face when I looked at Higgins. "It tells me I know nothing at all about the man and cannot help you." I stood up. "Thank you for coming by to tell me."

And then I counted the moments till she cleared out and I could get a handle on the guy I'd been near to loving not having been him at all.

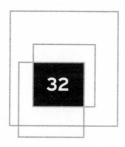

32

Ryan Hammond was Guthrie. How could he *not* have told me?

Ryan Hammond was Guthrie. What did that mean?

I wanted to jump on a Kawasaki and speed across town, roaring up hills, cutting through alleys, taking corners so fast the pavement would scrape my hip. I wanted the wind to sear my face. I needed to outrace my shock and anger and the mire of confusion.

I wanted to sit here and bawl.

Instead, I walked across Columbus Avenue into Chinatown, where you have to be alert on sidewalks jammed with elderly locals and tourists who stop abruptly to stare at dead chickens hanging in shop windows.

My Guthrie was Ryan Hammond. It was crazy to feel that I'd made love in the back of his truck with a stranger, but I couldn't shake that. *Same guy, just different name.* But he wasn't the same guy. Not at all.

Our whole relationship was based on not asking. Why are you changing the rules now?

Because you lied to me, you bastard!

I crossed Grant Avenue and cut down Kearney against the flow of one-way traffic. *Lied? Yes and no.* I'd known him ten or so years. By then he—Ryan Hammond—had been Guthrie for a decade. When did I expect him

243

to have told me? Right away? Hardly. When we first made love? *Oh, and by the way I'm using an alias?* Last Sunday, the day he died?

Last Sunday. *Maybe he would have if he'd met us that morning.*

I'd been in such an analytical mode in L.A., I'd stopped thinking of him here, last Saturday, the day before he died. But suddenly, I was back in the intensity of that day when he said he was near to loving me. And me, him. That day when he was desperate to talk to Leo, desperate to deal with something that was—How had he put it?—beyond absolving. He'd been so close to doing what he had to, so close to being with me. I couldn't bear to let myself linger on that, on what could have been for him and me. I had to keep walking, pushing the emotion behind.

But I remembered what I'd said, as we stood in the courtyard, his arms around me. I'd said: "I do know you. There's something we share—I can't put it into words, but with you I'm at home in a way I am with no one else. There's a reason for that and it's beneath the surface of who you are. I'm not about to give that up. No event is going to change it."

After that he went to Gabriella's to return something. To return something to a woman who was not his sister at all.

But Gabriella had insisted she never saw Guthrie.

Of course! She hadn't seen Guthrie—not her brother, Damon. If she had opened the door, it was to Ryan Hammond, a stranger. She saw a stranger who announced he'd taken on her brother's identity. Ryan Hammond, the kid lured by her vengeful brother into his burglary scheme.

I cut across the overpass to Portsmouth Square, zigzagged through the park, took a couple of alleys, and emerged on Polk Street, the old gay mecca back when Castro Street was merely a streetcar stop on the way to the Sunset District.

I thought of Guthrie's house in the canyon down south and I laughed. I'd wondered if Guthrie had shared the house with Ryan Hammond. It turns out they kept closer company than I could ever have imagined.

Those cylinders—chimneys—he built in the desert. He kept lowering himself down to see if he could deal with his fear. The night the real Damon Guthrie hired him for the burglary, the two of them climbed onto the roof. He—Ryan Hammond—was the one supposed to go down the chimney. Had he panicked? Looked down that dark chute and been paralyzed? Was that the reason he kept trying to prove to himself he'd outlived that fear?

It left me with one question, the same question that Higgins might have been asking herself, if she hadn't been so busy lording it over me.

I was nearly to Gabriella's house. I kept thinking of her entombed behind her blackout curtains, as Tancarro had said, in the once-lovely rooms she'd pine-paneled into a parody of 1950. Was that her own way of grieving for a rejected brother?

Had she been as outraged as I'd been a while back when a man had taken advantage of his resemblance to Mike? But if an actual impostor showed up at the door and announced he'd come into possession of Mike's wallet and driver's license and then he'd taken over his identity—I'd've been so furious I don't know what I would have done.

Guthrie isn't Mike. Gabriella's not you! I had to keep perspective. But perspective goes both ways. No matter how much Higgins had interrogated Gabriella, *if* she'd been able to at all, she could never see into this issue the way I could.

I walked through the Marina where the buildings had collapsed in the earthquake. I thought of Dad, whom I'd loved, who died with his guilt. And of Ryan who'd been overwhelmed by his, who'd been about to do what he could to make things right and then was killed.

245

I rounded the corner and was facing the Palace of Fine Arts, looking at the grassy expanse that had held the black convertible and his body.

I let myself pause only momentarily, then charged up the walk and rang Gabriella's bell.

The fog had been rolling in for hours. The dark sky suggested a later hour than 7:00 P.M., the time when residents of easy-access houses like this one were accosted by earnest young environmentalists and desperate religious peddlers, a time when answering the door rarely led to a good result. I balled my fist and pounded on Gabriella's door. Is this what Guthrie—*Ryan Hammond*—ended up doing? Did she let him in? "I know you're in there! I'm not going away! Open this door!"

If a guy showed up at Mom's house saying he'd slid into using Mike's identity because a cop stopped him and Mike had given him his license to hold and, well, now he wanted to give it back to her, give her Mike's identity back, Mom wouldn't have focused on the license or his rationale, she'd simply have told him to come in and then asked him the only question that mattered to her. The question that would lead to all the answers.

"Gabriella," I shouted, "where is your brother now? Where is Damon Guthrie?" *Where is the real Guthrie?*

Were those footsteps inside? I couldn't be sure. The wind was crackling the leaves in the neighbor's trees. I yelled louder, "Where is your brother?"

If this had been Mom's house, neighbors from both sides would have been heading toward me. Here, no one could see me over the fence. "Where is Damon!"

It was dark enough for lights, but there was no light escaping through her windows.

"Damon was up there on your roof! You called the police! He lowered himself down the chimney and then what? He didn't realize you'd closed

it off, did he? What did you do then? Call the fire department? The police? Did you press charges?" I wasn't even yelling any more, more talking
to myself than shouting at the closed door to the dark room. Over twenty
years ago, right before the biggest earthquake in a century—not a chance
there would still be a record of that cat-up-a-tree kind of call.

Wherever she was, she was inside and I was here in the dark and fog.
She could wait me out forever. "Fine! I'll just go have a look at that roof
myself."

I ran around the corner to the alley. Some kind of extension made the
fence higher. I leapt and grabbed for the top, but my hands slipped. I tried
again—nothing to get ahold of. There had to be something to stand on in
an alley.

Garbage cans. I was halfway down the alley when I found one and
wheeled it back.

I hoisted myself up, propping my elbows on the fence. Light shone at
the edge of the curtains in what must have been the kitchen; she was pulling them back, watching me. The roof would be manageable—two stories
up, with ramparts to grab onto. Back then Ryan had press-climbed a yew
tree and lowered a rope for the others, but now—

But the yew was still there! Thick, half-dead looking, taller surely, but
mostly decrepit. I could climb it.

This was crazy. What was I going to see, on the roof, in the dark?

I hoisted myself closer, unwilling to lower my feet into the mire of the
overgrown yard until I had to. Branches were bent, broken, as if someone
had pulled it—or climbed it—recently.

Only my guy would even attempt that. Because he'd done it all those
years before.

He was here asking the same question I was: Where is Damon Guthrie?
Why did he need to know? Guthrie may have owed him money, but no

way near enough to lead him—a guy who really didn't want to attract police attention—to climb up on the roof. Why was he so desperate to know?

He parked his convertible right here and climbed up on it and over the wall.

That's crazy!

Building three chimneys in the desert is crazy. Obsessed! Guilt-ridden!

After that, climbing up on the roof, *back* up on the roof, makes sense.

Also makes noise. Gives an assailant lots of time to grab a blunt object and hit you when you're vulnerable coming down.

Why *was* his body under the car?

What are cars for? To transport things from one place to another.

I could get up on that roof. There'd be evidence of his being there—fingerprints, threads, DNA. Evidence that would force Gabriella to talk. If I could make them—Higgins—go after it. *Fat chance!*

But I had to try. Keeping an eye on Gabriella behind the curtain, I felt for my phone.

Hands grabbed me from behind and slammed me hard, headfirst, into the wall.

33

"Is she dead?" Gabriella asked Tancarro.

I must have been unconscious. What brought me to was the thud from Tancarro dropping me on her living room rug. My head throbbed. My eyes were swelling shut. Through my lashes I could see her wiry frame draped in drab, heavy garments suitable to a house like this where she didn't turn on the heat. She was standing by a sofa facing a pair of leather chairs. It was a moment before I realized she was talking about me.

No one knew I was here. I could lie on this floor for days.

Or worse.

Was this how my guy—it was so hard to remember he was not Guthrie at all, but Ryan Hammond—was killed?

I stayed scrupulously still. Gabriella wasn't watching me; she was staring at Tancarro. But he wasn't letting me out of his sight.

I had to do something! Get his gun.

A gun! *His* gun? But Ryan Hammond hadn't been shot. He'd been hit with a pole, a poker, a cylinder—I stared at the big pistol—a pistol barrel?

"Shoot her now. Before she comes to." Gabriella sounded angry, terrified, desperate.

"Gunshot wounds leave blood. You want that sprayed all over your rug?"

"Move her. Put her in"—she pointed across the hall toward the room with the chimney and the walled-in fireplace—"that room. Won't matter in there. Just do it."

He shot her a look of disgust and resignation.

"Don't you dare—"

"Dare what? I'm here, aren't I? I've been here every time you've called for twenty fucking years. What more—"

"You're here because you conspired in a felony in which a man died."

Tancarro blanched. He gave an unconvincing shrug, turned, and looked ready to grab my feet and haul me, head smacking the floor, in the direction she was pointing. Very slightly, tentatively, I shifted my head. The room swam.

Tancarro was staring at my feet. He was looking at his gun, trying to decide if he could handle both. But he wasn't about to give her the weapon.

What did that mean? My eyes were swelling shut. My head throbbed so hard the room bounced.

"Go on! Dammit, Pernell, what're you doing—waiting, as usual?"

Ignore the pounding. Focus! What was going on with these two? No. No time to figure it out. I needed to startle them, jolt them off their track.

He turned toward her. "If you—"

Now or never! "Hey!" I snapped. "You can't kill me. You're on the Arts Commission!"

He stared incredulously, frozen for the moment. I clambered up. I had to lock my gaze onto something that wouldn't move—the armchair. Even so, a wave of nausea almost floored me.

"Sit down! Or he will shoot you now!" Gabriella yelled.

I longed to sink into one of the armchairs, let my head rest against its soft back. Like Ryan? Did he— But no. They hadn't killed him in here; there'd have been too much blood.

They didn't kill him in *this room*, but they did kill him. My chances—

Forget that! Focus on this moment. Right now, I needed to watch them both. I swung onto the bench of a spinet, landing hard, sending a new wave of misery through my head and stomach. But I kept my attention on them. Suddenly, I really was letting my thoughts and fears go, as I'd done sitting zazen. I was aware of the icy air, the stale smell, of myself, of them, of our connection. I was alert, waiting for my chance. Willing my eyes open, I stared at Gabriella and said, "Is this where Ryan Hammond sat before you killed him?"

Her gaze darted toward the hallway and back. "You're not—"

"—in a position to bargain? Au contraire. I am Ryan Hammond's girl-friend. I'm the one who knew he came here, remember? Why do you think I felt confident enough to knock on your door?"

"You're a fool," she said.

"Enough!" He hit the gun on a metal bowl. She jumped back. My head just about exploded. "Forget it, Gabi. We're not bargaining. Let's just get this over with. And you," he said to me, "get—"

"Gabi!" I said, "Where *is* Damon? Your brother? Goddammit, where is he?" My voice was loud, but their silence was way louder. They stared at each other, her dead pale, him with his jaw clenched, knuckles white against the gun butt.

"Where did he go?" I insisted. "Where *is* he? Did you break through the wall to the fireplace? Did you call the fire department? The police? What did you do?"

They looked like they couldn't speak.

"You did something!" I insisted.

They seemed frozen.

"You had to do something!"

Omigod! They'd left him there in the walled-in fireplace!

Suddenly I was shaking so hard I almost slipped off the bench. "The police!" There had to be an explanation. Some *other* explanation. I was grasping at straws. "You called the police. The guys heard the sirens while they were on the roof. That's why they scattered. You told me that, Pernell. Kilmurray told me. Didn't the police search the roof?"

"I thought"—her voice was almost inaudible—"I thought . . . the boys were gone. The police . . . came and . . . left."

"But they were here! Why didn't you have them check the roof? What harm—" She gasped.

But I knew the answer only too well. "The family! You didn't want it to become public that your brother was trying to break in. You didn't want to hurt the family. Of course, you *couldn't* hurt the family. How could you do that to your parents when they trusted you?"

Tancarro jolted toward me, but Gabriella's cry stopped him. I'd hit the mark with her.

I should have left it there, with her stunned, but I couldn't. I had to ask, "But after, you must've heard him in there? He must've yelled, pounded. You had to've heard him."

"No! *No!* I left. The house shook. I thought he'd dropped something down there. I didn't know what. I didn't think it was him, that he'd done something so crazy, even him. I thought he'd dropped a stink bomb or something. Something that would smell up the house. I was furious. I was scared. I'd had enough of him. I had to get out of here. I couldn't sleep here." She was staring at me, suddenly begging me to understand.

I nodded. "So you went to a hotel?"

"No, I slept in my office that night and the next night, too. And then the earthquake and I—I got sidetracked . . . Damon and his stupid prank. I never would have—" Gabriella seemed to shrink inside her heavy, ill-matched clothes. I tried to picture her as Pernell Tancarro had described her back then—an up-and-coming attorney, racing to court in an expensive dark suit and Italian high heels, a properly weathered leather briefcase slapping against her leg.

Twenty-one years ago. She'd spent twenty-one years in this house, slowly coming to suspect, and then knowing, her brother had died right there in the chimney he couldn't get out of. Where she had left him to die.

How had she lived with herself? How had she lived *here?* I thought of the guy I'd been near to loving that last day we'd been on the pier in Oakland. Him insisting he'd done the unforgivable, me unable to believe that, not of him. I'd buried my face in his chest, pulled him tight to me, and felt him shaking. He'd said, "I let him die . . . I walked away." I flashed on those chimneys he built in the desert, each more confining than the last. I could almost feel his dread as he lowered himself down inside, trying time after time to make himself stay, to experience even a bit of what he'd abandoned Damon Guthrie to. Each time scrambling out in panic.

I looked at Tancarro. "Why didn't Damon climb out?"

All the color was gone from his face. "Maybe the rope wasn't secured. It must have slipped in after him. He fell; he hit his head. He never came to at all."

No way you could have known. That's the story you made up to stave off the horror. So you don't have to think of your friend dying slowly in the dark. How soon did you get it? I wanted to ask. Did you wonder about him when he was coming to realize he was trapped? That time after time he must have tried to climb out and slid back down? When his legs gave out? When he clawed the bricks, screaming silently with his throat dry, his voice gone?

"Enough!" He motioned with the gun. "Walk!"

Slowly, I pushed myself up. My head nearly exploded.

"Move! There, across the entryway. Gabi, get the door."

Keeping her distance, she stepped around me and wrenched it open. The smell astonished me. It wasn't decay—not what I'd thought—but mold. All I could see through the doorway was boxes and dark-splattered papers piled, scattered, heaped higher than my head, filling a room twice the size of what she now used for her living room. A wall of paper sealing off the fireplace and her brother's body. I turned to Gabriella, stunned.

"Don't look at me like that! I had to live here, in this house, with him because he did that stupid, stupid, greedy thing! Him and his stupid friends and their stupid little plot. He was coming to steal from me. He died. It was his own doing. Not mine. But I'm stuck. I can't leave with him in there. I might as well be dead, too. And then he—your boyfriend—shows up—"

"You didn't have to kill him! He agonized over your brother. Why would he tell anyone?"

It was Tancarro who replied. "Maybe he wouldn't. But maybe he would. I couldn't take the chance. I've been chained to this place for twenty years. I've done my time. After all this, I'm damned well not going to jail. And I'm not spending the rest of my life worrying about it."

He shoved me into that awful room. My feet skidded on papers. I twisted, grabbed a box, and flung it at him. Then I lunged for his legs and brought him down hard. His head smacked the floor. The gun slid free. Gabriella lunged for it, but I scooped it up before her hands hit the floor.

"Move and I'll shoot."

They didn't doubt me.

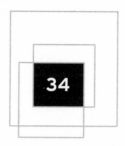

34

THE PREVIOUS NIGHT now seemed like a blur of flashing lights and police giving orders and racing around. I'd refused medical care—my head ached but I was damned sure it would ache a lot more if I was forced to spend hours in an ER. So, I'd ended up accepting police hospitality instead. And even with my brother Gary's help, I hadn't made it out of there till two in the morning.

When he finally dropped me off at the zendo, instead of going inside, I waited till he drove off. Then I walked slowly to the corner. I felt the damp, fresh, night air on my face and breathed in a faint garlicky aroma of tomato sauce, along with the exhaust fumes from a passing car and the sweetly rancid stench of garbage. Each of these familiar odors couldn't help but remind me of the great boon of just being alive. I wasn't thinking about Damon Guthrie in that chimney—but I wasn't *not*, either.

When I did go back to my room above the zendo, Leo's door was open. As if it were mid-afternoon instead of the middle of the night, he was sitting cross-legged on his futon reading what appeared to be an obscure Asian text printed on rice paper. It crackled as he turned the page. He was, of course, waiting up for me. I almost hugged him. I tried, but it's impossible to get your arms around a guy in that position without both of you ending up laughing. And I was even gladder about that. I put my hands together and bowed to him and he met my bow. Then I stepped into my room and flopped down on my futon and slept till noon.

When I finally got up, Leo was reading a different book. "Renzo's expecting us. Want to head out?"

"Great. I'm starving."

Then he added, "Various members of your family called. I told them you were asleep. They all said, 'No rush.'"

"Thanks." I was in no hurry either. They'd be relieved I was okay. They'd mask impatience while I rattled on about how now I understood why Gabriella didn't dare heat her house, why Guthrie/Ryan looked so good for a guy his supposed age—because Ryan was so much younger. They'd be polite as long as they could, but what they'd really want to do was talk about Mike. How could they not? I mean, whatever they'd been thinking, separately and together, his impending return had turned the world upside down. But, really, anything any of us might say would only be verbal nerves. We'd all be on eggshells until we actually laid eyes on him, till he was back and we could see how that realigned our stars.

I pulled on jeans and a T-shirt—a bright cab-yellow one that screamed: Alive!—and walked the half block to the café. When we arrived, Renzo was pouring espresso and a basket of his best pastries was on the table.

Leo hadn't asked about the last twenty-four hours, but that didn't mean he wasn't eager to know. I took a long, wonderful swallow of coffee and said, "I wanted to stay till the cops opened up that chimney. But not nearly as much as they wanted me out of the way."

He smiled and I had the feeling he was picturing Higgins's reaction to that request.

"It's probably just as well. I feel like the horror of it all will be with me forever. I understand why Guth—*Hammond*—could never pull free."

"Delusion."

"What?"

"You're indulging in delusion. You don't know what happened to Damon Guthrie in that fireplace. You can guess, even make a reasonable assumption, but you can never really know."

That was what I'd thought when Tancarro had speculated. But it was such a personally unsatisfying answer. Yet, now, I knew that in itself was the point.

"Leo," I said hesitantly, "can you tell me now what it was Guthrie—I mean, Ryan Hammond—was so desperate to discuss with you? What did he want to return to Gabriella? Just Damon's wallet and driver's license? Or was it"—I thought of Mom and Mike and all the years of his life she'd missed—"what he could tell her about what happened?"

"The *real* issue wasn't what he had to return . . . but what he was desperate to be given."

"Omigod, of course. He wanted an alternate explanation of what happened to Damon Guthrie." Suddenly I could see it all so clearly. "If only Gabriella would tell him Damon had gone to Tahiti or to jail or had become a monk! Any explanation but the one he was already haunted by."

Leo gave me some time to digest that ultimately depressing fact.

"Tancarro and Gabriella created fictional explanations. Kilmurray buried himself in drugs in Thailand trying for escape. Only Ryan Hammond wanted the truth."

Leo sat silent a few moments longer. Finally, he said, "Listen, I have a question. I asked him if he'd ever had trouble using Damon Guthrie's ID. Didn't Missing Persons check Social Security records? He said no. But how—"

"Higgins asked Gabriella about that. It was like she was personally offended that there was no missing persons' report. She really blindsided her. What happened, of course, is that in the beginning, Gabriella was so relieved to have her brother gone, the last thing she wanted was the police to drag him back. Ditto Tancarro. And then by the time they had real questions about him, they didn't dare make a report."

He shifted position. "What about your, uh, colleague, Blink?"

"Higgins really didn't want to discuss that. So, I'd say he's ridden off into the sunset. The law might be looking for him, but he'll be a low priority. He's probably been evading the law since before I was born."

"And the *Bullitt* car?"

"Drifted back into the realm of legend—its rightful place."

I finished my espresso and sat here in my favorite café, holding the warm cup, looking out at the cars sparkling in the sunlight as they whipped down Columbus. "You know, Leo, last night after Gabriella tried to lock me in that horrible room with her brother's remains, and I came up with her gun and called 911, I waited an eternity for the police to show up. When they finally came, I was so glad to see Higgins walk in I forgot what a pain in the ass she is."

"Things change," he said.

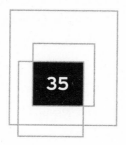

35

SOMETIMES EVENTS HAPPEN fast. Maybe it was John proclaiming that Dad was what he was and we'd all just have to accept that. No one believed him—he'd be struggling for the rest of his life to justify Dad's transgressions—but we were grateful, and impressed. Maybe it was Mike hearing about John. Or maybe Janice knew more about Mike's location than she'd let on. I didn't ask. Nor did I raise questions when she said she'd drive Mom and me up to Guerneville on the Russian River to meet him. If the rest of the family complained, Janice didn't let on. But I figured they understood. Mike was my buddy and protector, the one who made my dreams possible from the time I learned to crawl till the day he walked away. As for Mom, I could barely look at her now without thinking of the times, year after year, I had pictured her face on this day.

"He won't be the same," I said. We were sitting three across in the front seat of Janice's car; Mom and I were scrunched together because we had to be this close now, as if only our proximity was preserving this still unbelievable dream.

"We'll see."

I wanted to ask Janice if she'd talked to him, but I didn't do that either.

The sun was blaring off the August-low water as we sped along the River Road. The windows were all open and I had my hair tied back so it wouldn't snap in Mom's face. There was a vacation mood in the whole area, with the promise of rowboats, canoes, swimming behind the summer dams. The promise of good times ahead.

Janice slowed as we came into town and I could feel Mom tense.

The light at the Guerneville bridge turned red. Janice ran it. She cut left off Main Street and veered down a lazy commercial street, moving agonizingly slowly now. At the Veterans Memorial Hall, she made a left and then, suddenly—*finally*—pulled up to the edge of Johnson's Beach. The car jerked to a stop.

For a moment all three of us just sat. I hadn't asked them how many false leads they'd had over the years, how many moments like this had come to nothing. How hard it had been to let themselves hope again. We sat, preserving this moment of safety.

I opened the door and stepped out.

Across the narrow beach two canoes headed downstream, one slicing through the brown water, the other zigzagging as the paddlers laughed. On the sand, all the people looked suddenly alike. I stared but couldn't see.

None of them was Mike.

"Janice, are you sure . . ."

She didn't say anything.

"Omigod, there. There!"

I recognized his walk first, that loose-limbed stride with an odd catch in his right hip. His walk! I couldn't see his face; my eyes were tearing. I wanted to run faster than I ever had. But I slowed to let Mom catch up and she whipped right by me. When I looked up she was hugging him and he'd lifted her up like a little kid. Then I ran and wrapped my arms around him and felt the solidity of him really here.

After twenty years, we had really found him.

He wouldn't be the same. There'd be awkward times. But right now it was everything I had ever imagined it would be.

ACKNOWLEDGMENTS

AGAIN, I AM indebted to stunt coordinator and director Carolyn Day, to writer Linda Grant, and to my superb editors Michele Slung and Roxanna Aliaga. And, as always, to my agent Dominick Abel.